For Kathryn

Douglas Lindsay was born in Scotland in 1964 at 2:38a.m. It rained.

Some decades later he left to live in Belgium. Meeting his future wife, Kathryn, he took the opportunity to drop out of reality and join her on a Foreign & Commonwealth Office posting to Senegal. It was here that he developed the character of Barney Thomson, while sitting in an air-conditioned apartment drinking gin & tonic at eight o'clock in the morning. Since the late 1990s, he has penned seven books in the Barney series, and several other crime novels written in the non-traditional style.

Prologue

Breasts.

The body of the young woman lay on the kitchen table. The face, azurean white in the melancholic repose of death; the eyes, open and stark, staring blankly into whatever world of demons she had ventured; the body, lying to attention, as if on parade; and then the breasts. Small, firm, strangely upstanding in the fluorescent light of the kitchen.

What would happen if they were removed, now that the girl had been dead for over three hours? Would they fold into some amorphous mass, losing their singular beauty, or would they remain firm and shapely, their allure and elegance preserved?

The killer looked over the rest of the body. Until now the victims had all been men. In death their bodies were always brutal and ugly, repugnant flesh on the cusp of decay. But this girl, with her smooth, ghostly complexion, the neat, silvicultural thatch of thin blonde hair nestling snugly between her thighs, and her beautiful breasts, was so much more. It would almost be a shame to cleave into the luxurious pale skin.

Perhaps it would be simpler to send off an ear or a hand. A bland statement of release to the dear departed's family. A pleasant reminder of their daughter. Something for them to cherish in future years.

A delightful surprise, this girl, when a man had been expected. Hugo, she had said her name was. A final, pointless, damning lie. And the poor girl had been so disappointing in death. It was always the most sumptuous part of it, that horrified look on the face as they watched the cut-throat razor descend with elegant panache to the proffered neck. But this one. This girl. She had hardly looked interested.

Drugs probably. That would be it. So high on drugs that she'd hardly noticed. That was the trouble with people – the great bane of these times – there were just no standards any more.

It was time. And it had to be the breasts. It was so much more artistic. The killer smiled, ever the slave to the aesthetic, and, firmly clutching the right breast, pierced the skin with the eight-inch butcher's knife.

The English Are Bastards

There's nowhere worse than Glasgow on a freezing cold, dank, sodden day in March, especially when your car is in the garage undergoing repairs costing twice NASA's annual budget, and you are obliged to spend your day cutting hair. Greasy hair; pungent hair; hair riddled with insects; hair which cries out to be fashioned into a work of art, when the customer won't allow; hair which requires the use of a chainsaw, an implement long ago outlawed in barber shops. Hair of all sorts, vile, messy, contemptible.

Barney Thomson, barber, scowled. They were all bastards, every one of them that came into the shop. And if, on occasion, some left feeling like their head had just been raped, then they deserved it.

As he stood at the kerb waiting to cross the road for the final struggle up the hill, a passing van, hugging the pavement, sent a panoramic rainbow of water over his trousers and jacket; and he had no time to move before the rear wheels kicked up that little extra which propelled some more into his face.

He watched it speed off, thought of raising his fist, but sodden apathy got the better of him. There was no point. He hunched his shoulders even further and trudged across the road, imagining the van driver having a heart attack, dying at the wheel.

Sure, it rained everywhere in Scotland, he thought, one foot plodding in front of the other, it was one of the things that defined it as a place. But there was no other city as dour as Glasgow in the rain. Edinburgh – the rain made the castle even more dramatic. Same for Stirling. Perth, a land of kings, glorious in all weather. Dundee, Aberdeen, they were on the east coast, so if it wasn't raining then they wouldn't look natural.

It was just Glasgow. In the sun it looked good, and in the rain it was terrible. An awful place to be.

He was thinking that perhaps it was time to leave. Agnes didn't want to go, but then, he didn't have to take her with him. He could open up his own shop in one of the small towns up north. Fort William, Oban, Ullapool, wherever. Just away from here, and all these bloody miserable people. Like himself, the most miserable of the lot.

Two youngsters, duffel coated against the rain, school bags plastered onto their backs, gallons of molten snot turning their faces into cruel parodies of the Reichenbach Falls, scuttled past him on their way to some pre-school turpitude, and he thought of children. The barber's nightmare. He hated the lot of them, with their mothers looking at every snip of the hair, and talking all the time telling you what to do. And the kids kicking their feet up and down, making noises, incapable of keeping still. You'd spend twenty minutes just dying to give them a clip round the ear. But your hands were tied. Mothers should have to cut the hair of their own children until they were eighteen, he thought, and the only real smile of the day came to his lips.

He was nearly there, the long trudge almost over. He imagined himself to have been on a long trek across the Arctic. In euphonious celebration of his achievement, the rain increased its intensity so that it bounced off the pavement. He hurried the last hundred yards to the shop, but it was to no avail, and by the time he arrived his jacket had given up the ghost, his clothes were sticking to his skin like an over-reliant child, and his carefully nurtured bouffant hair had plummeted into a watery abyss. Neither of the others had yet arrived, and so he had to stand for another minute in the rain, fumbling to get the keys from his pocket before he could escape the downpour.

In the grey of early morning the shop was cold and lonely, and his heart sank further at the thought of the day ahead. He should have become an astronaut when he'd had the chance.

*

The television muttered in the corner. Wullie Henderson looked up from the Daily Record to watch the action. Aston Villa versus Derby County. Dire stuff, but football was football, and he'd reached the end of the sports pages.

They were filled with the usual things. Football, football, football, and an enlarged section on the England cricket team's latest test defeat. The size of the report was always directly proportional to the size of the defeat, he reflected, as the ball flew into the net from twenty-five yards, sparking a minor, but nevertheless engaging, pitch invasion.

He looked back and re-read the article on whether Rangers were about to sign Alessandro del Piero for £30 million, in an effort to still be participating in the Champions League come September, then folded the paper and laid it on the table. Took a cursory glance at the front page headline. 'The English Are Bastards'. Par for the course, he thought, as he tucked into his final piece of toast and marmalade. Beneath that story was a follow-up report concerning the latest murder in the city. The most recent in a series of grotesque killings, the work of one man, or so the police believed, which had been dominating the news for a couple of months. The English must really be bastards to keep that off the headline.

'You'll be late. It's nearly five to,' said his wife, not bothering to raise her eyes from the Daily Express.

Wullie Henderson looked at the television. They'd moved onto women's golf, two words that just ought not to be used in the same sentence. Time to go. Looked at his wife. Thought of the girl he'd met on Friday night in the Montrose, and wondered if she'd be there again this Friday. It didn't do any harm to fantasise, though he knew that he'd do more than that if he got the chance.

'Aye, I suppose you're right.'

He stood up, pulled at his jeans, was satisfied that he was beginning to lose some weight, then turned to the back door.

'Here you! You put a jacket on or you'll catch your death out there, so you will. It's pure bucketing down, so it is.'

'I've got one in the motor, and I'll be parking right outside the shop anyway. Keep your knickers on.'

'Aye, well, away you go,' she said to his back, and with a final grunt thrown over his shoulder, he was gone. Moira Henderson looked up from the paper to see the door close, and wondered whether to have another piece of toast.

The rain was hammering down as he stepped out of the door, and he ran to his car. A month earlier he would've been expecting trouble getting it started, but now, as he sat in his new Peugeot 306, his mind was more on how the rain would affect the Rangers-Motherwell game the following night.

The car started like a dream – which would actually be a pretty lame dream if you were to have it – and he set out on the five minute drive to the shop. It wasn't too far, but there were several strategically placed traffic lights, specifically positioned to hold him up in the morning, and he wondered to whom he could complain at the council.

(It was, in fact, a strange coincidence, that the person to whom he should complain was the girl he'd met in the Montrose the previous Friday night. Unfortunate, then, that by the coming Friday, when she would be waiting hopefully by the bar, Wullie Henderson would already be dead.)

By the time he pulled up outside the shop, the torrent of rain had eased, and he left his jacket in the car as he stepped out. There was a light on, which meant that one of the others had already arrived. Probably Barney. Chris would be late again. He was always late on Monday mornings, and Wullie knew he'd have to have a word with him. Some day.

He opened the door and walked in, the little bell ringing above his head, and Barney looked up from the Herald.

'Barney, how you doing?'

'Wullie. Not so bad, not so bad.'

'Good weekend?' asked Wullie, experiencing the sinking feeling that he always felt first thing on a Monday.

'Aye, it was all right, I suppose. You?'

'Aye, aye, fine.' He looked around the drab surroundings of the small shop which had been his workplace for over ten years. Was any weekend which just led back to this place really fine?

'I got soaked when I came in,' said Barney. 'Bloody rain.'

'Aye, terrible,' said Wullie. He looked at Barney, knew he had nothing else to say. The same brief conversation every Monday morning, with seasonal variations, and then they would hardly talk to one another for the rest of the week. No point in telling Barney about the girl in the Montrose.

They stared blankly for a few seconds then, with a nod, Barney looked back at his paper and Wullie went about his business.

★

Chris Porter stirred, his head encased in a pillow. His girlfriend had been sacked from her job as a Formula One driver by Tom Jones, the team owner, and he was in the middle of head-butting the Welshman, when he woke up. He smiled. That had been a belter of a dream. He would have to tell Helen later.

He rolled over, his eyes flickering open long enough to glance at the clock. Five past eight. It didn't register and he closed his eyes again, trying to slide back into the dream.

Shite. He opened his eyes, bolted upright. Shite. He'd slept through the alarm. The usual Monday morning event. Shite. He checked the clock again to make sure he wasn't rushing unnecessarily, then leapt out of bed and into the bathroom.

It wasn't that he ever did anything particular on a Sunday night, he reflected, as he washed all the parts of his body that seemed appropriate, randomly spraying water over the floor as he did so. It was just a natural aversion to Monday mornings. He knew it was a good thing that it was Wullie who was in charge and not Barney, or he would've been in trouble a long time ago.

He dressed with unnecessary flourish and flew into the kitchen, debating whether to accept the fact he was late and be even later by having cereal. Finding the fridge uncontaminated by milk, his mind was made up for him, and he sped to the front door and down the stairs with a sigh and an empty stomach.

He was still driving the same old Escort that his dad had bought for him in his last year at school and, after spluttering a little in the rain, it kicked into action and he set out on the ten minute drive to the shop, wondering if this was going to be the morning when he finally got his backside kicked for being late.

He arrived at twenty-five past eight, found a heaven-sent parking space right outside, and ran in. Barney and Wullie looked at him from empty chairs. There were no customers yet. A little prayer answered.

'What time d'you call this, Porter?' said Wullie.

Chris looked around the empty shop, slightly annoyed that he was out of breath after a ten yard run from his car. 'The time before any customers have arrived?'

Wullie raised an eyebrow. 'Aye, it's quiet now, but you should have seen the first twenty minutes of the day. Heaving, so it was. That not right, Barn?'

Barney shrugged, grunted, and went back to reading his paper.

'Won't happen again, Wullie,' said Chris, taking off his jacket and assuming his position.

'Aye, and you lot are going to win the cup this year.'

Chris smiled. 'Hey, we beat Morton three-nil on Saturday.'

'Yoo hoo!' said Wullie, raising his arms in celebration.

'Aye, you can laugh now, but you better hope you lot don't get us in the cup or you're in trouble.'

Wullie laughed again then stood up as the first customer of the day, his hair matted with rain, his face an atlas of misery, came through the door to the melodic tinkle of the bell.

'Aye, I'm shitting my pants, Chris. It's not as if you're going to get past Aberdeen in the quarter final, is it, Big Man?'

'You wait and see.'

Barney watched them from the corner of his eye. Football, football. It was all they ever talked about. It would be so beautiful one day to shut them up. What damage he could do with a pair of scissors. With a shake of the head, and further malicious reflections upon dark deeds, he returned to the gardening page.

Customers Must Have Hair

It was going badly. Exceptionally badly. There were voyages of the Titanic which had gone better than this. Barney caught the eye of the customer in the mirror, and did his best not to convey what he knew and what the victim had yet to realise. Sometimes the first haircut of the day can be catastrophic. A headlong rush to do good, which turns to bloody disaster. James IV at Flodden, the Charge of the Light Brigade, the Zulus at Rorke's Drift. It doesn't start out that way, but somewhere along the line it becomes a horror story. Grown men weep.

He surveyed his handiwork, realising the damage being cleaved by his own scissors. The man had asked for a straightforward short back and sides, a Frank Sinatra '62, but things had rollercoastered out of hand.

Ensuring he avoided his customer's gaze, he considered the two options open to barbers in such circumstances. One – keep cutting until all is recovered and the hair looks even. Unfortunately, this usually leaves the victim looking like a US Marine, and if it so happens that he thinks like a US Marine, you're in trouble. Two – cover his head in water, pretend your hair-dryer isn't working, and let the full devastation be revealed to him later on when he is sitting in work, his hair has dried, and his colleagues are having a field day. It's a lucky man who, under such circumstances, has a job which requires headwear.

The man who sat before him was of considerable stature. Seven feet tall, thought Barney. *Giant Kills Barber in Revenge Attack.* Option one was not viable. It must be number two, with the expectation that such a large man was unlikely to even ask for the hair-dryer in case anyone else in the shop might equate wanting your hair dried artificially with homosexuality.

Intricate and subtle are the politics of the barber shop.

He hesitated, but the decision was made. Imagining himself to be Clint Eastwood, he fixed a firm look in his eye and set about his work with as much conviction as he could muster.

Ten minutes later he breathed a sigh of relief as the slaughtered head retreated from the shop, the victim still unaware of the full horror which had been visited upon him, and curious as to why Barney had deposited a jug of water over his head. Barney made a mental note, to add to the list, to be certain to avoid the bloke in the street for the next few weeks.

He turned his attention to the bench. A man was waiting, but he recognised him as one of Wullie's regulars, so he nodded a slightly resentful acknowledgement and went about sweeping up the debris from the previous customer – noticing in the process that a disproportionate amount of it lay on the right hand side.

As he swept, he cast a wearied glance over his two colleagues, busy doing that barber thing: cutting hair and talking drivel at the same time. Chris was discussing the likelihood of truth in the rumour that Marilyn Monroe had had forty-three abortions; Wullie was grandstanding on the rights of man, as opposed to the rights of women, one of his common topics, to which Barney hated to listen. The words drifted across the short distance of the shop, and no matter how much he tried to switch off, the sound was always there, eating away at him. Like a cancer. Yes, that's it, he thought, a cancer.

'No, no, you see, I hate that,' Wullie said to a young lad. 'All this garbage about girls maturing faster than boys. It's bollocks.'

'You think so, Wullie?' said the boy, bright eyed, acne-blighted face, teeth yellowed by illicit teenage cigarettes.

Wullie smiled. There's nothing a barber likes more than some eager young sponge. 'Aye, of course it is. Think about it. The thing people equate most with maturity is sense of humour. One person's humour is another's schoolboy immaturity. Benny Hill, John Cleese, the Marx Brothers. For everyone that thinks they're funny, there's some eejit who thinks they're juvenile.'

'I hate Benny Hill,' said the boy.

Wullie nodded. 'Exactly. But he was the most famous British guy in America. You know,' he said, adding edge to the voice, 'that he ran for President against Ronald Reagan in 1980 and won nearly twenty percent of the vote?'

The lad looked impressed, nodding his head. Wullie continued before anyone could object, while deploying evasive scissor tactics to avoid cutting off the boy's ear.

'So that's the thing about comedy. What happens is that these young birds lose their sense of humour when they reach puberty, and boys don't, so they all think they're more mature than us. But they're not. They've just forgotten how to laugh, that's all.'

The lad's eyes had been opened. 'Jings, I never thought of it like that, Wullie.'

Wullie nodded, executing a neat manoeuvre around the left ear.

'Thing is, you can't really blame them, can you? I mean, if I'd had a pint of blood bucketing out of me once a month from the age of twelve, I'd have lost my sense of humour 'n all.'

The lad was impressed with Wullie's sensitivity for the female condition. 'Here, you're not one of these New Men, are you Wullie?' he asked, and Wullie smiled.

Barney rolled his eyes, shook his head and went back to his sweeping, an act in which he was deliberate and slow, as he was in everything he did. He had never had the knack of talking drivel to complete strangers. Certainly, he could talk about the weather with the best of them, or could cast an opinion on the repeated episode of Inspector Morse shown the night before – although the opinion usually belonged to someone else – but when it came to uncompromising asinine bollocks, he just didn't have it. He had been cutting hair for over twenty years, and yet, in this respect, he remained an amateur. Still, on this imagined Day of Days, he had something up his sleeve.

The door to the shop opened, accompanied by a gay tinkle from the bell. It was a Sad Man. Barney groaned. The 'few pathetic strands of hair' brigade. Men for whom hair is something which happens to other people. Men who grow a few strands of hair to a length of several metres, wrap it tenuously around their scalps, then wonder if people notice.

The Sad Man looked at the man in the queue, who gestured that he was waiting for Wullie, then walked towards Barney. Barney ushered him into the chair, ran a discreet and well-trained eye over his baldy napper, and wrapped him in the cape.

'What will it be then, Sir?'

'A short back and sides'll be just fine, Big Man.'

A short back and sides. What a joke. Barney looked at his hair, and dreamt of being able to cut it off at its roots. He lifted a pair of scissors, and they itched in his fingers. Twitch, twitch, twitch, eager to cut. Had to control the muscles in his fingers, the thoughts in his head. He sighed, put the scissors back on the worktop and lifted a comb. Might as well do as he was bid. As usual. One day he would have his revenge on all these bastards.

He combed the hair several different ways. He wasn't a fast worker, but he could have had this hair cut and the guy out of the shop in under a minute. But they never appreciated that, these Sad Men, so he knew to spin it out for at least twenty. Make him think he had a decent head of hair on him. A dream maker, that's what he was. He felt like Steven Spielberg as he pondered the tools of his trade. Scissors, brushes, combs and razors, before deciding on an electric razor. Might as well pretend he had to shave the back of the neck and round the ears.

On a normal head of hair that would be good for at least five minutes per ear. He'd been told at barber school that he would resent ears at first, so much would they get in the way, but in time that resentment would pass and he would come to love and cherish the ears, like you did any other more straightforward part of the head. However, it had never happened for Barney. His resentment of ears went beyond rationality, and he knew he would never be cured of it. And, as always, even though there was little to be done with this Sad Man, Barney got himself into a tangle of arms and legs as he attempted to negotiate the elaborate folds of skin and cartilage.

However, ten minutes into the cut things were going smoothly. He was making it look as if he had much work to do, the Sad Man seemed happy, and there had been minimal conversation. Barney looked around the rest of the shop. Chris was reading the paper, Wullie had just finished telling his next customer of Florence Nightingale's prodigious number of lesbian affairs.

Barney smiled. Now might just be the time to drop his bombshell, show the others he could compete on level ground. Show them that when it came to talking shite he was right up there with the two of them.

He had no interest in football. He hated it with something approaching passion, if so dour a man could feel passion for anything. Grown men as little boys. A war substitute. But even though he knew nothing of football, he had done something grand. That weekend he had looked at the league tables. He now had a little knowledge.

'Hey, any of you ever read these lonely hearts messages?' said Chris from the bench, the paper rustling in his hands.

Barney turned round quickly, nearly depriving the Sad Man of his right ear. God, would they ever shut up?

'Listen to this. *Single woman, late 30s. Interesting looks. Likes gardening, books and quiet nights. Seeks Marty Feldman lookalike.*' He laughed, was joined by Wullie and his customer. 'Interesting looks? Bloody hell, she must be a stankmonster if that's the best she can do.'

'Ugly bird, left on the shelf, more like,' said Wullie.

'And these guys are just as bad,' said Chris. *'Forty-six year old aesthete...* What's an aesthete again?'

'I think it's someone who changes his y-fronts twice a day,' said Wullie.

'They probably meant athlete. It'll be a printing error,' said Wullie's customer.

'Aye, right,' said Chris. *'Forty-six year old athlete seeks attractive woman in early twenties.* Bloody hell, I bet he does. *For long walks, gin and tonic as the sun goes down, Corelli's Concerto Grosso in G Minor, Wordsworth, and Renaissance architecture.'* He shook his head. 'What a flipping bampot.'

'What are you saying?' said Wullie. 'You don't like Corelli?'

'Not sure,' said Chris. 'Was he the Juventus centre-half the Rangers tried to sign?'

Chris laughed and returned to reading the paper. Barney simmered. He waited to see if Chris would say something else, thinking, 'just shut up for five seconds'. Got ready to talk his own bit of drivel. Opened his mouth, smiled.

'Listen to this one,' said Chris, laughing. *'Mature woman, mid-80s, looking for love. Skilled in Eastern lovemaking. Seeks man in 20s/30s for nights of passion. No cranks.* Mid-80s! Can you believe it? Cheeky old midden.'

'There's some strange folk out there,' said Wullie. 'Bet she gets loads of replies. Good luck to the gallus old cow.'

'Eastern lovemaking?' said Wullie's customer. 'You think that means she's shagged someone in the back of a motor in Edinburgh?'

The others laughed, Barney fumed, annoyed at himself for listening. Mid-80s. Incredible. It could've been his own mother, and he shivered at the thought.

Silence again. This time he would seize the moment.

'What d'you make of those Rangers, eh?' he said to the Sad Man, slightly louder than was necessary, and he cast an eye over the rest of the shop to see the reaction he had elicited. Chris was laughing at the paper, and ignoring him; Wullie glanced over, but no more. Barney looked back to the customer.

Sad Man shrugged. 'What about them?' he said. 'Don't really follow it myself.'

He caught Barney's eye in the mirror and looked convincingly back. He was lying. He'd been a season ticket holder at Ibrox for over seventeen years, but he was aware of Barney's conversational deficiencies and there was no way he was talking to him about anything. Even the Rangers.

Barney had little reply, as he was already almost at the cusp of his knowledge; so he lurched into his usual silence. All that waiting for nothing. Feeling spurned, he hurried through the rest of the haircut, managing to stop himself cleaving off several feet of hair emanating from behind the right ear.

Five minutes later, the Sad Man handed over his cash, an extra fifty pence included, and walked out into the light drizzle of morning feeling like Robert Redford.

Barney watched him go, shaking his head with every step. If he ever got to run the shop he would have a sign put in the window. *Customers Must Have Hair.* He sneered and looked at the waiting area. The next customer up, he shuffled his razors and contemplated whether or not to mention the fact that he knew Rangers were five points clear at the top of the league.

*

The day dragged on, following its usual course. Barney only cut about half the amount of hair as the other two, partly because he was a lot slower, partly because few people sought him out in particular ahead of the others. It wasn't until late in the afternoon that he felt able to broach the subject of football again, and with an almost mathematical inevitability he was caught with his pants down.

It was a big bloke, a labourer from a site down by the Clyde. He was wearing a Scotland top, making Barney feel confident in starting a football conversation. Once again he bided his time, then chose his moment with a flourish, foot firmly in mouth, when all else in the shop was quiet.

'What d'you make of those Rangers, eh?' he said, not quite as cocksure as before, but still with a glint in the eye.

'What about them?' growled the Scotland strip.

Displaying the kind of blinkered enthusiasm which allowed Custer to stop for a KFC and a doughnut at the Little Big Horn, Barney failed to spot the warning signs.

'Five points clear at the top of the league. Some team, eh?'

The Scotland strip grunted. 'They're shite. Lost their last three games now. Pile of pish, so they are.'

Barney hesitated, but he bravely determined to battle on, like the German tanks in the Ardennes, until he ran out of fuel.

'Aye, but you know, five points clear at the top of the league. Can't be bad, eh?'

'They're still shite. They're only five points clear at the top of the league because everyone else is even more shite than them.' He looked at Barney. This was a man who ate babies. 'What do you know about football anyway?' he growled.

Barney swallowed, scissors trembling in his hands. Unable to think of an answer, he quickly resumed some gentle snipping, a layer of tension now descended on his little area of the shop. For once he did not dither over a cut and, while ensuring that he did not make a hash of it, sent the Scotland strip packing as quickly as possible. He left with a grunt and all his change in his pocket.

As the door closed behind him, and Barney breathed a sigh of relief, Wullie laughed and spoke to him for the first time since twenty-five minutes past eight that morning.

'If you're going to tell someone how good the Rangers are, try not telling a Celtic fan next time, eh Barney? We don't want a riot in here.'

He laughed again and was joined by everyone else in the shop. Barney, suitably embarrassed, retreated to the hiding place that was his natural reserve, and plotted his usual plans of revenge.

Bastards. They were all bastards.

He looked out the window at the massive figure retreating into the distance, and dreamt of him falling into a manhole, breaking his neck.

The rain thundered down with ever greater intensity. The skies were dark; occasional ferocious streaks of lightning rendered the clouds. The street lights were already on, fighting a losing battle against the gloom. Barney bent low over his brush, sweeping with slow deliberate strokes, and thought of dark deeds. Deeds to match the weather. Deeds which fate would force his hand to commit within the week.

The Lure Of The
Flashing Blue Light

It rained all the way home. It always rained all the way home when Barney had to walk back from the shop. A phone call to the garage at four o'clock had produced the usual mutterings about a 'big job', and an estimated time of readiness of sometime the following morning – and so he had stepped out into the raging torrent without even making the effort to cover up. Head bowed, spirit broken, besieged by ill humour.

He lived in a top floor flat in a tenement at the university end of Partick, one of the old houses, with huge rooms, and ceilings higher and more ornate than the Sistine Chapel. The kind of place which years ago had fostered a warm community spirit, but no longer in such times as these. Barney viewed all those around him with varying degrees of contempt and suspicion – his neighbours were no different.

He hung his soaking jacket on the hook behind the door and trudged wearily into the kitchen. Agnes was making an uninteresting dinner, with one eye glued to a prosaic Australian soap on the portable television. As Barney clumped in, Charlene was having a fight with Emma's sister's ex-boyfriend's girlfriend Sheila, who was pregnant by Adam's gay lover Chip.

'Good day at work, dear?' she asked, her eyes never leaving the television.

He grunted, took a glass from a cupboard, went to the fridge and poured himself some wine from a carton. Chilean Sauvignon Blanc, flinty with a hint of apple; good length; full-breasted; serve with fish or chicken, or perfect as a light appetiser. He took a long and loud slurp and belched. Put the back of his hand to his mouth in some affectation of manners, then pointed at nothing in particular.

'You know what really pisses me off?' He looked at her expectantly, assuming her interest, although long years of indifference should have told him to expect otherwise.

'What, dear?' she said eventually.

'It pisses me off, all these bastards,' he waved his hand, ''scuse the French, who come in there every day and insist on one of they two wee shitbags cutting their hair.' The voice rose a fraction in agitation. 'I mean, do these people, these bampots, actually think that Wullie or Chris is going to give them a better haircut than I am, eh? Eh?' He stabbed his finger in the air, unintentionally pronging a passing fly.

'Yes, dear,' she said. Troy had finally told Charlene that Cleopatra was pregnant by Julian.

'Exactly. I mean,' he continued, slight bubbles of froth beginning to appear at the side of his mouth, a string of spit suspended between top and bottom lip, 'how long have these two been cutting hair? Five, maybe six years. All right, maybe ten for Wullie. So what? Look at me. Twenty years I've been cutting hair,' he said, scything the air with his hand in time with each syllable, 'and I'm bloody good at it.'

'Yes, dear.'

'Bloody right. And look at those two muppets. They couldn't cut the hair off a…off a…' He searched the air for a suitable analogy, finding it as Charlene slapped Tony in the face and told him that there was no way that she and Beatrice could be half-sisters, '…they couldn't cut the hair off a drugged mammoth. No they couldn't. Bloody useless the pair of them. You know what they do?'

'Yes, dear?' She wasn't listening, but the tone of his voice had wormed its way into her subconscious, so she knew to sound inquisitive.

'I'll tell you. They just bloody talk about football all day. As if it's important. Who gives a shite about football? It's a lot of pish. Or that Wullie just stands there and comes out with all sorts of garbage. Did you know,' he began, attempting an impersonation of Wullie and missing by several miles, 'that Cary bleeding Grant had an affair with Randolph Scott? Big bloody deal! As if anybody's going to believe that shite. I mean,' he said, rising to his subject, while his voice descended to Churchillian depths, 'I mean, look at all that's going on in the world. The country's going down the toilet. There's wars and strikes and death.' He clutched the breast of his shirt with his right hand. 'What's happening to the Health Service? Transport? Eh? What about that stuff? There's some bloody heid-the-ba' running about Glasgow slashing folk and cutting them up. What about that? What's the bloody polis doing about that? And what do they two talk about? Football!'

'Yes, dear.' Charlene was now convinced that Troy and Beatrice were having an affair and that Bethlehem wasn't her brother, while some savoury pancakes which Agnes had magicked from the freezer twenty minutes earlier quietly burned on the stove.

Shaking his head and grumbling in a low voice, Barney polished off the glass of wine and began pouring himself another.

'Where's my dinner?'

'Programme'll be finished in a couple of minutes, dear.' Had Bill really lost his voice, or was he just doing it so that Charles wouldn't realise that Emma still loved Tom?

Barney grunted loudly and wandered off into the sitting room. He flicked on the television, found the snooker on BBC2 and within five minutes was sound asleep.

*

The rain struck relentlessly against the window of the dingy little office. Detective Chief Inspector Robert Holdall stared gloomily at the water cascading from the gutters outside and wondered what other disasters could befall him. As he had occasion to do most days, he tried to remember what it was that had made him want to be a policeman in the first place. Action, adventure, glamour, women. Obviously it'd been none of that, so what had it been? A vague desire to fight the forces of evil? Something like that. He'd had the thought in the past that it was because of the sixties Batman TV series, and had spent a lot of time since persuading himself that it wasn't that at all. That would be just too sad. Thwack! Biff! Blam! Love your tights...

The lure of the flashing blue light, that was all. Just the lure of the flashing blue light. He could be driving an ambulance.

There was a knock at his door and a young constable walked into his office. Not long removed from school, the dregs of adolescent acne still clinging wildly to his face, barnacles to a boat. He closed the door behind him and stood before Holdall, nervously awaiting the invitation to talk.

'Constable?'

'Sir. The results from the lab are negative, sir.'

Bugger.

Why are you thinking *bugger*, Holdall? Of course the results are negative. You're not dealing with an amateur here. You're dealing with some seasoned killer who knows what he's doing. And who's intent on mocking you every step of the way.

'All right, Montgomery.' He wondered as he said it if this really was Constable Montgomery. 'Will you ask MacPherson to come in here, please?'

The constable nodded and disappeared back through the door, leaving a trace of Clearasil in the air. Holdall leant back in his chair, put his hands behind his head, his feet up on the desk. Where did they stand?

Five murders. No corpses, just body parts mailed through the post to the victims' families. Never anything from the package to help them trace the killer. Always postmarked from a different town in Scotland; always a note sent to the police at the same time, each one more laden with derision than the one before. When he caught the guy, which he was sure he'd do, before going through the formalities of making the arrest, he was going to kick his head in.

The door opened and Detective Sergeant MacPherson walked into the room. He was a big man, who had in his day played full-back for West of Scotland, but after being sent off for the eleventh time had decided to save his brutality for the job.

Holdall watched him as he entered the room. He liked him, enjoyed the Barbarian pleasure of working with him. It made him feel safer, if nothing else. And for all his brawn and thuggery, he was a good man. Intelligent with it.

'Take a seat, Sergeant. Won't keep you long. I presume you'll be wanting to get home.'

MacPherson shrugged his giant shoulders. 'There's some football I wouldn't mind watching. It's not that important.'

'That English Premier league stuff?'

'Aye.'

'Don't know how you can be bothered with it. Seems like a load of shite to me.'

He looked away from MacPherson, took his feet off the desk and swivelled round, so that he was side on to the other man. MacPherson knew what was coming, sat and waited patiently for it. Another examination of the facts. Another run through the salient information. Another drive down the road to nowhere. They were in exactly the same place they had been since the first murder, and all there was for them to do was talk. However, he understood Holdall's need to do it.

'Roberts tell you about the lab report?' said MacPherson.

Roberts! Bugger. That was it. Who was Montgomery? Felt a slight redness in his face as he remembered. WPC Eileen Montgomery.

'Aye, aye he did,' said Holdall, shaking his head. He put his hands down, clasping them on his stomach. Felt like he should be giving some leadership to the investigation, but the tank was empty. He had no ideas.

'Where does it leave us, Sergeant? Where are we at?'

MacPherson considered.

'We're in a pile of shite,' he said.

Holdall smiled. That was just about right.

MacPherson continued his recap of events.

'We're nowhere. We've got some eejit running around Glasgow committing indiscriminate murder, then visiting other parts of Scotland to send back a slice of body. No connection between the victims, other than that they've all been men. Don't know if there's any significance to that. Certainly doesn't appear to be a gay thing, and hard to imagine a woman doing all this stuff. But you never know, can't rule it out. Not these days. Anyway, nothing to link the places the body parts have been getting sent back from...'

'Which have been?'

'Pitlochry, Edinburgh, Kingussie, Largs and Aberdeen. We've checked out hotel guest lists in those places for the nights that the packages were posted, but there hasn't been anyone who stayed in more than one of them. We've spoken to everyone from Glasgow who stayed overnight in these towns on the relevant dates, but they all had their reason for being there, and there was nothing suspicious. There've been a few people that we can't trace, and it could be that he left false names and addresses, but it could also mean nothing. There's no reason why someone couldn't have got the train to any one of they places and back again in the same day.'

Holdall nodded, then grunted.

'That's about it, isn't it, Stuart? Everywhere he goes is on a main rail route, so we can maybe assume that he's been taking the train. So that narrows it down.'

'Sir?'

'All we have to do is arrest everyone in Glasgow who doesn't have a car.'

MacPherson smiled. The idea appealed. Too bad it wasn't practical.

'Anything else, Sergeant?'

MacPherson marshalled his thoughts, then continued in his low voice.

'There's no connection with the body parts that he's sending back. So far we've had an ear, a right hand, a right hand and left foot together, a left leg, and then on Friday we had a head.'

Holdall shook his head, still unable to comprehend the awfulness of the crime. Killing someone, beheading them, and then mailing the head back to the family, when they'd probably still been under the impression that the bloke had run away to Blackpool for a few days. Couldn't think about it too closely. You couldn't do that on this job and stay sane.

'This is a sick bastard we're dealing with, Sergeant, a sick bastard.'

MacPherson nodded, continued talking.

'So far we've no idea what he's doing with the remainder of the bodies. Certainly, if he's got rid of them, we don't know where.' He paused, thinking for a second or two. 'I don't think there's anything else, sir.'

Holdall shook his head, staring wearily at the floor.

'No, Sergeant, you're right. There isn't. We've got some sick bastard carving up the citizens of Glasgow, they're expecting us to do something about it, and we haven't the faintest idea what that is.'

For a fleeting second MacPherson felt pity for him. He knew he took his cases personally. But it was all part of the job, and Holdall had been doing it long enough to accept the weight of expectation.

Holdall turned round in his chair, placed his hands decisively on the desk, looked MacPherson firmly in the eye.

'There's nothing else for it, Sergeant. Take the list off the system of everyone in Glasgow who owns a car, and then arrest everyone else.'

MacPherson raised his eyebrows, until the look on Holdall's face told him he was joking. Of course he was. If they did that they would have to arrest too many councillors currently off the roads on drink driving charges. The stink would be unbelievable.

They smiled and, with a wave of the hand, Holdall dismissed the Sergeant from his office.

'Have a good evening, Sergeant. Who's playing?'

MacPherson thought about it then shrugged. 'Who cares? Football is as football does, eh, sir?' He turned and walked from the office.

Holdall nodded. 'You can't say fairer than that,' he said to the empty room. He looked out at the Gothic darkness of early evening, the rain now hammering against the window. Allowed his chin to slump into the palm of his hand. 'Fuck,' he said softly, before rising slowly from the chair.

Death Row

Barney looked on proudly as his finest haircut of the month walked from the shop. The lad had wanted his hair cut by Chris, but there had been too many people in the queue ahead of him, forcing him to settle on Barney. And he had shown him what real barbery was all about. The haircut had been a peach. A non-technical short back and sides job, low difficulty certainly, but executed with beautiful panache nonetheless. Even and neat on the top, tapered to geometric perfection around the ears and the back of the neck. Barbery at its finest, he thought to himself, from one of the best exponents of the art in the west of Scotland.

He glanced at the other two to see if they'd noticed, but Chris was too busy discussing the on-going plight of Partick Thistle, while Wullie was contemplating the exact nature of the relationship between Laurence Olivier and Danny Kaye. Barney shrugged. If they were too busy discussing trivialities to notice real genius, then that was their problem.

He turned and surveyed the shop, feeling good about himself. A warm glow. Like the pilot who lands the plane in a storm without a bump, or the teacher who discovers the one pupil in a thousand who understands triple differentiation, the barber who carries out the perfect haircut has reason to be proud.

It was a small shop. A row of four chairs along one side next to the great bank of mirrors, and a long cushioned bench along the other, upon which the customers awaited their fate. Wullie worked the chair nearest the window, Chris next to him, then there lay an empty chair, occasionally filled on busy Saturdays by a young girl moonlighting from an expensive hairdressers in Kelvinside. At the back of the shop, working the fourth chair, was Barney, and he resented it. Behind him was a small alcove, making the room into a slight L-shape, where there was a fifth seat, a seat which hadn't been worked since the great hair rush of the late seventies, when every man in Britain had wanted a perm, so that they could look as much of an idiot as everyone else. It was some surprise to Barney that he had not been relegated all the way back there.

There'd been a time when he'd had possession of the coveted window seat – for some fifteen years in fact – but he'd been ousted late one Friday afternoon in a bloodless coup. Wullie had been after the chair for some time and, using the fact that his father owned the shop to his advantage, he'd executed a manoeuvre that had relegated Barney to the back of the room. It'd been the talk of the shop for some time – the talk of hushed voices – but gradually the affair had quietened down, as Wullie had known it would, and they'd settled back into a steady routine.

However, it had widened the gap between Barney and the other two men. They shared no interests whatsoever and consequently no conversation. And they also shared very few customers, most of them preferring to go to the younger men. Barney was left with a few old boys whose hair he had been cutting for years, a few men who didn't care, and the odd stray first-timers who didn't know any better.

He looked over the queue of ten people crammed onto the seat and realised there were none who fitted any of the required categories. They would all be waiting for one of the other two bastards. However, he still had the post-dream-haircut glow about him. Surely at least one of them would have surveyed the majesty of the hair on the bloke who had just left. Surely brilliance such as that would not go unnoticed.

He looked at the row of men, each with their private thoughts about the ordeal awaiting them. A mini-Death Row. Some sat with anticipatory relish, some were nervous, some were angry, present only on the instructions of their wives. Or mothers.

'Who's next?' said Barney, with the confident air of a fighter who takes on all comers.

Like a row of disciples denying all knowledge of Jesus under the scrutiny of an awkward centurion, most of the ten stared blankly ahead, ignoring him as best they could. The two or three nearest him felt obliged to shake their heads, although only one of them could do it while looking him in the eye. Barney gave them an incredulous stare, but since they were all ignoring him, it was wasted. A change in strategy was required.

It is frequently effective for the unemployed barber to remorselessly select individuals who may well crack under the pressure of personal attention. Another useful lesson from Barber School, which Barney had never forgotten.

'You, my good man,' he said pointing to the chap at the head of the queue, 'come on.'

He had chosen unwisely, however, for this was not a man to be browbeaten. He looked Barney in the eye, unconcerned about such things as direct appeals.

'It's all right mate, I'm going to wait for Chris, thanks.'

Bloodied, but not yet beaten, Barney nodded. 'Fair enough.' He pointed to the next in line. 'You then, my man, on you come.'

The man shuffled his feet and stared at the floor, remembering the words of his wife as he'd left the house; 'Here you, mind and no' let that old bastard at your hair, 'cause you know what he did the last time, and if you come home and you've no' got your hair cut, I'll be like that, so I will, I'll be like that, get back out there. See if you spend that money down the boozer, I'll be like that. I will.' Finally shook his head.

Barney rolled his eyes, gritted his teeth, looked like he was going to punch someone. Did his best to remember the lessons he'd learned from years past, and kept his cool. Perseverance, that was what was needed. Someone would eventually crack. He just had to make sure it wasn't him.

He gestured to the next chap, who noiselessly gestured towards Chris. Barney gritted his teeth again. He wasn't coping with this at all well. One more. He'd try one more.

'Here you, what about you?' he said to the next in line, his temper beginning to spill over.

The man ignored the tone of voice. 'No thanks mate, I'm just going to wait for Wullie, if that's all right.'

The final straw, settling gently on the camel's back. Forgetting everything he'd learned at Barber School, Barney cracked.

'No, it bloody well isn't all right.' He stared angrily up and down the row of embarrassed faces. 'Not one of you, eh? Not one of you is willing to get your hair cut by me? Am I that bad?'

He pointed towards the closed door. 'Did you not see that haircut I just did. Bloody stoatir, so it was. And you're all going to wait for these two,' he said, sneering. 'It's three-thirty now. If you all wait for them, some of you aren't going to get your hair cut at all. I've just pulled off one of the finest haircuts this shop's seen in months, and yet you all just sit there like bloody sheep.' He stared them up and down. 'Well?'

He was aware of the beating of his heart, the redness in his face. Began to feel a bit of an idiot, but something drove him on. Searching for the one who looked the most sheepish, the most likely to crack under pressure.

'You!' he said, pointing. The chap turned reluctantly to look at him. 'Aye, you, young man. How about you? I'll do you a nice Gregory Peck, something like that.'

It was a lad of about seventeen and, with pleasure, Barney realised that he was about to give in. He would have his chance to show the rest of these bastards what a decent haircut looked like.

'Look Barney, if they all want to wait for Chris or me, then that's fine. You can't have a go at the customers. Someone else will come in shortly'

Slowly, Barney turned and looked over at the window. Wullie stood wagging a pair of scissors in Barney's direction. Barney stared back. His heart beat a little faster.

The bastard. The total bastard. That he should have humiliated Barney in front of all these customers.

He stood with his feet spread. An aggressive stance, ready for a fight. Wullie was having none of it. He murmured something to his customer and took a few paces towards Barney. He spoke in a quiet voice, but it was a small enough shop that there was no way that anyone could miss what was said. At the last second, and with a fine sense of diplomacy, Chris turned on his hair-dryer to create some background noise.

'Look Barney, don't think that I'm embarrassing you in front of the customers. You're embarrassing yourself. And them. If they don't want to come to you, it's no bother. Just leave them to it. Gregory Peck, for fuck's sake.'

Barney grumbled something about not leaving them to it, without having the guts to really say it.

'I'll talk to you about it later, Barney, if that's all right with you.'

Barney stared at Wullie, the anger boiling up inside him, but contained for all that. He nodded a bitter nod, sat down in his chair, roughly lifted the paper, and made no attempt to read it.

The moment had passed, but tension still hung thick in the air. Barney looked at his paper for a few seconds, then turned the corner down and glanced menacingly over at the row of men sitting trying to ignore him.

It was the first time he'd felt so humiliated since the window seat debacle, and while he'd eventually let that one pass, there was no way he was going to let Wullie talk to him like that in front of all these bloody goons.

Chris silenced his hair-dryer – much to the relief of the man at the other end of the warm blast – then the only sound in the shop was the quiet snip of two pairs of scissors going about their business. Finally the man at the whim of Wullie's hand asked him if he'd read the gossip about some film star of whom Barney had never even heard, and slowly the shop returned to normal. The quiet hum of pointless chatter, interspersed with electric razors and the gentle flop of hair to the floor.

Then, with the elegant timing of a Victorian watch, the door to the shop swung open. Ten pairs of eyes looked expectantly. The possibility that here might be someone to assuage their guilt. It was a man in his late twenties, unaware of the cauldron into which he had just walked. Quietly closed the door, took his place at the end of the queue.

Barney laid down the paper, stood up, brushed down the seat, lifted the cape, looked the man in the eye. He didn't immediately recognise him. A good sign.

'All right then, my good man. All these others are waiting, so you're next in line.'

Unaware of the expectations weighted upon his shoulders, the man did not even hesitate.

'That's OK, mate, I'm just going to wait for Wullie.'

Barney stood, cape in hand, a bullfighter without a bull. He stayed calm. Bit his tongue, although the sight of Wullie staring at him out of the corner of his eye did nought but increase the desire to explode. He placed the cape back over the chair, deliberately lifted the paper, and once again sat down. Just before his backside hit the seat, he paused, looking once more at the customer.

'Are you sure now, my friend, there's a long queue?'

The man nodded. 'Aye, I'm all right, mate, thanks. There's no rush.'

'Very well.'

Barney slumped into the seat, seething quietly within. He hated all these bloody customers. Who did they think they were anyway? Complete bastards the lot of them. But no matter how much he hated them, it did not tie the shoelaces of how much he hated Wullie and Chris. Those smug bastards. He would have his revenge.

He didn't know how, but somehow he would. He was sure of it. He looked along the shop at Wullie, and then past him out of the window. It was a dark day, the rain falling in a steady drizzle, as it had done all afternoon. Doleful figures passed by, hunched against the wind and rain, unaware of the injustices within the shop past which they scuttled. But some day they would find out. Some day, everyone would know about what went on in the shop. Some day soon.

*

Robert Holdall slumped into his seat with the enthusiasm of one settling into the electric chair. Another press conference. The Chief Superintendent was forcing them on him almost daily. He would have liked to have argued that they were stopping him from doing his job, but he had so little to go on that the only thing that they were getting in the way of was his afternoon tea and sandwich.

He was accompanied as usual by the burly press officer, a woman of quite considerable stature, who exercised an amount of control over the press that no man had ever managed. And as Holdall readied himself to read his prepared statement, she silenced the packed room with a couple of dramatic waves of her right arm. This was a woman who ate large mechanical farm implements for breakfast.

Holdall stared gloomily at the words written down in front of him. God it was short. Of course it was. They had nothing to say to these people. What could he tell them? That they were thinking of arresting everyone in Glasgow who didn't own a car? Of course not. And so he had written down three sentences of total vacuity. A nothing statement, forced on him by a bloody-minded boss. He would liked to have seen him sit there and read out this garbage.

He finished staring at it, looked up at the collected press. Aw shite, he thought, there are even more than usual. Maybe a few up from England. He made the decision quickly and without any prior consideration. To Hell with it, he thought, give them something a bit more solid than this piece of vacuous mince.

He cleared his throat and, pretending to read from the paper in front of him, began in his low, serious press-voice.

'Ladies and gentlemen. I shall be necessarily brief today, which I am sure you will understand when you hear what I have to say.' He paused briefly. Shit. What was he going to say exactly? Cleared his throat again, took a drink from the glass of water at his right hand, then jumped into the blazing inferno, eyes open. 'Late last night, officers from this station came into possession of a valuable piece of evidence, the exact nature of which I am not yet at liberty to divulge. It has given us a very definite direction of inquiry which we are now pursuing with all possible vigour.' Not bad, he thought. Optimistic, but vague. Don't blow it. 'Given the nature of this new information, we are hopeful of a major development in this investigation, some time in the next forty-eight to seventy-two hours.' Christ, what are you saying? You idiot. Shut up, and don't say any more. 'I am afraid that I am unable to disclose any more information at this time, but you can be assured that when these anticipated further developments have taken place, you will be notified in the usual manner.'

He closed his mouth, blinked, looked up. A brief second and the room had erupted in a cacophony of noise. He sat looking like a stuffed fish, while Sgt Mahoney did her best to calm the crowd. Eventually, after some time and with much difficulty, the room had returned to rest, and the sergeant pointed a yellowed finger to a man with his arm raised, near the front of the crowd.

'Bill Glasson, Evening Post,' he said, a look of surprise upon his face. It was the first time he'd been called at a press conference in fourteen years, and he had no idea what question to ask. He knew they were not going to get anything more out of the guy, but they were obliged to shout at him. It was their job. When the tumult erupted he had been asking what the inspector had had for breakfast that morning, just so he could add to the clamour. A new question was needed, however.

'So,' he said, thinking frantically, 'you say you have some idea who the killer is. Do you know exactly who the killer is?'

Holdall shook his head. What a crap question, he thought. He could have sworn that, before, this bloke had been asking him something about breakfast.

'I'm sorry, but I'm not at liberty to discuss any information other than that which I have just given to you.'

When it became obvious that he wasn't going to say any more on the matter, the clamour immediately started up again, and after a minute or two, was quietened down. Enough of this, thought Holdall. What's the point? If I go on with this, I'll just end up saying something even more stupid than I already have done.

He muttered quietly to the sergeant that he would only take one more question and, when she announced this to the crowd, there was an even more extravagant commotion and frantic waving of hands. She selected the most innocent looking one, a young blonde haired woman sitting in the centre of the room.

'Greta Burridge, the Mail.' Greta Burridge swallowed. Third day on the job. She had her question to ask, however. 'So, Chief Inspector Holdall, does this mean that the rumours that you intend to arrest everyone in Glasgow who doesn't own a car are unfounded?'

*

Holdall sat at his desk, his head firmly buried in his hands. He still hadn't come to terms with what an idiot he'd been. Looked at his watch. Another forty minutes, and then he would have a meeting with the Chief Superintendent. He was going to have to explain himself. As always, he couldn't help thinking of the time he'd been dragged to the Headmaster's office when he was fourteen, after exploding a small bomb in the music teacher's sandwich box.

And he hadn't had an explanation for that either.

Alas, Poor Nietzsche, I Knew Him, Bill

The rain streamed against the windows. The old wooden frames rattled in the wind, the curtains blew in the chill draught which forced its way into the room. Ghosts and shadows. Outside, the night was cold and bleak and dark, to match Barney's mood as he sat at the dinner table. He pushed the food around his plate, every so often stabbing randomly at a pea or a piece of meat pie, imagining that it was Wullie or Chris. All the while Agnes looked over his shoulder at the television, engrossed in a particularly awful Australian soap, taped from earlier in the afternoon. The food grew cold on their plates, as Dr. Morrison told Nurse Bartlett that she would never be able to have children, as a result of the barbecue incident at Tom and Diane's engagement party, and Barney gave forth on what he intended to do to take his revenge upon his colleagues.

'I'm going to get they bastards if it's the last thing I do. I mean it.'

'Yes, dear.' Agnes's mind was on other things.

'I mean, who the hell do they think they are, eh?' He stabbed a finger at her. 'I'll tell you. Nobody, that's who they are. They're nobody. And I'm bloody well going to get them.'

'Yes, dear.'

There was a mad glint in Barney's eye. The possibilities were endless, the bounds for doing evil and taking his revenge unfettered, limited only by his imagination; a very tight limit, as it happened.

He had been thinking it over since the afternoon's humiliation, and the more he dwelt upon it, the more he liked the idea of murder.

Murder! Why not? They deserved it. You should never humiliate your colleagues in front of the customers. Wasn't that one of the first things they taught you in Barber School? But these young ones today. They never even bothered with any sort of hairdressing education. Five years of high school learning sociology and taking drugs, and they thought they knew everything. They lifted a pair of scissors and started cutting hair as if they were preparing a bowl of breakfast cereal. It just wasn't that simple. It was a skill which needed to be nurtured and cultivated. Like brain surgery, or astrophysics.

The trouble was that they were all bastards, every one of them. Not just Wullie and Chris, but every other cretin who'd ever lifted a pair of scissors in anger. But not for much longer. It was payback time.

'What d'you think? Stabbing? Shooting? Poison even?'

'Yes, dear,' she said, absent-mindedly nodding.

He brightened up. Poison. Brilliant. Agnes was good for bouncing ideas off sometimes. 'Aye, you're right. Poison's the thing. I don't know anything about it, but I'm sure I can find out. I'm sure I can. What d'you think?'

'Yes, dear.'

'Aye, it shouldn't be too difficult.' Murderous plans raced through his mind, a manic smile slowly wandered across his lips. 'One of they slow acting ones, so I can stick it in their coffee during the day, and they won't die until much later.' He rubbed his hands together. 'Brilliant idea. Bloody brilliant.'

There was some illuminated corner of his mind telling him that he wasn't being serious. Not murder. Surely not murder. But it was good to think about it for a while. Thinking about it wasn't the same as doing it.

'Yes, dear,' said Agnes. Was Doreen really a lesbian or was she just pretending she loved Epiphany so she could get close to Dr.

Morrison without Blaize becoming suspicious?

Without any further stabs of conscience, Barney tucked into his pie, chips and peas, all the time plotting his wild revenge. It was sad that it had to come to this, he thought, but they had brought it upon themselves. Particularly that bastard Wullie.

Another thought occurred. Perhaps he could poison some of the customers as well. They were asking for it, most of them. He got carried away for a second on a rollercoaster of genocide. Calmed down. He was Barney Thomson, barber, not Barney Pot, deranged dictator. Still, the thought was there, if it ever became necessary. A lot of them deserved it, that was for sure.

His mind began to wander to a grand vision where he was in the shop with two other barbers, neither of whom anyone would go to, while there sat a great queue of people all waiting for him. He would take three quarters of an hour over every haircut, and annoy as many of them as possible. Heaven.

He was reluctantly hauled from his dreams by the telephone. He stopped, a forkful of chips poised on the cusp of his mouth, and looked at Agnes. Her eyes remained glued to the television, oblivious to the clatter of the phone.

'You going to get that, Hen?'

She scowled. 'Can't. Faith and Puberty are about to have it out with Bliss.'

Executing his trademark eye rolling and head shaking routine, he tossed the fork onto the plate and stood up to get the phone, hoping it would be a wrong number.

'What?'

'Hello Barney, it's me.'

He breathed a sigh of relief. It was one of the few people from whom he didn't mind receiving a call, his drinking and dominoes partner, Bill Taylor. This would be a call to arms.

'Oh, hello Bill, how you doing?'

'Not so bad, not so bad. And you?'

'Oh, can't complain, can't complain.'

They discussed trivialities for a few minutes, such as Bill's brother Eric having told his girlfriend Yvonne that he loved Fiona. Finally, however, Bill got to the main item on the agenda.

'Fancy going out for a few pints the night?' he said.

'Oh, I don't know, mate. I need to see my mother. She'd be a bit upset if I didn't go. You know what they're like, eh?'

'Well, how about a couple of pints before you go. I'll meet you down the boozer about half seven, eh?'

'Aye, that shouldn't be too bad. Can't stay too long though.'

'Aye, aye.'

Barney said his goodbyes and trudged back into the sitting room. He tried to ignore the television while he polished off his dinner, then he slumped into the armchair and fell asleep. He dreamt of poison and of long prison sentences and of chain gangs and electric chairs, and then he awoke with a start at just about the time he needed to.

As he left the house, the aftermath of dinner remained where it had been for over an hour, while Chastity and Hope attempted to bundle Mercury into the boot of a car, in what he assumed to be an entirely different soap from the one he'd suffered earlier.

'I'm going to the boozer, then Mum's. All right?'

'Yes, dear.'

'I'll be back about ten.'

'Yes, dear'

He waited for some more reaction, waited in vain, then walked out, slamming the door as he went.

*

'Aye, well that's all very well,' said Bill Taylor, brandishing his pint, 'but who is to categorise depth? Eh? Everyone is capable of depth. Nietzsche said, "Some men consider women to be deep. This is untrue. Women are not even shallow." Well, to me that's a load of mince. Now, I'm no feminist or nothing, but I've got to say, even women can say stuff that's deep too. Most of what they come out with is pants, but it doesn't mean they can't say something intelligent every now and again.'

Barney nodded in agreement. 'I never realised that you were a student of Nietzsche?'

Bill grunted, burying his hand in a bowl of peanuts. 'I wouldn't go that far. Obviously I've studied all the great philosophers, but I'm definitely not a fan of Nietzsche.'

'Me neither. Typical bloody German. Spent his life writing about some kind of master race, then he went off his napper, reverted to childhood, and spent the last ten years of his life in an asylum, playing with Lego and Scalextric, pretending to be a cowboy. To be perfectly honest, they nineteenth century German philosophers get on my tits.'

Barney wondered about himself. Why was it that when he sat over a pint and a game of dominoes in the pub, he could talk pish with the best of them, but when the chips were down, and he really needed to, there was nothing there? Like the guy who could hole a putt from any part of the green, until someone offered him a fiver to do it.

'My friend,' Bill said, his mouth full of peanuts, 'you don't need to tell me about German philosophy. I'm as aware as anybody else of its failings. And let's face it, when it comes down to it, all German philosophy amounts to is "if in doubt, invade it." Aye, that's it in a nutshell, so it is.'

'Well, well, Bill, I never thought I'd hear you talk like that. Certainly Germany was guilty of horrendous imperialism during the first half of the twentieth century, but that's not necessarily indicative of the past two hundred years.'

Barney executed a swift manoeuvre with a double four and lifted his pint.

'Is it not? That's a load of shite. You can't just dismiss fifty years as not indicative. Especially when it is,' said Bill.

Barney paused to take another sip of beer, studying the state of their game of dominoes. It was turning into a bloody tussle, good natured but life-threatening. He was about to make his next move and expand his thoughts on German imperialism, when he paused briefly to listen to what two young women were saying as they walked past their table.

'So I says to her, that's not right, Senga. I'm like that, Neptune's the planet that's the furthest from the sun at the moment. All right, Pluto's further away most of the time, but Neptune's got a pure circular orbit 'n that, while Pluto's got an elliptical one, so that for some years at a time, Pluto's orbit takes it nearer to the sun than Neptune, 'n that. I'm like that...'

The voice was lost in the noise of the bar as they moved away. Barney and Bill looked at each other with eyebrows raised.

'Unusual to find,' said Barney, 'a woman with so much as an elementary grasp of astronomy.'

Bill raised his finger, waving it from side to side. 'As a matter of fact, I was discussing the other day with this girl in my work called Loella, the exact...'

'You have a girl in your work called Loella?' asked Barney.

'Aye, aye I do. And as I was saying, Loella and I were talking about anti-particles. I was under the impression that a photon had a separate anti-particle, but she says that two gamma rays can combine to produce a particle-anti-particle pair, and thus the photon is its own anti-particle.'

'So, what you're saying is that the anti-particle of an electron is a positron, which has the same mass as the electron, but is positively charged?'

Bill thought about this, slipping a two/three neatly into the game. 'Aye, aye, I believe so.'

'And a woman called Loella told you this?'

'She did.'

The two men jointly shook their heads at the astonishing sagacity displayed by the occasional woman, then returned with greater concentration to the game. They both tried to remember what they had been talking about before the interruption, but the subject of German imperialism had escaped them and Bill was forced to bring up more mundane matters.

'So, how's that shop of yours doing, eh, Barney?' he said, surveying the intricate scene before him, and wondering if he was going to be able to get rid of his double six before it was too late.

Barney shook his head, rolled his eyes. 'You don't want to know my friend, you do not want to know.'

'Is there any trouble?' asked Bill, concern in the voice, although this was principally because he'd found himself looking at a mass of twos, threes and fours on the table, and sixes and fives in his hand.

'Ach, it's they two bastards, Wullie and Chris,' said Barney. 'I don't know who they think they are. Keep taking all my customers. It's getting to be a right blinking joke.'

Bill nodded. In the past he had been on the receiving end of one of Barney's one hour fifteen minute *Towering Inferno* haircuts, and in the end had been forced to move from the area to avoid subjecting himself to the fickle fate of his friend's scissors.

'They're good barbers, Barney.'

Barney stopped what he was doing, the words cutting to his core. Dropped his dominoes, placed his hands decisively on the table. Fire glinted in his eye. A green glint.

'And I'm not, is that what you're saying, Bill? Eh?'

Bill quickly raised his hands in a placatory gesture. 'No, no, Barney, I didn't mean it that way, you know I didn't.'

'Like hell you didn't. Et tu, Bluto?' said Barney, getting within inches of quoting Shakespeare.

'Look, mate, calm down, I didn't mean anything. Now pick up your dominoes and get on with the game.'

With a grunt, a scowl and a noisy suck of his teeth, Barney slowly lifted his weapons of war and, unhappy that Bill had seen what he held in his hands, resumed combat.

The game continued for another couple of minutes before Bill felt confident enough to reintroduce the subject. The quiet chatter of the pub continued around them, broken only by the occasional ejaculation of outrage.

'So what's the problem with the two of them, Barney?' he asked gingerly.

Barney grumbled. 'Ach, I don't know, Bill. They're just making my life a misery. They're two smug bastards the pair of them. Getting on my tits, so they are.'

Barney was distracted, made a bad move. He didn't notice, but Bill did. Bill The Cat. Suddenly, given the opening, he began to play dynamite dominoes, a man at the pinnacle of his form, making great sweeping moves of brio and verve, which Barney wrongly attributed to him having had a glimpse of his hand.

'So what are you going to do about it?' said Bill, after administering the *coup de grâce*.

Barney, vanquished in the game, laid down his weapons and placed his hands on the table. Looked Bill square in the eye. They had been friends a long time, been through a lot. The Vietnam war, the Falklands conflict, the miners' strike. Not that they'd been to any of them, but they'd watched a lot of them on television together. And so, Barney felt able to confide the worst excesses of his imagination in Bill.

He leant forward conspiratorially across the table. This was it, a moment to test the bond to its fullest.

'How long have we been friends, Bill?' he asked, voice hushed.

Bill shrugged. 'Oh, I don't know. A long time, Barney.' His too was the voice of a conspirator, although he was unaware of why he was whispering.

Barney inched ever closer towards him, his chin ever nearer the table.

'Barney?' asked Bill, before he could say anything else.

'What?'

'You're not going to kiss me, are you?'

Barney raised his eyes, annoyed. Didn't want to be distracted at a time like this. 'Don't be a bloody mug, you eejit. Now listen up.' He paused, hesitating momentarily before the pounce. 'Tell me Bill, do you know anything about poison?'

'Poison? You mean like for rats, that kind of thing?'

'Aye,' said Barney, thinking that rats were exactly what it was for.

'Oh, I don't know...' said Bill. Then, as his rapier mind began to kick in and he saw the direction in which Barney was heading, he sat up straight. He looked into the eyes of his friend. 'You don't mean...?'

'Aye.'

'You've got rats in the shop!'

Barney tutted loudly, went through the headshaking routine, then slightly lifted his jaw from two inches above the table.

'No, no! It's not rats I want to poison.' He took a suspicious look around about him to see if anyone was listening. 'Well, it is rats, but the human kind.'

This took a minute or two to hit Bill, and when it did it was a thumping great smack in the teeth. As the realisation struck, there came a great crash of thunder outside and the windows of the pub shook with the rain and the wind. He stood up quickly, pushing the table away from him, almost sending the drinks to a watery and crashing grave.

This momentarily dramatic display attracted the attention of the rest of the bar, who had, up until then, been sedately watching snooker on the TV. Barney panicked, fearing his plan would be discovered before he had even begun its formulation.

'Sit down, Bill, sit down for God's sake.'

Bill looked down at him, horror etched upon his face for a few seconds, then slowly lowered himself back into the seat. The two men stared at each other, trying to determine exactly what the other was thinking, trying to decide how they could continue the discussion. Bill was clearly unimpressed with Barney's idea. Barney, absurdly, wondered if he could talk him into it.

'Look,' said Barney eventually, attempting to sound hard and business-like, although Bill knew he was soft, soft as a pillow, 'I want to know if you can help me or not.'

The look of horror on Bill's face increased tenfold. 'Commit murder? Is that it? Murder?'

Barney looked anxiously around to see how many people had noticed Bill's raised voice. Fortunately, the rest of the bar had returned to more mundane interests.

'Look, keep your voice down.'

Bill leant forward, once again regaining the mask of the grand conspirator. 'You can't seriously be thinking of killing Chris and Wullie? They're good lads. For Christ's sake man, I know Wullie's father.'

Barney shook his head. He had chosen the wrong man.

'Huh! Good lads my arse. They'll get what's coming to them.'

'But why?'

Barney thought about this for a second or two. It was a reasonable question, demanding a good answer. He fixed his gaze on Bill. 'Because they're asking for it.'

'You're not making any sense, Barney, and whatever you're planning, I don't want any part of it, d'you hear me? Keep me out of it.'

He rose from the table again and started to put on his coat. Barney felt chastened, looked up anxiously.

'Very well, Bill. I'm sorry you feel that way,' was all he said.

Bill pulled on his cap, nodding shortly to Barney as he made to go.

'We never had this conversation, eh, Bill?' said Barney.

Bill looked him hard in the eye. Was there an implied threat in the voice? If he didn't help him, could it be that he'd be included in Barney's murderous plans? Another potential victim? Deep down, however, he could not believe that Barney was serious. Still waited for him to say that it was all a joke.

'I don't know about that, Barney, I really don't know,' he said. Their eyes battled with each other – two weak men – and then Bill turned and walked from the pub, out into the squalid storm of the night.

The New Merlot

Holdall sat looking out of the window. Evening rain spattered against the glass. Street lights illuminated the rain in shades of grey and orange. There was a tangible silence in the room. The silence of a courtroom awaiting a verdict; the silence of a crowd awaiting a putt across the eighteenth green.

The Chief Superintendent read the latest report on the serial killer investigation, fumbling noiselessly with a pipe. The only light in the room was from the small lamp on the desk, shining down onto the paper which the old man was reading. It cast strange shadows around the room; the old face looked sinister under its curious glare.

Chief Superintendent McMenemy had been on the force for longer than anyone knew, and his presence in the station went beyond domination. 'M' they called him, and no one was quite sure whether it was a joke. There was no Moneypenny, no green baize on the door, but he was a considerable figure. A grumpy old man, much concerned with great matters of state. And perhaps his senior officers liked the implication; if he was M, then they must be James Bond – although in fact, most of them were 003s, the men who mess up and die in the pre-credit sequence of the movie.

He put the pipe to his mouth and sucked on it a couple of times while attacking it with a match, eventually managing to get it going. Tossed the box of matches casually onto the table, looked at Holdall.

There was nothing to be read in those dark eyes – Holdall shifted uncomfortably in his seat. Long, unnerving silences, another of his trademarks. He continued to suck quietly on his pipe, finally pointed it at Holdall.

'Well, Robert, what have you got to say for yourself?'

Holdall tried to concentrate on the question. It was a good one. What did he have to say for himself exactly? He couldn't say the truth – that he'd felt like a bloody idiot giving the press conference and had made something up so that he wouldn't look stupid. Apart from anything else, it was destined to make him look even more stupid when he couldn't produce the promised serial killer, and he had to explain that one to the press.

He looked into the massive black holes of M's eyes, wondering what to say. M grunted and picked up the report so that he could toss it back onto the desk.

'You've got the whole country thinking we're just about to collar someone, when as far as I can see we're no nearer making an arrest than we were at the start. What in God's name were you thinking, man?'

Holdall stared at the floor, trying to pull himself together. Be assertive, for God's sake. The one thing the old man hated was a bumbling idiot. Straightened his shoulders, looked him in the eye. Tried to banish the picture of Mrs Holdall brandishing a frying pan, which had inexplicably just come into his head.

'I thought maybe we should try and sound positive for once. We've spent two months coming across as losers, sir. It's about time people started thinking that we've got some balls about us. If we haven't come up with anything in the next few days, we'll have to say that our enquiries in this respect have come to a dead end. But at least we'll look as if we've got some spunk, and that we're putting something into this investigation. Certainly the shit'll be on our shoes the next time someone is murdered, but until then we have to look as if we're getting somewhere.

'We know nothing about this killer, sir. Why he's doing it, what motivates him… It could be that he won't kill again. Who knows? Or it could be that we come up with a lead in the next few days. We need to show some assertiveness. Try to create some momentum.'

He looked into the impassive face, the eyes which hadn't moved from Holdall while he'd talked, the expression of stone. Now M turned his seat round so that it faced the window, and he stared at the night sky, the dull orange reflection in the low clouds. His pipe had gone out and he once more began to fumble with the matches.

Holdall waited for the reaction. The fact that he hadn't immediately exploded was a good sign. He'd half expected to be out of a job already.

Eventually, after several minutes of working the pipe, followed by ruminative smoking, M turned back to Holdall, holding him in his icy stare. He considered his words carefully; when he spoke, he spoke slowly.

'Well, I'm not sure about this, Robert, and I'd rather you'd talked to me about it first. But on reflection, perhaps it wasn't too bad a strategy. Of course, if pieces of dismembered body start turning up in the post tomorrow morning, like confetti at a wedding, then we're in trouble.' He stopped, pointed the pipe. 'You're in trouble.'

He swivelled the chair back so that he was looking out of the window again, showing Holdall his imperious profile. M toyed with his pipe, tapping it on the desk.

'It might be a good idea if you came up with something solid in the next two days, Robert.'

'Yes, sir.'

He added nothing and Holdall shifted uncomfortably in his seat wondering if he'd been dismissed. Never rise until you've been told, however, he said to himself.

Finally, M turned, a look of surprise on his face that Holdall was still there.

'That will be all, Chief Inspector.'

*

Mrs Cemolina Thomson was eighty-five, and lived alone in a twelfth floor flat in Springburn. Smoked eighty cigarettes a day, an obscure brand she'd discovered during the war, containing more tar than the runways at Heathrow; spent her days watching quiz shows on television. Donald Thomson had died when Barney was five years old, and ever since she'd attempted to rule the lives of her children. Her eldest son had long since escaped her clutches, leaving Barney to face the brunt of her domineering personality. Her attitudes had not so much progressed with the century through which she had lived, as regressed to some time between the Dark Ages and the creation of the universe. She was a white, Protestant grandmother with a bad word for everybody.

Barney let himself into the flat, and was immediately struck by a smell so rancid it turned his stomach. His first grotesque thought – perhaps his mother had lain dead in the flat for some days, the smell her decomposing body. He steeled himself for the stumble across her rotting flesh, but knew that that wouldn't be it. He had talked to her the night before. Even his mother's crabbed body would not decompose so quickly – certainly not in the damp chill of Scotland in early March.

The first rooms off the hall were bedrooms, and he looked into those to see if she was there. However, as he neared the kitchen, he realised that was where the smell most definitely emanated from. Quickened his pace, burst through the door.

Cemolina stood stirring a huge pot of steaming red liquid, wearing an apron; curlers in her hair. He wondered whether the stench was coming from the pot or from the horrendous stuff women stick in their head when they do a home perm. Decided it was too bad even for that. Must be the pot.

'What the hell are you doing, Mum? That stuff's minging!'

She turned her head. Beads of sweat peppered her face at the effort she was making, her face flushed.

'Hello, Barnabas, how are you? Nearly finished,' she said, turning back to her strange brew.

Visibly wincing, as he always did at the mention of his name, he walked over beside her and looked down into the pot. It was a deep red, thin liquid, bubbling slightly. Up close the stench was almost overwhelming, but Barney did not withdraw.

'What on earth are you making, Mum, for God's sake?'

'What does it look like?' she barked, unhappy at his tone.

'I honestly haven't the faintest idea. What in God's name is it?'

She tutted loudly, bustling some more. 'It's wine, for God's sake, surely you can see that?'

He stared, new understanding, even less comprehension. Maybe that explained it, but he knew nothing about viniculture.

'Is this how you make wine?' he said.

She stopped stirring, looked him hard in the eye, lips pursed, hands drawn to her hips. Nostrils flared. He knew the look, having suffered it for over forty years, and prepared to make his retreat.

'Well, I don't know about anybody else, but it's how I make wine. Now away and sit down, and I'll be with you in a few minutes.'

He nodded meekly, made his exit and closed the door behind him. Glad to escape the kitchen. Went into the sitting room and opened up the windows letting the cold, damp air into the house, clean and refreshing. Stood there for a couple of minutes breathing it in, trying to purge the stench of the kitchen, then withdrew into the room and sat down. Found the snooker on BBC2 and settled back on the settee.

He didn't have long to wait before his mother walked into the room, red-stained apron still wrapped around her, a bustle in her step. Tutted loudly when she saw the open windows, closed them noisily, then sat down to light herself a cigarette. Sucked it deeply, two long draws, then with a shock realised that there was snooker on television.

'For Christ's sake, what are you watching this shite for? *Whose Pants!* is on the other channel,' she said, grabbing the remote and changing it over.

Barney rolled his eyes, looked at his mother and thought that he might as well not be there. She sat engrossed in the television, while a variety of celebrity undergarments were brought on and the contestants attempted to identify them from the stains. She had finished her second cigarette by the time the adverts arrived. Lowering the volume, she turned to look at her boy.

'Why are you making wine, Mum?'

She shrugged. *Not all questions in life have answers*, she thought. 'I didn't have enough sugar to make marmalade,' she said, and pulled hard on her newly lit cigarette. 'So, how are you? You're looking a wee bitty fed up?'

He sat back, staring at the ceiling. Could he talk to his mother? Probably not. He'd never been able to before, so why should he suddenly be able to start now? Mothers aren't for talking to; they're for obeying and running after. At least, that's what his mother was for. Iron hand in iron glove.

'Ach, I'm just a bit cheesed off at work and all that, you know. It's nothing.'

She drew heavily on the cigarette. 'Oh aye, what's the problem?'

'Just they two that I work with, they're really getting to me. Keep taking all my customers, so they do. Pain in the arse, to be quite frank.'

Now Cemolina shook her head. Lips pursed, eyes narrowed. Saw conspiracy. Believed Elvis was abducted by aliens on the instructions of the FBI. 'It doesn't surprise me. Yon Chris Porter. He's a Fenian, isn't he? Can't trust a bloody Tim.'

Barney shook his head. 'No, mum, the other one's just as bad.'

She looked surprised. 'Wullie Henderson? He's a fine lad. Goes to watch the Rangers every week, doesn't he?'

Barney nodded. Felt like he was in the lion's den. Even his mother put great store by football. 'Maybe he does, Mum, but that's not the point.'

'Oh, aye. What is the point, then?'

'I don't know. They take all my customers. Make me look bloody stupid in front of everyone. They're all laughing at me.' He stopped when he realised that he sounded like a stroppy child with a major humph, lip petted, face scowling. Cemolina hadn't noticed. Either that, or she was used to seeing him like this.

'So, what are you going to do about it then?'

Barney stared at the floor, wondering what to say. Felt he had to obey the golden rule of not confessing murderous intent to your mother – notwithstanding the *Norman Bates Exception*, when you and your mother are the same person – and his villainous ardour had been partly quashed by Bill's horrified reaction to his nefarious scheme. There was little point in talking to her about it. And who was he fooling anyway? He wasn't about to kill anyone. He was Barney Thomson, sad pathetic barber from Partick. No killer he.

He shrugged his shoulders, mumbling something about there being nothing that he could do. Sounded like a wee boy.

'Why don't you kill them?' she said, drawing forcefully on her cigarette, as far down as she could go.

He stared at her, disbelief rampaging unchecked across his face. 'What did you say?'

'Kill them. Blow their heads off, if they're that much trouble to you. Your old dad used to say, "if someone's getting on your tits, kill the bastard, and they won't get on your tits any more".'

Barney looked at her. Staring at a new woman, someone he'd never seen before. His mother. His own mother was advising him to kill Wullie and Chris. Stern counsel. She couldn't be serious, could she? Was that the kind of thing his father used to say? He remembered him as kind, gentle; distant memories; soft focused, warm sunny summer afternoons.

'D'you mean that?'

She shrugged, lit another cigarette. 'Well, I don't know if they were his exact words, it's been about forty year after all, but it was something like that I'm sure.'

'No, not that. D'you really think that I should kill them? Really?'

'Of course I do. If they're upsetting you that much, do away with them. You've been in yon shop a lot longer than they two heid-the-ba's. You shouldn't let them push you about. Blow their heads off.'

A huge grin began to spread across Barney's face. He had found a conspirator. A confidante in the most unlikely of places.

'I can't believe you're serious.'

'Why not? They're bastards, aren't they? You says so yourself. Especially yon Fenian, Porter.'

'Wullie's worse.'

She looked sad, downcast. 'I don't know. A good Protestant lad gone wrong.'

Barney gazed upon his mother with wonder. That her mind was now undoubtedly caught in a tangled web of senility was completely lost upon him, so delighted was he to find an enthusiast. He was about to broach the subject of poison, when she realised that the adverts had long since finished. She held up her hand and returned her gaze to the television.

The presenter, an annoying curly-haired man with thick Yorkshire accent, was holding up a gigantic pair of shorts, festooned with numerous revolting stains. A caption at the bottom of the screen gave a choice of four celebrities. The giggling girl, all lipstick and false breasts, partnered by Lionel Blair, pressed the buzzer, giggling some more. 'Pavarotti!' she ejaculated, and with a 'Good guess luv, but not correct this time. A big hand for that try though, ladies and gentlemen', from the presenter, the audience erupted.

And so the show continued for another ten minutes, before with a 'thanks for watching, ladies and gentlemen, please tune in next week when once more it will be time to Name That Stain!', it was over. Cemolina lowered the volume again, turned back to Barney, the look of the easily satisfied on her face.

'So, you're going to blow their heads off?' she said, her look giving a stamp of approval.

Barney stroked his chin in murderous contemplation. 'I was, eh, thinking of poison. D'you know anything about it?'

Cemolina grabbed the arms of the chair, lifting herself up an inch or two. She was a slight woman, but still she presented an imposing figure, especially to the weak son.

'Poison!' she shrieked. 'Poison, did I hear you say?'

Barney flummoxed about in his seat for a second, a landed fish. Recovered his composure enough to speak, although not enough to stop himself looking like a flapping haddock.

'What's wrong with poison?'

Her head shook like a tent in the wind. 'It's womany for a start. You'd have to be a big jessie to want to poison somebody. Did I bring you up as a girl? Well, did I?'

'No, Mum,' he said.

'No, you're damned right I didn't. Act like a man, for pity's sake. You've got to give it laldie, Barney, none of this poison keich. Blow their heads off. Carpet the floor with their brains. Or get a hammer and smash their heads to smithereens.'

'Mum!' There was a growing look of incredulity on his face, horror in his voice. He had long known that everyone had their dark half, but he'd never really thought that everyone included his own mother.

Cemolina looked aghast. 'You want them dead, don't you? You says so yourself, so what are you blethering about?'

'Aye, aye, I do, but something simple. I don't like mess.'

She screwed up her face, waved a desultory hand. 'Well, I didn't think you'd be that much of a big poof. I just thought that if you were going to do it, you might as well have some fun while you're about it.'

Barney looked at his mother with some distaste. Maybe she was mad. But then, it had been him who'd been thinking about killing them in the first place. She had merely added some enthusiasm to the project.

'Ach, I don't know, Mother. I'll have to think about it. I certainly don't think that I could beat anybody's head to a pulp.'

She scowled at him and turned her attention back to the television to see which quiz show would be on next.

'I cannot believe you're being such a big jessie. Your father would've been black affronted, so he would,' she said, turning the volume back up. 'Black affronted.'

'Yes, Mum,' said Barney.

He couldn't do it. Not anything violent. He knew he couldn't. Perhaps, however, he could get someone else to do it for him. A hired hand. There was a thought. And as the opening strains of *Give Us A Disease* started up, he sank further into the soft folds of the settee and lost himself in barbaric contemplations.

A Pair Of Breasts

Margaret MacDonald glanced up at the television, which had been droning away in the background all morning. They were running over the previous night's football results. She raised her eyebrows. Rangers had lost two-nil at Motherwell. Typical. That was why Reginald had been in such a foul mood when he'd come in last night. And still this morning. Stomping around like a toddler who'd been woken up too early, and then charging out the door without saying a word to her. God, men were so pathetic.

Her eyes remained on the television, but she wasn't watching. She was thinking about Louise, as she had been for the past three days. It wasn't like her to just vanish. Nearly twenty now, and there had been plenty of times in the past when she'd gone off for the night without letting them know where she was. But three days.

Felt that nervous grip on her stomach, the tightening of the muscles, which she'd been experiencing more and more often. Gulped down some tea, tried to put it out of her mind. It wasn't as if she didn't have plenty of other things to think about.

The doorbell rang. She jumped. Looked round in shock, into the hall, could just make out the dark grey of a uniform through the frosted glass of the front door. Swallowed hard to fight back the first tears of foreboding. It was the police. The police with news about Louise.

The doorbell rang again. Feeling the great weight resting upon her shoulders, she rose slowly from the table, inching her way towards the door. Whatever she was going to find out wouldn't be true until she had opened that door and had been informed. Her hand hovered over the key; she wished she could suspend time; wished she could stand there forever, and never have to learn what she was about to be told.

She turned the key, slowly swinging the door open, the first tears already beginning to roll down her cheeks.

'You all right there, hen, you're looking a bit upset?'

She started to smile, and then a laugh came bursting from her mouth. A big, booming, guttural laugh which she had never heard herself make before. She put her hand out, touched the arm of the postman.

'I'm sorry, Davey, it's nothing. I thought you were going to be someone else, that's all.'

'Christ, who were you expecting? The Pope?'

She laughed again, and for the first time looked past him. It was a dark and murky morning, the rain falling in a relentless drizzle. The winds of the previous day had abated, but still it was horrible, as it had been for weeks.

'God, it's a foul morning to be out, Davey.'

The postman smiled. 'I'm not in it for the weather, hen.' He rummaged inside his bag and pulled out a small parcel. 'There's this and a few letters. I'd better be going.'

She took the post from him, looking through it to see if there was one with Louise's handwriting. Looked up to see Davey MacLean already walking down the road, hunched against the rain, the hood of his jacket drawn back over his head.

'Thanks, Davey. I'll see you later.' He responded with a cool hand lifted into the gloom and then, the Steven Seagal of his trade, went about his business with a certain violent panache.

She closed the door, retreated into the kitchen, shivering at the cold weather. Dropped the letters onto the table – nothing from Louise, fought the clawing disappointment – and studied the parcel.

She wasn't expecting anything, didn't recognise the handwriting. Postmarked Ayr. Ayr? Who did she know in Ayr?

Then suddenly it was there. A horrible sense of foreboding. A cold hand touching her neck, making the hairs rise; the chill grip on her heart. She let the package fall from her fingers and land on the table. Her stomach tightened, she began to feel sick. Walked slowly over to the drawer beside the sink and lifted out a pair of scissors. She started back to the table, but suddenly the vomit rose in her throat, and she was bent over the sink, retching violently, as the tears began to stream down her face.

The Accidental Barber Surgeon

It came sooner than Holdall had feared. Every morning he'd sit in his office waiting for the phone to ring, the angry herald of more news of stray body parts popping through someone's letter box. Every time the phone rang he'd assume the worst, and given what he'd told the press the evening before, he was even more fearful this particular morning.

However, fate did not even bother to tease him. There came no endless stream of calls concerning more mundane matters, leading to the dramatic one confirming his worst fears. The dreaded call arrived first, and within three minutes of him sitting at his desk.

A woman in Newton Mearns, a woman with a missing daughter, had received what appeared to be two breasts, neatly packed into a small wooden box, that morning. So she had turned up on the doorstep of her local police station, hysterical, and who could deny her that, demanding to speak to the bloody idiot who'd been on television the previous night implying that the police had as good as got their man.

The policeman on duty had done his best to calm her down, and had then put the call through to Holdall to tell him the grim news. And to ask him what the hell he'd meant when he'd talked to the press the previous evening.

When the call had come down from McMenemy's office, Holdall had not been the least surprised. Ill became those who were summoned up there two days running.

*

The rain was falling in a relentless drizzle against the window of the shop, the skies grey overhead, the clouds low. Every now and again someone bustled past the shop front, their collar pulled up against the cold wind, a dour expression welded to the face.

The shop was near deserted, as it had been most of the day. Wednesdays were usually slow, and with the cold and miserable weather, this day had been even worse. Barney had had to do only two haircuts all day, both of which had been ropey; one indeed, so bad that he thought it might lead to retribution. He hadn't liked the way the man had asked Wullie for Barney's address on his way out, and had been surprised that Wullie had claimed ignorance on the matter. Nevertheless, it was a day for keeping his head down.

At three o'clock Wullie had offered Chris the chance to go home early, telling Barney that on the next quiet day he could take his turn of an early departure. After that there were only three more customers, all of whom had wanted Wullie to cut their hair. Barney had sat and read a variety of newspapers then had finally given in to the boredom and had fallen asleep, his dreams a web of exotica.

He awoke with a start to slightly raised voices, dragged from a screaming drop down a black, bottomless shaft. Barney stretched, yawned, squinted at the clock. Two minutes past five. Time to go. Thank God for that.

He stood and stretched again, busying himself with clearing up, not something that would take very long. Took his time, however, doing as many unnecessary things as possible, not wishing to leave before Wullie. He listened to the idle chatter from the end of the shop and was not impressed.

'Now 16th century Italian art,' said Wullie, as he put the finishing touches to a dramatic taper at the back of the neck, 'there's the thing. Full of big fat birds getting their kit off. It doesn't matter what the painting's about, in every one there's always about five or six huge birds with enormous tits.'

The customer nodded his own appreciation of 16th century Italian art as much as he could, given that there was a man with a razor at the back of his neck.

'I mean,' Wullie continued, after pausing to pull off some intricate piece of barbery, 'you've got some painting of a big battle scene or something, or a nativity scene for Christ's sake, and they'd still manage to get in some great lump of lard, bollock naked, legs all over the place, dangling a couple of grapes into the gob of another suitably compliant naked tart, with nipples like corks, and her lips pouting in a flagrantly pseudo-lesbian pose. I love it, so I do. It's pure brilliant.'

'Even so,' said the customer, holding up his finger as Wullie produced a comb to administer the finishing touches, 'I still don't think it's a patch on modern art. That's got far more life and soul to it than a bunch of birds with their kit off.'

Wullie stopped combing, looked at the man as if he was mad.

'You're joking? I mean, fair enough, if they painted a bit of paper completely orange, then put a red squiggle in the middle of it and called it *A Boring Load Of Crap That Took Me Two Minutes And Isn't Worth Spit*, then that'd be fine. But they don't. They'll do that, then call it *Sunrise Over Manhattan* or *Three Unconnected Doorways*, or *I'm A Pretentious Wank So You've Got To Give Us Three Million Quid*. Piece of bloody nonsense.'

'No, no you've got it all wrong. These things have got a depth and soul to them that the likes of you can't see. If you can't see what an artist is saying, then it's because you're not in tune with the guy. That's hardly his fault.'

Wullie shook his head as he dusted off the back of the neck.

'Come off it. Any nutter can splash paint onto something and call it *Moon Over Five Women With Hysterectomies*,' – Wullie was indeed a new man – 'or something like that. My two year-old niece could do it, and she wouldn't get three million quid.'

'Of course not,' said the man, as Wullie removed the cape from around his neck and handed him a towel, 'and that's the point. If just anyone does it, it doesn't mean anything. The artist, however, is expressing himself, is letting you see what's inside. It means something because it comes from within, from his soul. That's what gives it heart, and that's why people are willing to pay money for it. Artists bare themselves to the public.'

Wullie thought about this for a second or two. The man stood, brushed himself down.

'A fine defence of modern art you've constructed there,' said Wullie eventually.

'Aye, thanks,' said the customer, fishing in his pockets.

'However, it's a complete load of pants.'

The man produced a five pound note from his pocket.

'You're not listening to me, Wullie.' He paused, stared at the ceiling, tried to think of how he could best get his point across. He was not used to such rigorous debate. Reaching for his jacket, he found what he was looking for. 'Let's put it this way. Say some wee muppet playing at St Andrews hacks out of the rough at the side of the green and it flies into the hole. Now, it may seem like a great shot, but let's face it, he didn't have a clue what he was doing. You know he's lucky. But if Tiger chips from the rough and it flies into the hole, you know he meant it. It's a thing of beauty. It's art. The execution and the outcome are the same, but the intentions are different. That's what it's all about.'

He stopped on his way to the door, holding out his hands in a gesture of 'there you have it'.

'Are you saying,' said Wullie, 'that Tiger Woods is the same as one of they bampots who throws paint onto a picture?'

The man laughed.

'I'll never win. See you next time, Wullie, eh. See you, Barn.'

The barbers said their goodbyes, Barney grudgingly, then Wullie turned to start his final clearing up for the day after fixing the *Closed* sign on the door.

Still muttering at the discussion which had just finished, Barney completed the minutiae of clearing his things away. Now that Wullie had finished, he felt free to go. Naked Italian women; these people didn't half talk some amount of mince.

'Can I have a word, Barney?'

Barney looked up; Wullie walked towards him and sat in the next seat up from his. Barney looked into Wullie's eyes and sat down, suddenly feeling a tingle at the bottom of his spine. It could've been the label on his Marks and Spencer's boxer shorts, but he had the feeling that it was something worse.

'Wullie?'

Wullie was staring at the floor. Looked awkward, like a seventeen year-old boy not wanting to tell his father he'd written off his new Frontera San Diego. He struggled with himself, then his eyes briefly flitted onto Barney and away again.

'Em, this isn't very easy, Barney. I'm not really sure how to say this,' he said. Looked anywhere but into Barney's eyes. Barney stared, a look of incredulity formulating across his face. He couldn't be going to say what he thought he was, could he?

'I'm afraid we've hired a new barber, Barney. It's an old friend of my dad's who's just moved into the area. You know, my dad wanted to give him a job and...'

Barney switched off, knowing what was coming. He couldn't believe it. Felt a strange twisting in his stomach, a pounding at the back of his head. Cold, wet hands. The gutless, gutless coward, making himself out to be merely the messenger of his father's decision, rather than the instrument of it.

How the hell could they let him go? He was the only one in the place who could give a decent haircut. Certainly he was better than these two young idiots, surely everyone could see that? But of course, Wullie would have been telling his father something completely different. Maybe his mother had been right; poison wasn't good enough for him, not violent enough.

'...so, you can work here for another month if you like, or we'll understand if you want to leave now, and we'll keep your wages going for the rest of the month. You don't have to make any decision right now, but if you could let us know in the next couple of days.'

Not once had he been able to look Barney in the eye, and then he sat, an attempted look of consolation on his face, eyes rooted to the floor.

Barney was in a daze, a thousand different thoughts barging into each other in his head. Could not believe it had happened, could not believe that they had had the nerve to do this to him. He was by far the most superior barber of the lot of them. This was ridiculous. His immediate thoughts were of violent retribution. Vicious, angry thoughts involving baseball bats, sledgehammers and pick axes.

But he couldn't show his hand. Not yet. He had to be calm about it. If he was going to avenge this heinous crime, he had to be calculating and cold; he had to pick his moment. Cool deliberation away from the scene of the crime was required. And as he sat staring angrily into Wullie's eyes, which remained Sellotaped to the floor, he decided that he would have to stay in the shop, however great the feeling of humiliation, however great his desire to leave.

'I'll stay for the month,' he said abruptly.

'What?'

Wullie looked up at him, for the first time, surprised. He hadn't expected an answer so quickly, hadn't expected the one he'd been given and, moreover, he'd been thinking about the phone call to the shop that morning from Serena, the girl from the Montrose. Wondering if that was her real name, anticipating Friday night; vague intimations of guilt.

'I'll stay for the month.'

Wullie stared briefly at the floor again. He and his father had assumed that Barney would just take his leave. Hadn't reckoned on an awkward month with Barney still in the shop. He looked up.

'All right, that'll be great. You're sure now?'

'Aye,' said Barney, almost spitting the word out. Managed to contain his wrath. Fingernails dug into palms. Wrath would have to be for later.

'Right then. That's great, Barney. I'll let my dad know.'

That's great, is it? You've just stabbed me up the backside with a red hot poker, and you think it's great because I accepted it. Fucking bastard. He thought it, didn't say it.

Wullie attempted another look of consolation, succeeded only in a tortoise-like grimace. Went about his business.

Barney stood up to clear away a couple of things which didn't need clearing away. Didn't want to immediately storm out of the shop, knowing his presence would unsettle Wullie. Didn't want him to be at ease any earlier than he should be. Although, should he ever be at ease?

As he lifted an unnecessary pair of scissors from his workplace, he realised his hands were shaking. Didn't want Wullie to see what effect it was having on him. Steadied himself, lifted a cup to get a drink of water. Filled it at the sink next to his workplace – Scottish tap water, the sweetest tasting drink; that was what he'd always thought; not today however. But as he raised it in his still trembling hand, the cup slipped free. Struck the edge of the sink surround and disgorged its contents, some over Barney, mostly over the floor. He muttered a curse. The water ran over the smooth tiles of the floor, a mocking river of humiliation to his disgrace. Mumbling a few other appropriate words which came to mind, he grabbed a towel to dry himself off. Wullie looked over at him and started to walk into the rear of the shop.

'I'll get a mop, Barney,' he said.

Like burning someone's house down, then offering to replace the welcome mat, thought Barney.

'Don't bother, I'll do it in a minute,' he growled, but Wullie felt the restlessness of the guilty and scurried off to retrieve the mop anyway. Barney shook his head and began to clear away the final few things lying around his work area. He lifted the pair of scissors again and studied them, his eyes drifting to Wullie, his back turned to him in the storeroom at the rear of the shop.

What damage I could do with these, he thought, but he knew he never would. If he was to avenge this crime, it would have to be by some subtle act of treachery, not a brutal and bloody stabbing.

He still held the scissors as Wullie emerged from the storeroom with the mop, walking towards him. Barney pursed his lips, tried not to appear too angry.

'Look, Wullie, it's all right. I said I'd get it.'

'I'll just give you a hand, Barney, it's no bother.'

Fine last words.

Wullie stepped forward to start clearing up the water, not noticing it had run so much towards him. His first step was firmly placed into a pool of lying water on a smooth tile, and his foot gave way. He attempted to regain his balance, and in doing so fell towards Barney. Barney raised his hands to catch him. Automatic reaction.

Wullie slumped heavily onto Barney and his outstretched hands. Neatly, exactly, with medical precision, the scissors entered through Wullie's stomach and jagged up under his rib cage. He rested in Barney's arms for a few seconds, then pulled back to look at him, an expression of stupefied surprise on his face.

He lurched back, blood pouring from the wound, the scissors embedded in his stomach. Fell back against the chair, which toppled backwards, allowing him to slump down onto the floor. His back rested against the bottom of the chair, his eyes stared blankly one last time up at Barney, then head fell forward onto his chest.

Barney stared mutely down at the body on the floor and the pool of blood spreading across the tiles. His face mouthed silent words of horror, his voice a hushed croak of wind, and finally when it found some substance, it was the weak and desperate voice of the frightened.

'Fuck,' he said.

Garbage Removal

Holdall stared blankly out of the window, wondering why it had stopped raining. It deserved to be raining. It had been an awful day, the sort of day when it bloody well ought to rain, because any other type of weather was completely inappropriate.

He'd been annihilated by McMenemy early on, and given instructions to set about investigating every missing persons case that had been reported in the past week, interview every family, and to follow up every new one that came in, anywhere in the West of Scotland. So he had been sent out on the rounds, and worst of all, Robertson had been put in charge of the investigation. Detective Chief Inspector Brian Robertson – the biggest bastard on the force. *Think yourself lucky you're not suspended*, McMenemy had said to him. Quite the reverse, Holdall had thought.

The day had been spent trailing round Glasgow, wet and dreich and unremittingly miserable, interviewing a series of women whose sons had unquestionably run off to London, and one man whose wife had, without any shadow of a doubt, fled the country with her boss. Her husband, however, was still holding out some hope that she'd been brutally murdered, and was optimistically checking the post every morning.

The day had indeed been long, and then, having returned half an hour earlier, Barney'd had to face Robertson to be given the latest update on the case and his instructions for the following day. Which bore a remarkable similarity to his instructions for the day he'd just endured. Any more than a week of this and he'd be resigning.

I may resign anyway, he reflected as he stared out of the window, noticing with some satisfaction that the rain had just begun to fall again.

*

Quiet descended upon the shop. The body lay inert and slouched, propped against the toppled chair, the blood slowly spreading across the floor. Barney stood over it, staring dumbly at the bloody scene. His mind was numb, his feet anchored to the spot, even as the blood began to spread towards them.

'Shit,' he said eventually. It hung in the air, awaiting addition. 'Shit, shit, shit, shit, shit.'

The blood about to touch his shoes, he jumped away from it, started pacing around the room. His heart thumped loudly, he began to sweat, his face beaded with perspiration, flirting dangerously with panic. He had killed Wullie. God, he'd killed Wullie. He might have been a gutless bastard, but he hadn't meant to kill him. Not yet, anyway. If he had been going to do it, it would have had to have been on his terms. Why hadn't Wullie just let him clear up the water himself? The bloody idiot. And why had he had to sack him? If he hadn't done that, this wouldn't have happened.

The memory of that, the dismissal, nudged at him again, the feelings of annoyance returned. Maybe it was Wullie's own fault. It was true. If he hadn't sacked him, it wouldn't have happened. Good logic.

He stood on the far side of the shop beside the door, staring at the corpse, the steady flow of blood now beginning to ease. Don't feel bad about it, part of him was trying to say, Wullie got what he deserved. Think about it, it was true. If he hadn't been such a gutless little coward, then he wouldn't be dead now. Perhaps the punishment didn't quite fit the crime, but then what had he been about to do to your life, Barney?

He stood for some minutes arguing with himself over the rights and wrongs of Wullie lying in a pool of blood. Suddenly it hit him – he was going to have to tell someone about it. He would have to call the police, he would have to tell Wullie's wife, Moira. It wasn't just about him and Wullie. There were other people involved. The guilt began to grow. He tasted the blood, felt it damp on his hands. Thought about Macbeth.

What was he going to say to the police? Well, officer, he'd just sacked me and although I didn't mean for this to happen, I do think you can see that it was perfectly justified. Very well, Mr Thomson, the officer would say, we'll let you off just this once. But don't murder anyone else.

Of course not. Of course it wouldn't be that easy. And once the police found out that Wullie had intended to sack him, as they surely would from Wullie's father, then they would be more than willing to believe that Barney had meant to kill him.

The phone rang.

His heart stopped beating for some seconds, while it clattered up through his mouth, hit the ceiling and bounced off the floor a few times. He got over the shock, gathered himself together; the phone was still ringing.

He stared blankly at it. 'Shit, what do I do? If I answer it, it places me at the scene of the crime.'

Somewhere in Barney's head there was a calm, calculating half, trying to get him under control. It was that which had reminded him of Wullie's treachery. It was that which now tried to drag him back from the precipice of panic.

'You work here. That places you at the scene of the crime.'

He stared at the phone, trapped in his indecision, the ringing persistent. He still had much to decide upon and this was forcing him to a decision too quickly.

'If I don't get it, I can say I left the shop around five with Wullie still here.'

'Don't be a fool,' his other half replied. 'What if someone sees you leave the shop now? You're caught for a liar. You're bound to go down.'

'But why should I? Why should I go down? I didn't do anything. Not intentional, like.'

'Come on, you fool. No one's going to believe that. If you leave the shop and let the body lie, you've had it. Answer the phone. If it's someone looking for Wullie, say he's already left.'

Barney hesitated. Had to be done, though.

Slowly he walked over, lifted the receiver.

'Henderson's?'

'Oh, hullo, Barney, it's Moira. Is Wullie still there?'

His heart crashed frantically out through his ribs, cannoned off the wall and, after bouncing several times around the room, eventually returned to rest, shaken and battered.

Wullie's wife. It was Wullie's wife. Shit, shit, shit. Stay calm, Barney, stay calm.

'Eh, no, Moira, he's not. He, eh, just left a couple of minutes ago. He shouldn't be too long, you know.'

'Right, thanks then, Barney. Goodn...'

A thought suddenly occurred to him and in his fright he did not ignore it. Give yourself more time, Barney.

'Oh aye, Moira, I forgot. He said he was going to do a bit of shopping or something before he went home.' Not bad for off the cuff, he thought.

'Shopping? What shopping's he doing? Wullie's never been into a shop in his life!'

'Eh, I don't know, Moira, he didn't say.' Maybe it hadn't been so brilliant after all.

'Oh God, I wonder what he's up to now. I'll kill that eejit when I see him, so I will. He's pure dead.'

Appropriate, but you won't have to. The dark, clinical half of Barney, which was beginning to emerge almost as an independent being, interjected into his thoughts – get off the phone before you say anything else stupid!

'Aye, right, well, I'm sure it's nothing, Moira,' he said.

'Aye, well it better not be, or I'll skelp his arse for him.'

'Aye, right. Goodnight, Moira.'

'Aye,' she said, and then she was gone.

He hung up the phone and slumped down into his seat, relief washing over him in great waves. He'd handled it reasonably well and he'd managed to get himself a little more time.

Then the waves washed away and once again he was high and dry. His eyes fell upon the corpse, lying in the pool of blood. Blood; how odd it looked. Much darker than he imagined it would be. Maybe it was just the low lighting in the shop. That low lighting for which he had been profoundly grateful in the past, when, after dark on winter days, atrocious late afternoon haircuts had gone unnoticed.

Maybe now he would get to keep his job. A smile wandered aimlessly across his mouth, stopping as it went, to linger on the spoils of victory. They'd need the new barber to cover for Wullie, so they wouldn't have any reason to sack him. Smashing. At least that was something. Only, however, if he could avoid being arrested for murder.

Harsh truth: he was going to have to do something with the body which lay before him. Whatever he did, he would have to be analytical and cold. This was not Barney. He needed this new, unrealised dark half to think for him. He sat back, attempting to focus. No time to waste, and whatever had to be done, would need to be done quickly. Finally, after staring blankly at the body on the floor for some time, his dark half arrived on a gleaming white horse, followed by a large posse.

'Now, Barney, you've got to be clear about this.' Barney sat back to listen, not really sure who was doing the talking. 'If the body is discovered here in the shop, then you've had it. You'll be charged with murder and you'll spend the next fifteen years in jail. You're going to have to dispose of it. You have to clean up all traces of blood from the shop and remove your bloody clothes.' Barney looked at himself. God! He'd hardly noticed – the huge patch of blood where Wullie had fallen against him. 'Once he's reported missing, the polis'll call, so there can't be any traces of murder. And you're going to have to be quick about it, so get to work.'

Barney stared at the corpse a little while longer, deciding what had to be done. His independent self thinking for him, as if he had been possessed. Finally, his mind put straight on the matter, he set to work with feverish determination, thinking all the time that the police were about to come bursting in through the door.

They kept some large black plastic bags in the back of the shop, for the general detritus of the day – hair clippings, rubbish, corpses – and in these he wrapped up the body, binding it tightly with string. As is always the case with new murderers, he was surprised by the weight of the corpse and how difficult it was to manhandle, but still he was able to work efficiently and quickly; more quickly than he'd ever cut anyone's hair. He cleaned the blood that had collected on the outside of the bags, then placed the body beside the door awaiting removal. Then there were the traces of blood to be removed, the large pool of it, and all the other smudges and marks which had been spread around the floor and the furniture.

Forty minutes later he stood beside the door and surveyed the shop. It looked good. It looked like it was supposed to look. *Barber Clears Away Dead Body In Record Time.* All traces of the murder were gone and he had cleaned up Wullie's workplace and removed his jacket to make it look as though he'd departed as normal. Over a hundred and fifty pounds in his wallet, another small bonus to bring a smile to his face. All that remained to tell the tale was the bulky black package on the floor and the blood on Barney's clothes. There was nothing he could do about that until he got home but he was able to cover up the worst of it with his jacket.

All looked well and only one immediate problem remained. How to get the body out to his car, unseen. It was just after six o'clock, a busy hour, but the street in which the shop stood was off the main road and usually quiet.

He turned off the lights, opened the door and poked his head out into the street. There was one car driving past and the main road seemed busy, but there were no pedestrians in the immediate vicinity. All seemed clear. He had little option anyway. He had to risk it.

He walked up the road to where his car was parked, giving a small prayer that it had been returned that morning, and reversed it back down the road so that it was directly outside the door. Opened the boot, took another few furtive looks over his shoulder, went back into the shop.

He looked around once again in the near dark, the light from the street throwing strange shadows into the corners; a final check to make sure that everything was normal; turned his attention to the plastic bags. First of all he attempted to lift the body onto his shoulder, a task at which he completely failed. Resigned himself to dragging it along the floor. Lifted the bags firmly at one end, making sure to grab the body through the plastic so as not to tear it, and started walking backwards out of the shop, into the murk and the drizzle, pulling the dead weight.

'Oh, hello there, Barney, how are you?'

For about the fifteenth time in an hour Barney's heart pushed vigourously against the restraining tissue around it.

He looked up. Charlie Johnstone, one of the shop's regulars. Shit, shit, shit. Why hadn't he checked the road again before he'd dragged the body out? Too impetuous.

He lowered the body to the ground, stood to look at Charlie. Fully expected him to say at any second, 'Here, is that not Wullie inside those bags there?'

'Oh, eh, hello Charlie. How's it going?'

Potential crisis point. Charlie stopped to chat.

'Ach, not so bad, not so bad. Mind you, these headaches I've been getting are an absolute nightmare, so they are. They're killing me. And Betty, Betty, well, you don't want to ask about her.' Shook his head a few times and then continued before Barney had the chance not to ask about Betty. 'Awful trouble with yon trapped nerve in her shoulder, so she has. Awful trouble. Aye, and she had a bit of bother with her eye, you know, her cataract, but I suppose we've been lucky really, and I shouldn't complain...'

Barney felt compelled to interrupt, even if it meant drawing attention to what he was dragging from the shop. The longer he stood there, the more chance there would be for a police car to drive by; a police car with a corpse detector.

'Look, I'm sorry Charlie, but I'm in a bit of a hurry here.'

'Oh, aye, aye. Sorry about that.'

He looked down, saw for the first time what Barney was dragging out of the shop. A look of curiosity passed fleetingly across his face. Applied his hands to his sides, widening his stance.

'Here, that looks like a bloody big thing, so it does. D'you want a hand with that?'

Barney shook his head. Groaned inside. 'Eh, no, no, it's fine, I'm all right, thanks.'

He bent to lift the sack, making sure to grab hold of the body again, while Charlie watched. There was little concealing the act now, so he decided to get on with it and hope that an arm, or some other appendage, did not spring free. As he did so, he began to think of another eventuality. What to do with Charlie if he realised what was going on. There were still plenty of pairs of scissors in the shop.

He pulled the sack to the edge of the pavement, laid it behind the car. Stared at it, wondering if he was going to be able to lift it up over the high edge of the boot. Charlie bustled over.

'Here, let me help you with that. Looks bloody heavy, whatever it is.'

Barney shrugged, felt the tightness in his chest. He had to accept the offer, began to make mental preparations for taking care of Charlie, should the need arise. For how could he fail to realise what it was that he was lifting into the boot? Maybe he should just go back into the shop and return with a pair of scissors, embed them in some suitable part of Charlie's body and then bundle his corpse into the boot as well.

Closed his eyes, breathed deeply. Felt the tremble all over his body. Hands shook.

He looked into the boot. Never. There was never enough room to put two bodies in there. The back seat then. He cast an eye over his shoulder to see if there was anyone abroad who might see what was going on.

Charlie studied the black bags, gently kicked them. Used to play wing-half for Queen's Park. Long time ago. God, thought Barney, surely he must realise that this is Wullie, or a body of some description. He must.

'Look, just a minute Charlie,' said Barney, taking another look up the road, 'I've got to get something from the shop. I'll just be a second.'

He walked quickly back through the door, lifted the first pair of scissors which came to hand at his own workplace, then returned to the street. Half expected to find Charlie kneeling beside the bags, tearing them apart to reveal Wullie's dead face, contorted in perpetual wonder. Barney prepared to wield the scissors.

However, Charlie stood alone, staring up the street, idly whistling some aimless tune. Might have been Verdi, might have been Manic Street Preachers, might have been Bob Dylan. Barney slipped the scissors into his pocket. There was no need to do anything stupid yet.

Charlie turned to him and smiled. 'Wullie's not in the shop is he, letting us two do all the work?'

Barney swallowed, tried to smile, didn't answer.

'Right then, you ready Charlie?'

'Aye, aye.'

The two men grabbed the ends of the bags and, with some effort, managed to lift them up, shovelling them over the edge of the car and into the boot. The bags at Charlie's end started to tear but the body slumped down into the boot before anything was revealed. It came to rest with the feet at Barney's side still protruding over the edge, and he had to bend the legs to fit the whole thing in – the body already less pliable than he thought it would be.

They were both breathing hard as Barney quickly closed the boot to prevent Charlie looking at the bags any further.

'Bloody hell, Barn, what was that thing? Jings, it felt like a body or something.'

Barney coughed loudly, attempting to cover up the involuntary splutter. Automatically his hand drifted into his pocket, his fingers fell on the cold steel of the scissors. Cold, cold steel.

'Oh, it's eh, it's just some rubbish, you know, that we've collected, and I'm taking it to the dump.'

Charlie smiled and nodded. Simple Charlie. Used to play wing-half for Queen's Park.

'Rubbish? Bloody heavy rubbish, Barney. I don't know what kind of rubbish you collect in that shop.' Gave Barney a wink and a nudge. 'Sure you haven't been having arguments with Wullie or Chris, eh?'

Barney tightened his grip on the scissors. 'Don't be daft,' he said, attempting a smile. 'It's just, well you know, stuff.'

Charlie winked extravagantly again. 'Aye, right. Stuff. Your secret's safe with me, son.'

Barney nodded, grimaced slightly. Thought: God Barney, the guy's joking, he doesn't realise anything. But the hand in his pocket was ready to strike. He looked up the road, the coast was clear. The opportunity was there. Wait. Just wait to see if he said anything else.

'Thanks for your help, Charlie. I've really got to be going now.'

Charlie had the collar of his jacket pulled high up over his neck, so that was one point of entry removed. The eye socket, that would be a sure-fire place to do it.

'Aye, aye, all right. I'll be seeing you, Barney,' and with a wave he walked off towards the main street. Barney watched him go, his whole body aching with relief.

'Here, Barney,' said Charlie from the end of the street, 'Wullie's not in the shop, is he, I was needing to speak to him?'

Barney didn't answer. He couldn't. He stood and stared, feeling the rain on his face. Charlie waited a second for the reply, and when he didn't get it, he waved and disappeared around the corner.

Barney groaned, but there was nothing he could do about it now. Charlie hadn't realised anything. There had been no hint of suspicion about him. Nothing.

As he walked back into the shop to return the scissors, the phone started ringing again. He gave a little jump. Whoever it was, he was in no mood to talk. He quickly left the shop and locked the door behind him. There was a lot of thinking to be done.

*

He drove home as calmly as he could. He was not relaxed, however; his steering was wayward, his gear changes were edgy, and his avoidance of old people crossing the road, at best, uncertain. His thoughts were consumed with what he was going to do with the body. And as he drove the short distance home, he resolved to tell Agnes. He would have to. He needed someone to talk to, and if he could trust anyone, surely it was her. And perhaps she might even have body disposal experience that he was unaware of, he reasoned to himself.

He arrived home, parked the car outside, left the bloody booty of his misfortune congealing in the back and tramped upstairs. When he walked into the sitting room, his dinner was waiting patiently and cold on the table, while Agnes watched television.

He removed his jacket and stood in the centre of the room, his clothes soiled with blood, a look of grim desperation on his face. A chainsaw would not have looked out of place in his hands.

'There you are. Where've you been? Your dinner's been ready for ages,' said Agnes, without looking round. Blane and Liberty were getting married and everyone was waiting for Sobriety to object.

He stood for a second before answering, waiting to see if she would turn to look at him, something which under normal circumstances he would've known she would never do.

It rose within him, a pressure cooker waiting to explode, until he could keep it in no longer. 'I've killed Wullie,' he blurted out.

Agnes gasped. It wasn't Sobriety who'd objected. It was Bleach.

'Yes, dear,' she said finally, after coming to terms with the fact that Bleach was pregnant by Blane, when everyone had believed that she'd been artificially inseminated with Rock's semen.

'Are you not listening to me? I've killed Wullie!' His voice had become a desperate plea for help.

'Oh, aye, dear? What did you do that for?'

He took a step nearer to her. She wasn't looking at him, but maybe she was listening at last. 'I didn't mean to. It was an accident. I swear to God, I didn't mean to.'

Agnes briefly turned and looked at him. 'Don't worry, dear, I'm sure he'll have forgotten all about it in the morning.'

Barney dropped to his knees, put his hands to his face. Finally, the magnitude of what had happened was coming to him, the idiocy of what he'd done. He had killed a man. Maybe not intentionally, but he had killed him, and now he was plotting to dispose of the body. Whatever trouble he'd been in when he'd started had now increased a hundredfold.

Why had he not just phoned the police and explained what had happened? Nobody would have suspected him of murder, why should they have? He was known as a reasonable man. Just because he'd been about to lose his job was no reason for him to kill anyone.

He started sobbing, loud retches coming from deep within, his chest heaving and the tears tumbling down his face. He bent over, putting his forehead to the floor, started banging his hands on the carpet. With no force, however, just a quiet, pathetic gesture of desperation. The first time he had cried since the death of his father.

'Shh!' Agnes waved a desultory hand, as she turned the volume of the television up with the other. Lance and Billy Bob were arguing over which one of them had first refusal on Flame.

Barney quietened down, but remained on the floor, sobbing softly, his head in his hands. Then slowly, a small voice began to come to him, a small instinctive voice nudging at his subconscious. The small voice which everyone hears whenever there is a problem which they cannot resolve. 'Go to your mum,' it was saying. 'Go to your mum.'

Maybe that was right, maybe that was the thing to do. She'd been almost gung-ho about killing the two of them, perhaps she would know what to do now. It seemed ridiculous, but he needed help, advice at the very least, and it wasn't as if he had too many options. He would go to see his mother.

He struggled to his feet, looking sadly at the back of Agnes's head, then trudged into the bedroom. He changed his clothes and put the bloodstained ones into a plastic bag, which he secreted at the bottom of the wardrobe. He walked back into the sitting room, a sense of purpose having crept unawares back into his stride.

'I'm going to my mother's.'

'Yes, dear.'

And as Barney walked from the house, Charity and Monogamy were trying to pick a dress for Cerease to wear to the christening of Cream and Hamper's daughter, Tupperware.

Forgive Me, Mother,
For I Have Sinned

There is a time of definition in the life of every man when the pieces fall together or events take place to shape the future. It might happen suddenly or it might be a gradual process, a build up of things over weeks or months. Sometimes when it occurs he will be unaware that it is doing so, until one day he looks back and realises that his life has altered completely, for better or worse. It could be that he has fallen in love. It could be that some outside event changes his whole attitude to life, so that he views everything from a different perspective, and then indeed is life new. It could be that someone dies, creating a hole in his life that cannot be filled. It could be a new job, or a new car, or a new interest of any kind. Or it could be that he accidentally stabs his boss to death with a pair of scissors.

Barney's life was changing, he knew it was happening, and there was nothing he could do about it. He tried telling himself that this was what he'd wanted, that he had planned to kill Wullie anyway, but deep down he knew there was no way that he'd have been able to do it, had fate not forced his hand. And now he prepared to turn to his mother. Forty-six years old and still the same solution to his problems as he had had forty-four years previously when he'd broken a toy or spilled tomato ketchup on his bib.

He was still contemplating the fickle hand he'd been dealt when he walked into his mother's house. He called out to announce his arrival, a shout which was, as usual, greeted by silence. He could hear the television playing in the sitting room and imagined she would be engrossed in some dreadful quiz show.

He opened the door, immediately started coughing as the great wall of cigarette smoke swept into his lungs. It was always the same on days when she'd been sitting watching television all day and it was only very rarely that she ever opened a window; in itself something that was only ever likely to happen between the end of June and the beginning of September.

He walked into the room, extravagantly waving his arms in front of him, still coughing loudly.

'For God's sake, I wish you'd open a blooming window in this place if you're going to smoke so much, Mother,' and he walked between her and the television to pull back the curtains and let in some fresh air. Cemolina scowled at him but she was more concerned with the television and *Give Us Your Body Fluids*.

He stood by the window breathing deeply, as much for show as clean air, before moving back into the room when he realised that she was paying him no attention. He slumped down into a seat, leant forward, rested his forearms on his knees, looked keenly at his mother. He stared at her for a while, hoping she would notice him. However, her attention was undivided. This show was her favourite. Finally, he felt bound to speak.

'Mum, I've got to talk to you. I'm in trouble.'

She didn't answer for a while, then eventually lifted a dismissive hand, waving it in his direction.

'Shh! Not when they're trying to guess whose fluids these are. Who d'you think? This bloke says Alfred Hitchcock, but I thought they looked more like Robert Altman's. What about you?' She turned, gave him a brief look.

Barney faced the realisation that all the women in his life were more interested in television than they were in him.

'Mum, I need to talk. I'm in trouble. Real trouble.' He hesitated, but he had her attention at last. 'I've killed Wullie.'

Her eyes widened, her jaw dropped. The expression held on her face for a few seconds and he definitely knew he had her complete attention when she lowered the volume of the television. If he wasn't mistaken, there was a glint in her eye, a smile forming upon her lips.

'Wullie! You've killed Wullie did you say?'

'Aye, aye I did. Christ, Mum, I'm in real trouble. Real trouble,' and he ran his hands through his hair and looked at her with desperation. Comfort me, his face said, I need it.

'Jings! Well done, I didn't think you had it in you.'

'What?' he said. Despite the night before, it wasn't the reaction he'd been expecting.

'Well, you wanted to, didn't you? You said you wanted to kill him. I'm proud of you.' She paused, reflected. 'Although, d'you not think it would have been better if you'd taken care of the papist first? Can't stand they bastards, so I can't. Bastards the lot of them.'

He looked upon her with wonder. How could she take it so lightly?

'Well, then, how did you do it? What was the instrument of his destruction? And don't tell me it was poison or I'll be right upset, so I will.'

When the scales fell from his eyes, they did so quickly and dramatically, cascading and tumbling away in a frantic rush. He looked upon his mother in a new light. She was mad. Of course she was. Completely mad. Perhaps it was senility but if he thought about it, he was sure he could think of examples of her madness throughout the years. She'd always been insane but since it'd been with him all this time he'd come to take much of her behaviour as normal. But this wasn't normal.

All the plans and schemes and silly ideas she'd had. He had liked to think of her as vaguely eccentric, perhaps even extravagantly eccentric, but it was more than that. Worse than that. And now, what about this reaction? How could she possibly be enthusiastic about him killing Wullie? Killing anybody? What mother could be so welcoming about her son committing such an act?

What was he doing here and what advice could he possibly get from her that would be of any use? Christ, he'd been a fool. He'd been a fool to tell her what he'd been thinking in the first place, and he was a fool to come here tonight with a bloody corpse in the boot of his car.

'Accidentally. With a pair of scissors,' he mumbled, wondering why he was bothering to tell her.

She tutted loudly, displeased at the lack of drama in the description.

'Was there a lot of blood?'

'Aye,' he mumbled. 'A lot of blood.'

He stared at the floor. He had no business here. There were no great answers to his problems to be found in the home of his insane mother. He was going to have to solve them himself.

'What have you done with the corpse?' she asked, the glint returning to the eye. He didn't notice, so much attention was he giving to the carpet. His heart had sunk. He was scared.

'It's downstairs, in the boot of the car. Wrapped in several large plastic bin liners.'

'Crike! Bring it up then. I'll make soup!'

Barney looked up, aghast. 'Mother!'

She smiled, had the decency to look slightly embarrassed, but he knew it was feigned. They cast a quick glance at the television as the presenter produced a bag of thick, lumpy green liquid, but Cemolina was too intrigued with Barney's predicament to raise the sound. Barney turned away from the TV with a look of disgust. Cemolina came with him, her finger momentarily twitching over the volume button.

'Well, what are you going to do with it then?'

He let his head hang low, enveloped, as he was, with dejection. 'I don't know, Mum, I really don't know.'

She stared at him; he stared at the ground, there being very little else for him to say. He had to leave and get on with things, but when he got outside there was a body which he was going to have to dispose of and he had no idea how he was going to do it.

Slowly he dragged himself out of his seat and stood up.

'Look, Mum, I really ought to be going. I shouldn't have come here and brought you into this. It's my problem to solve...'

'Now, none of your nonsense,' she chided, 'you sit right back down and we'll talk this through, all right? I'm your mother and I'm here to help.'

He paused at her words, grudgingly lowered himself back into his seat, his reluctance to get help from his mother fighting his desperate need for help from anywhere.

'Now, tell me everything that happened and we'll see what we can do.'

Barney stared at her. What options did he have? He hardly had any friends with whom he could share the story. Wondered if he could go to the Samaritans; didn't think they had a murder line. So maybe it would do him some good to tell his mother, even if there was nothing she could do to help him. And all the while, something at the back of his mind was hoping that she would advise him to go to the police and get it over with. It wasn't a decision he could possibly make for himself, but he knew it'd be the right thing to do.

He laid the story out for her, trying not to miss anything out. For almost all of it she sat quietly taking it in, except for pitching in to suggest that he really ought to have killed Charlie Johnstone when he'd had the chance. When he was finished he was distraught and rested his head back against the seat, trying to stop the tears spilling over onto his face. His hands were shaking and now that he had related it all and confronted the full awfulness of his situation, he was close to panic.

He opened his eyes to Cemolina bending over him and forcing a large whisky into his hands. He took it and shakily lifted it to his mouth. God, it felt good. Talisker, he thought, although he was no expert. Probably been there since his father died. Breathed deeply as it burned its way down his throat.

Cemolina settled back into her seat.

'What d'you want me to do, Barnabas?'

He leant forward, resting his forearms on his knees.

'I don't know, Mum. I can't ask you to do anything. What am I going to do, that's the question?'

'Why don't you bring the body up here, son? Let me take care of it.'

He stared at her, a wild look in his eye. It was ridiculous. What could his mother possibly do with a human body? But no matter how ridiculous it seemed to him, he loved the idea. If she took the body, he was free of it. He could wash his hands. It would be wonderful.

'But what are you going to do with Wullie that I can't?'

She bustled.

'Never you mind. Just comfort yourself with knowing that I can take care of it. You can always rely on your old mother. Now you run downstairs and bring the body back up. And mind and try not to let anyone see you, this time.'

★

Half an hour later Barney was driving home, feeling moderately relieved. Felt like a weight had been lifted. Noticed other cars on the road; remembered to use all the gears. He had no idea what his mother intended to do with the corpse, but whatever it was she had in mind, she'd had a reassuring look in her eye and enough confidence in her voice to put him at ease. It wasn't over yet but the immediate worry of the corpse was gone. It had given him plenty of time to worry about all the other problems which would arise.

On his way home something made him drive past the shop. Just a hunch, a vague feeling of unease. Didn't know what he expected to see. Wullie's ghost, perhaps, his face pressed against the window, his features contorted in eternal agony. However, the shop front stared darkly and mundanely back at him. Quiet, deserted.

Deathly quiet.

He walked into his flat at just after ten o'clock. Surprised to be confronted by the sounds of silence, rather than some abysmal Australian or American Deep South soap. Stopped and listened before he walked into the sitting room but there was nothing. Maybe Agnes had gone to bed already but something told him it wasn't going to be that. The hairs on the back of his neck stood to attention, his skin crawled. Panic.

Tentatively opened the door to the sitting room, expectations of a massive police presence behind the door. The television was on but with the sound turned down. Agnes sat, cup of tea in her hand, concerned look on her face; next to her on the settee was Moira, Wullie's wife, tear in her eye, cup of tea untouched on the table. They looked at Barney as he walked in the door and such was their relief at seeing him that neither of them noticed that he, as the ancients used to say, completely bricked himself.

They didn't say anything; watched closely as he removed his jacket, letting it fumble out of his hands and fall to the floor. He came into the room and sat down in a seat opposite them, not wanting to say anything. Didn't want to betray his secret. Felt like he had blood all over him and the word *murderer* carved into his forehead.

Agnes finally spoke. The silence could not be allowed to extend for the entire evening. Quick look at her watch. Twenty minutes until *Rectal Emergency Ward 6*.

'Moira's here,' she said.

Barney nodded. Aye, I can see that.

'She's pure dead worried, so she is, and I says, you know, maybe she should be worried.'

Barney nodded again, tried to look interested but not overly concerned. Telling himself to behave as if he didn't know why Moira was here. Act natural. He was nervous; felt like the slightest hint might give him away. Had to ensure that there was nothing in his demeanour that would strike a discordant note. Act natural,

Barney, act natural. Thought of the Beatles. *They're gonna put me in the movies.* Wasn't the Beatles who wrote it. Who did it first?

'Barney?' said Moira.

'I didn't do it' he blurted out, fingers gripping the seat.

'What?' said Moira and Agnes in unison.

He closed his eyes, tried to take hold of himself. Don't be such a bloody dunderheid, Barney. They don't suspect you of anything. Why should they? Just be calm and don't put your foot in it. He opened his eyes. Determined to play the part; the grand conspirator.

'Oh, sorry, nothing. I thought, well, I don't know. I was thinking about something else. In a daydream, you know.' He paused, tried to regain his composure. 'What's the problem Moira?' he asked finally, his voice just about steady enough for them to not notice the difference.

'It's Wullie, Barney, he didn't come home the night. Are you sure he didn't say anything else when he left the shop? Just that he was going shopping, is that all?'

Barney thought. Tried to look like he was giving the question serious consideration; trying to compose himself. Had never felt so uncomfortable in his life. Fighting the urge to blurt out the truth but knew he'd already gone too far for that.

'Aye, that was all,' he said eventually. 'He left about quarter past five and said something about going to the shops. That was it, you know.'

Moira waited for something else, but Barney was finished. How could he give her more hope than that? She'd lost her husband, although she didn't know it. Her head dropped into her hands and she started crying in gentle sobs. Agnes moved closer, put an arm around her shoulder.

'What kind of mood was he in, Barney? Did he seem to be all right, you know? Think about it, 'cause Moira's pure upset, so she is.'

Barney stared into space for a while, casually lifted and dropped his shoulders. Hoped it was casual. 'Aye, well, you know Wullie. He just looked like he normally does, you know.'

'You don't think he's been nabbed by yon serial killer, do you? That's what me and Moira have been talking about.'

Barney scoffed, nearly choked on it. At least he could honestly deny that one.

'No, no, don't be daft. He hasn't fallen into the hands of any serial killer. Don't worry about that.'

He decided it was time to look unconcerned, make them think they were over-reacting. Which was exactly what he would've thought, if he hadn't just stabbed Wullie in the stomach. He stood up, stretched, yawned.

'Look, Moira, I wouldn't worry about it. He's probably just gone down the boozer and had a few too many. You know what he's like, eh? You know Wullie.'

She shook her head slowly, mumbling through the tears. 'No, no, it's not like him. Not Wullie, so it's not. A Friday night, aye, but never during the week. Not my Wullie.'

Barney waved this away, casual, dismissive, but the next question hit him harder. Full in the face at about a hundred miles an hour.

'D'you not think we should phone for the polis?' said Agnes.

The polis! He hadn't really thought of that yet. He knew it would come to it but not yet. It was too early for the polis to be involved. God, Wullie could genuinely be sitting down the pub for all anyone else knew.

'Eh, no, no, not yet. I think that might be a bit hasty, you know. Wait and see what happens. Maybe if he hasn't shown up by the morning, give them a wee call. I'm sure he will but, so I wouldn't worry about it.'

'D'you really think he's all right, Barney?' Moira said to him through her tears. Desperately seeking reassurance.

Barney looked into the damp eyes, was finally overwhelmed by guilt, to the point of not being able to reply. Mumbled some attempted words of comfort to her, squeezed her hand, muttered that he was tired.

He walked to the bedroom, an air of unconcern about him; the great lie. And when he got into the room, he collapsed on the bed and wept.

When Did You Last
See Your Enthusiasm?

Holdall stared disconsolately at the list of names. Another six people had been reported missing by the morning. Another six groups of worried relatives he had to trawl round, whose minds he would have to try to put at ease. God, he hated Robertson. The man was a complete eejit and if ever he had the chance to get his own back, then he'd bloody well take it. And if it involved several blunt instruments and a lot of blood, well all the better.

He looked at the names and the ages, trying to decide by looking at them what might have happened. As usual, four of the six were teenagers. The options were numerous for this lot and dying at the hands of a serial killer was unlikely to be one of them. They could be lying in a gutter somewhere creamed out of their faces from the night before; they could be on the bus to London with £150 in their pocket and a collection of ridiculous dreams in their head; they could be lying in some bed somewhere enjoying again all the things which they had enjoyed the night before (lucky, lucky bastards); or, and at this he brightened up a little, they might be lying dead in a ditch, by their own hand. And at least two of them would've probably already reappeared by the time he got to their homes. There was always that as consolation.

He studied the other two on the list. A thirty-eight year-old woman with seven children, aged between eighteen and two, all of whom still lived at home. There appeared to be no particular father figure. Big mystery, he thought, and mentally crossed that one off. She would be back in a day or two, feeling guilty and angry that the kids had called the police.

One remained. A man in his late twenties. Ran a barber's shop, lived with his wife, no children. This one wasn't so easy to dismiss. He might've gone out and got drunk, ended up in some woman's bed somewhere, but he should have turned up by now.

Maybe this was it. For all he scoffed at this ridiculous goose chase, there was a fair chance that he would come across victims of the killer at some stage. They would, of course, already be dead by the time he began to investigate their disappearance, a small flaw in the great plan, but perhaps they might stumble across some clue. The exercise itself wasn't a waste of time, but he resented Robertson having given it to him.

He looked out of the window, at the rain hitting steadily off the glass. Of course it was. This was Glasgow in March. It always bloody rained.

The door to his office opened, Detective Sergeant MacPherson came in, his face the usual mask of taciturnity. The two men nodded. MacPherson placed some papers on Holdall's desk.

'When'll you want to start out this morning, sir?' he asked, having withdrawn a few feet.

Holdall sighed heavily, stared at nothing. The horror of going out. He didn't even want to think about that yet. Wet and cold, concerned mothers and children. Jesus. He thought some more, his mind on a variety of things, and just as MacPherson was beginning to shuffle his feet and glance at his watch, Holdall looked up, made up his mind.

'Let's give it half an hour, eh, Sergeant? I think I need a good deal of coffee and something to eat before I can face the rigours of the day, if rigours they're to be.'

MacPherson nodded, issued a short 'very good, sir', and marched out of the door, a hundred things to do in the next half hour.

Holdall sat back, laced his fingers behind his head, stared at the ceiling. How long could he do this before he'd tell them to stuff their job? So, it'd be a blindingly stupid thing to do and Jean would be unbelievably annoyed at him, but he was damned if he could put up with much more of this. He could find something else to do, it couldn't be that difficult.

Maybe he could set up his own private detective agency. That might not be a bad idea. Sure, he'd have to start with small time stuff. Divorce cases and missing children. He winced at the thought. But it wouldn't be long, surely, before he'd be getting into adventures, mixing it up with glamorous women and being sent on the hunt for golden falcons and the like. God, that'd be the life. Maybe, he reflected, Jean wouldn't be able to handle it. She'd maybe even leave him, but hey, he thought, what the heck. There'd be plenty more babes out there given what he'd be doing. He'd watched enough private dick shows on the TV to know that it would be one stunning chick after another in that job. Heaven.

His eyes fell on the list in front of him and the pile of papers which MacPherson had placed on his desk. With a weary sigh, and wondering if MacPherson would have taken the hint and instigated a cup of coffee on his behalf, he turned off his dreams and looked at the reports at his right hand.

*

'And when did you last see Stuart, Mrs. Hutchinson?'

The woman stared over her cup of tea at the wall, trying to remember. 'Tuesday,' she said eventually. 'Tuesday about eight o'clock. Aye, that'd be about right.'

MacPherson nodded, looked at his notepad. Holdall was sitting beside him, quietly sipping a cup of tea, doing his best not to listen to any of what was going on. The chief inspector's trick – let the sergeant ask all the questions while pretending to be coolly paying attention at his side.

'And you expected him back about when?'

'Oh, well, I don't know. He says he was just going down the boozer, you know, and I'm like that, don't you be too late and all that, you know. Expected him back about eleven.'

MacPherson nodded, appeared concerned. 'So, if you expected him to return at about eleven o'clock on Tuesday, why did you wait 'til this morning to report him missing? Did you not think about doing it yesterday?'

She took a loud slurp from her cup, placed it on the table.

'Well, you know officer, I just assumed he'd scored with some bit of skirt and buggered off back to her place. It wouldn't be the first time that's happened, you know.' She smiled weakly at MacPherson, he nodded back. 'I was a wee bit worried by yesterday afternoon, but I don't know, I just didn't like to bother anyone, you know. I mean, I remember once when Missus Thingwy from down the road reported her wee boy missing and if it wasn't just the thing, but he turns up...'

Holdall interjected. Strained patience; teeth ground together.

'All right, Mrs. Hutchinson, can we just stick to the story?'

'Oh aye, aye, no bother,' she said.

MacPherson scribbled something else in his notebook.

'Look Mrs. Hutchinson, you've done the right thing by reporting your son missing now and you're not putting anyone to any trouble.'

Like hell she's not, thought Holdall, as he began to drift away from the conversation.

'Now, can you tell us who he usually met down the pub and if you've been in contact wi...'

There was a noise at the front door, followed by the sound of footsteps marching into the house. Holdall rolled his eyes extravagantly, stood up. The prodigal son, he thought. No point in delaying; might as well get out of the damn house before she killed him.

MacPherson joined him as the door to the sitting room opened and a young man of around nineteen walked into the room. He stopped, stared at the two strangers, looked at his mother. His mouth opened but he didn't get as far as formulating a sentence.

'Where the bloody hell have you been, eh? I've been worried sick, so I have, but no, you wouldn't give a shite about that, would you? You're too bloody busy thinking about yourself and to Hell with everybody else! And look what you've made me do, you stupid bastard. I've called the polis, so I have. I'll probably be in trouble now but you'll not give a shite about that, will you? No, you bloody won't. You're just too busy thinking about yourself. Bloody Hell, to think that I raised you from nappies. And what thanks do I get?'

She paused for breath, started talking again before anyone else had time to speak.

'Look, I'm really sorry about this, officers, wasting your time and all that. Can I not offer you another biscuit?'

Holdall and MacPherson held out their hands in unison to refuse, inching slowly towards the door. Following the biscuit refusal, the mother turned once more upon her son.

'Well, don't stand there like a bloody great pudding. Where have you been?'

He shrugged and stared at the floor. 'I just met this girl, Mum, you know. She was really nice. Anyway, I spent the night with her, nothing happened! And then we went away for the day yesterday. Millport.' Ah, Millport, thought Holdall. Land of Fantasy. Or was he confusing it with California? 'I tried phoning but, honest I did, Mum, but you weren't in. Then I ended up spending the night last night 'n all.' He turned to Holdall. 'How, am I in trouble?' he said.

Holdall shook his head and laid his hand on the lad's shoulder. 'No, son, you're not in trouble.' He smiled and began to walk past him. Stopped, looked the boy in the eye. 'Was she a babe?'

Stuart Hutchinson – The Hutch to his friends – looked surprised, then the smile broke onto his face.

'She's a wee stoatir,' he said.

Holdall grinned and turned to the mother. 'We'll see ourselves out, thank you, Mrs. Hutchinson.'

He walked from the sitting room with MacPherson at his heels and as they opened the front door they could hear the woman begin to berate her son in earnest now that they'd gone. They stood out in the light rain for a second, looking at the dank and depressing street before them. Lost in thought.

'This is a lousy job, Sergeant,' said Holdall, beginning to trudge towards the car.

'Bloody right it is,' replied MacPherson, following on, his stride nevertheless the more purposeful.

They got into the car and MacPherson studied the list he was carrying with him.

'Just one more to go, sir. A William Henderson. The barber.'

Holdall winced at the thought that this one might prove to be more serious than the others, started the engine and drove off into the gloom.

Interview With A Barber

Big Billy McGoldrick was in danger of getting his ear cut off, so animated was he becoming in the discussion, constantly trying to turn his head to look at Chris.

'But why,' he said, 'why is it that our teams can't beat anyone in Europe? Christ, we lose to them all these days. Teams we'd have pumped the pants offa twenty years ago. All they wee pish teams. Now we're the wee pish teams.'

Chris studied the back of McGoldrick's head, executed a couple of smooth moves, the scissors sizzling in his fingers, then straightened up, catching his eye in the mirror.

'Cause, and this is what I keep trying to tell you, they play cultured football, not like our kick and rush game. With us it's all heads down and last one in the penalty area's a big poof.'

McGoldrick shook his head, narrowly avoiding a scissor in the ear. 'Aye, all very well, but why can't we play cultured football, if they can do it? It's places like Turkey and Latvia we're talking about here for Christ's sake, not Brazil.'

'Because the fans wouldn't stand for it. Nobody in Scotland wants to see cultured football, do they?'

'Are you saying that I don't like cultured football?' McGoldrick said, straightening his shoulders and slightly raising his head, changing forever the course of the growth of his hair.

'Who does in Scotland?' said Chris, already beginning to make the necessary adjustments. 'I mean, look. Do any of us really want to see our team come out and fanny about in the midfield like a bunch of Jessies? It's not the Scottish mentality. If the Thistle haven't scored after about ten minutes, we're all baying like dogs for them to blooter the ball up the park as hard as possible. That's what Scottish football's all about.'

McGoldrick looked doubtful, but Chris was flowing, the barber in his element.

'It's typical of the generally aggressive nature of Scottish behavioural patterns. It's like if two blokes get into a fight in a pub. What do they do? Do they glass each other, or do they pass the ball about in midfield?'

McGoldrick held up his hand and made to reply, but Barney switched off, tried not to listen to the rest. He was in the middle of a haircut and had already committed two or three too many stinkers today; didn't want to do any more.

He was attempting to embrace denial but it wasn't easy. Combined with worry about what Cemolina would do with the corpse and worry about what he would say to the police when they finally showed up, as he was expecting the inevitable, his head was a mess. Much the same as most of the customers he'd dealt with this black day.

Moira had phoned the shop that morning to say there was still no sign of Wullie, and had asked Chris if he knew of anywhere he might have gone. If Chris was worried about Wullie's disappearance, he wasn't showing, telling himself that Wullie had probably just gone off somewhere, got drunk, and fallen in with some woman. He would stagger home later that day, an apologetic look on his face and a stream of spectacular excuses pushing each other out of the way in order to be first to get to his mouth.

Barney surveyed the task in which he was currently embroiled, and wondered about how hideously wrong it had already gone. The man had asked for a Charlton Heston '86, always a tricky proposition, but especially so since Barney's hands were shaking;

involuntary spasms, sporadic bursts. Barney had been tempted to suggest that his customers take out ear insurance before they sat down. Thought, however, that if he had nothing to do but sit and brood he would feel even worse.

Of the customers that had come in looking for Wullie, some had immediately departed on finding him not there and the rest had mostly gone to Chris. There were a couple who'd reluctantly agreed to be prey to Barney's fickle hand, being rewarded with hair which received a fright every time it looked in a mirror.

It had been a long morning, and Barney was in the middle of his Charlton Heston, when he finally got what he'd been expecting. Two men walked into the shop, their coats buttoned up against the rain. They looked miserable and unhappy, but it wasn't the usual misery of men coming to get their hair cut. They stood for a few seconds looking at the barbers and then one of them walked forward, his hands fishing around in his pockets. Finally he produced his card, holding it up between Chris and Barney.

'Chief Inspector Holdall, Maryhill. I wonder if I could have a word with you two gentlemen?'

'Is it about Wullie?' asked Chris. The police, instant worry. Same for Barney, but for different reasons.

'Yes, it's about Mr Henderson.' Holdall waved a hand at Barney and Chris, moved to sit down. 'The two of you finish what you're doing, and we'll speak to you then. It shouldn't take too long.'

They sat down at the end of the queue. The two customers ahead of them looked nervous at the closeness of the law and shuffled as much as they could towards the other end of the long bench. Finally the strain became too much for one of them and he stiffly rose and walked quickly from the shop. MacPherson looked suspiciously after him. He'd arrested people for less, but Holdall quelled his enthusiasm with a wave of the hand. Whatever reason the man had to remove himself from the presence of the police, it wasn't their problem. If they chased every idiot who looked suspicious… and he let the thought run away.

Barney, meanwhile, was considering doing the same thing, but managed to talk himself out of it. Instead, he attempted to concentrate on the haircut which he was committing. Fortunately, in a Charlton Heston '86, there's more blow-drying and brushing to be done than scissor work. Consequently, after he laid down the scissors, the very instruments of death from the previous evening, he found that his hands stopped shaking, and the work with the hair-dryer became altogether more straightforward. So much so, that to his dismay, he finished his job off before Chris. Thought: bugger. He'd be first to interview, but there was nothing he could do about it.

The customer seemed reasonably content with his thatch – he knew a girl in his local who went mad for men with Charlton Heston '86 haircuts – and after thrusting an extra couple of pounds into Barney's hand, walked suspiciously past the police and out of the shop. Barney swallowed hard, tried to compose himself the best he could, and turned to face his tormentors. Couldn't open his mouth, not yet trusting his vocal cords, but stood in front of them looking like a stuffed fish.

Holdall and MacPherson walked towards him.

'Is there somewhere we can talk?' said Holdall, doing his best to keep the disinterest from his voice.

Barney waved his hand towards the door at the back of the shop, in off the alcove, behind the fifth seat – a place of mystery for the customers who never got to see what went on within – and he led them into the room. It was not large; used mostly as a store room, although there were a couple of chairs so the barbers could nip out and take a break should the work allow. There was a large window in the back of the room, with bars across, looking out onto a grim and tiny courtyard, where the rain fell on dirty and cracked stones. Barney looked through the bars, considered that this could be his fate, and turned to the policemen after they had closed the door.

MacPherson produced his notebook, prepared to start. Holdall pulled out one of the seats and prepared to look bored. The shop and this back room depressed him and he was beginning to think that he couldn't blame one of the barbers for wanting to run away from it.

'Mr Thomson or Mr Porter?' asked MacPherson.

'Thomson,' muttered Barney, still not entirely trusting himself to open his mouth.

'Why don't you take a seat, Mr Thomson?'

'I prefer to stand, thanks.' Barbers were used to standing.

'Very well.'

MacPherson studied his notes. Barney tried to prepare himself to do his best to hide his guilt. This was just routine, he said to himself, routine. They had to speak to him; he was the last person who would say he saw Wullie. It didn't mean they suspected anything.

'Mr Thomson, this is just a routine missing persons inquiry. Moira Henderson has reported her husband missing since late yesterday afternoon. Now, she told us that you were the last person she knows to have spoken to him. Is that correct?'

Barney considered his answer, as he would do after every question; all the better to avoid self-incrimination.

'Aye, aye, that's right. He, eh, left here about quarter past five, as far as I can remember.'

'And did he say where he was going?'

Another pause. 'No, no, he didn't. He just said something about going to the shops, but he didn't say which shops, you know. He asked me to lock up, then he left. That's all really, I think.'

MacPherson made a couple of scribbles in his notebook, lifted his head to look at Barney.

'He didn't mention going anywhere else, or going away or anything?'

'No, no, nothing like that.'

'And was it normal for Mr. Henderson to go to the shops after work?'

Barney shrugged, almost too hastily. Held it back, looked noncommittal. 'I don't know. I didn't really know what he did outside the shop, you know, we weren't really friends.'

MacPherson raised his eyebrow, looked at Barney in such a way as to make him feel extremely uncomfortable. Barney tried to think of what he had just said and how it might have been incriminating.

'You *were* not really friends, Mr Thomson?' MacPherson's voice was low and hard, Holdall looked up with some interest. What was he doing, he wondered. 'Surely you mean, you *are* not friends? Or d'you suspect something might have happened to Mr Henderson which you're not telling us about?'

Barney let a laugh ejaculate from some unknown region of his throat, an attempted dismissive, apologetic laugh, which unfortunately sounded as if he had just murdered someone and been caught with the scissors in his hands.

'Aye, aye, of course. We *are* not friends. That's what I meant. Slip of the tongue. You know how it is, eh?'

MacPherson slowly lifted an eyebrow. Mr Spock never looked so cool. 'How what is, Mr Thomson?'

Holdall watched his sergeant with some fascination. MacPherson was taking the piss out of the barber, trying to make him as uncomfortable as possible. He shrugged. Why not? It was one of the few pleasures left to the police; to put people to as much discomfort and unease as they could. And, he had to admit, there was no better exponent of the art than MacPherson.

'Oh, you know, nothing. You know how it is when you get interviewed by the polis. You always get worried, even when you haven't accidentally stabbed someone with a pair of scissors,' – *what are you saying!* – 'which of course I haven't, and well, you know, and you, eh, know how it is.' He finally shut up, stood with a stupid grin on his face.

Holdall watched with wonder, found himself almost bursting out laughing. MacPherson was a genius. Here was some poor sap who had nothing whatsoever to do with the guy disappearing and the sergeant had him acting like he was in the dock on a multiple murder charge.

MacPherson stared thoughtfully at him; tapped his pen on the notebook. Brilliant, thought Holdall, brilliant.

'And where was your colleague, Mr Porter, when Mr Henderson left the shop?'

Barney relaxed. An easy one, thank God. 'He'd gone home early, at about three o'clock, because we were so quiet. Wullie sent him home.'

'And does that happen often?'

Another easy one. Holdall smiled. Another calm before the storm, if he wasn't much mistaken. Relax them, then grab them by the balls. Terrific fun.

'No, no,' said Barney, easily. 'I don't know what happened yesterday. Just a quiet day, I suppose.'

'So, how many customers were there in the shop?'

Jings, this is a dawdle, thought Barney, an absolute dawdle. 'Oh, I don't know. Maybe fifteen all day. Not many.'

MacPherson nodded, scratched behind his ear with the pen. Time to crank it up again. Holdall knew what was coming, enjoyed the show.

'And do you and Mr Henderson get along all right, seeing as you're not really friends?'

Shit, what did he say now? He could hardly lie, because they could easily find him out from Chris. The truth it would have to be, however incriminating.

'No, I don't suppose we did get…do, do get along very well.'

'Why is that Mr Thomson? Everyone else we've spoken to seems to think he's a nice enough guy. What's so different about you?'

Everybody else they've spoken to! Who the hell could that be? Holdall almost guffawed. This was wonderful. The *Godfather, Part II* of police interviews. Hard, powerful, but cracking entertainment. Wait until the lads down the station heard about it. MacPherson was a genius.

'Eh, I, eh, don't really know. Just a personality clash, I suppose.

Different generations, interested in different things, you know. Something like that.'

MacPherson nodded, looked doubtful.

'I don't like football,' muttered Barney in his defence. Quite the wrong thing to say to MacPherson, who looked at Barney as if he suspected him of being a master criminal.

Barney heard his heart beating faster and faster, hoped they would be done with him soon. What else could they have to ask him, after all?

'We understand that Mr. Henderson is about to ask you to leave the shop. Had he done that yet, Mr. Thomson?'

Barney's mouth opened slightly, the return of the stuffed fish look, hook in upper lip.

Oh God! Answer that! They must have spoken to Wullie's father. Bloody hell, if they knew that, maybe they'd suspect him of anything. Maybe they'd already spoken to Charlie Johnstone. Maybe they were about to arrest him...

A thought struck him, uncomfortable, unpleasant. Why were two detectives doing a routine missing persons inquiry? Surely it should be a couple of uniforms. They must already suspect something. Shit, shit, shit. What was he going to say? Only one thing to do. Deny everything!

'Jings, I'm sorry to look shocked, you know, but I hadn't heard that, no. They were going to sack me? Who told you that?'

He looked hopefully at the sergeant, wondering if his acting had been of sufficient merit. MacPherson studied his notebook, raised his eyes.

'We understand from Mr Henderson's father, a Mr James Henderson, that he intended to tell you yesterday.'

Barney shook his head, mumbled a denial, stared at the floor; a child with crumbs around his lips denying having broken into the biscuit tin.

MacPherson raised the eyebrow once more, then scribbled something else in the notebook. Decided to put Barney out of his misery. Certainly he was acting a little suspiciously, but then so would anyone if you treated them the right way. They were looking for a serial killer, not some boring old barber who wet his pants the minute the police hoved into view.

'I don't think there's anything else for the moment, Mr Thomson. We may want to speak to you again, however. You're not thinking of going anywhere, are you?'

Barney stared at him, eyes wide. No, he hadn't been thinking of going anywhere, but now that he'd mentioned it. It was obvious. That'd be the easiest way out. Run away! Disappear up to the Highlands or down to England. Or France even. Just get out of Glasgow.

'No, I'm not going anywhere.'

'Right then, Mr Thomson. When you go out, will you ask your colleague to come in here, please?'

Barney nodded, tried not to show the smile of relief which itched to burst free all over his face. Nodded at Holdall, walked back into the shop.

'Brilliant, Sergeant,' said Holdall smiling, when the door was closed, 'you took the piss out of that guy something rotten.'

MacPherson looked quizzically at him. 'What d'you mean, sir?'

Holdall didn't answer and stared disconsolately at the floor.

Barney walked back into the shop, relief smothering him. For all their questions, the police obviously didn't suspect him of anything. And why should they? He was also comforted by the thought of running away from it all; imagined a variety of exotic locations. America would be a good one; he didn't think they played football there.

Chris was half way through a regulation short back and sides, and almost finished a half-hearted discussion on how Partick Thistle could best go about winning the league. He looked at Barney as he came through the door.

'They'd like a word with you now, Chris,' he said.

'Aye, OK.'

'D'you want me to finish that off?'

The customer's strangled cry of *no!* was cut off by Chris's acceptance, and Barney, with new lightness in his heart, new vigour, went about his business with a whistle on his lips and a nimbleness in his fingers. Suddenly he was a man transformed, in all his relief almost able to forget his troubles. He polished off the haircut to general satisfaction and had started on another before Chris emerged back into the shop, a worried look on his face, the police close behind.

They nodded at Barney as they walked past, then they were gone, out into the morning rain. Chris and Barney looked at each other. Barney didn't know what the look said; no words were exchanged.

An hour and a half later they found themselves alone in the shop, having worked their way through half a dozen customers. Barney was feeling rather pleased with himself, as he grabbed a look at his paper. In quick succession he had executed a *long at the back, short at the sides*, a *not too much off the top, tapered at the sides and back*, and a *Bobby Ewing '83*. They had each, in their own way, been immaculate haircuts, barbery out of the top drawer, smooth, elegant and polished. A trio of satisfied customers, the money from the healthy tips still jangling in Barney's pocket. Had this been America there would have been loud whoops and cheers, and cries of *good hair!*, and he and Chris would have exchanged high fives and banged heads. Barney imagined the word would already be going around Partick – "Want good hair? Barney Thomson's your man."

The door opened and a young lad entered. He nodded at the two barbers. 'Wullie not in today?'

'No, he's got the day off,' said Chris. 'I'll do your hair if you want to sit down.'

The lad hesitated, looked a bit embarrassed. 'No, it's all right, I'll go to this other bloke, if that's OK?'

Chris didn't care. 'Aye, sure, no problem, mate.'

Barney did, however. He lowered the paper and looked at the

boy as he walked over. He was delighted. This was the kind of thing he'd always wanted and it hadn't taken long. Maybe he should've killed Wullie ages ago.

Stood up, offered him the chair.

'Hello, young fellow, how's it going?' Tried to keep the enormous grin from his face. Didn't entirely succeed.

'All right, mate,' said Allan Duckworth, 'how about you?'

'Aye, aye, can't complain, can't complain.' He swirled the cape around dramatically, draped it over the customer and reached for the towel to put at his neck. 'So, what will it be the day, my friend?'

'Oh, you know, just a haircut,' he said.

Just a haircut. Music to the barber's ears. *Carte blanche* to do as you pleased. What could be easier? The smile on Barney's face increased by another inch or two on either side as he picked up the electric razor.

'What d'you make of those Rangers?' he said after a minute or two. 'Lost four games in a row now, eh? Really struggling.'

'Aye, but they're still six points clear at the top of the league.'

'Five.'

'Five, is it?'

'Aye. But you know, they're only that far ahead because everybody else is so crap.'

'Aye, you're right about that.'

And so the conversation continued, and so the day continued. Barney cut more hair than he had had to do in a single day for many a year and he loved every minute of it. Quite forgot about Wullie, other than to be glad he wasn't there to take business from him. And customer after customer left the shop with hair from the Gods; hair for which movie stars would have paid hundreds of dollars, for only four pounds plus tip. People would recall this day for years and how they had been privileged to have had their hair cut by a man at the zenith of barbetorial invention.

They had seen the final customers off by ten past five. Chris had grown more and more uneasy during the day as no word had come from Wullie; his initial lack of concern giving way to worry. Imagined all kinds of disasters but never the truth.

He exchanged few words with Barney and after everyone had gone, told him to leave and that he would lock up. Barney accepted and, after clearing away the fallen hair around his chair, put on his jacket and walked from the shop. It had been a glory day for him, the best that he could remember. And any day which he didn't round off by stabbing someone would from now on be viewed as a success.

But as he stepped out into the bleak rain of an early March evening, he was forced to return to the real world. He was going to have to face the consequences of his actions. He had to go and see Cemolina and discover the gruesome truth of how she had disposed of the body. He hadn't worried about it all day because he hadn't thought about it. Now, however, the time was at hand.

And however bad he imagined it was going to be when he got to her house, it was nowhere near as bad as it actually was.

The Freezer Full Of Neatly Packaged Meat

Barney stood on the threshold of his mother's door, giving himself pause, trying to come to terms with the ill feeling he had about what lay within. Jodie Foster in *Silence of the Lambs*. It was not just his mother's *soup* remark which still rang in his ears; something else, a sense of grave foreboding.

He opened the door and walked into the flat, calling out her name. There came no reply but that was not unusual. However, there was an ominous feel to the house. Silence. No television played in the sitting room, no other sound. He sensed death; could smell it. Perhaps she was out on her grotesque errand, he thought. Yet somehow he knew it was not that.

He walked quickly along the hall and into the sitting room. In the dark, at first he saw nothing, because he wasn't expecting to see what was there. Then he realised that his mother was lying sprawled on the floor, her head resting at an awkward angle. A cup lay spilled at her side, its contents splashed across the carpet; a murky brown stain all that was left of a milky coffee, three sugars.

He stared at her, rooted to the spot. Shock. Then through the gloom, he saw her eyelids flicker, dashed to her side and knelt down.

'Mum! Mum! Are you all right?'

Bloody stupid question, thought Cremolina, of course I'm not all right. But she had not the strength to say it. Her life was fading quickly, the strain on her heart intolerable. Had he come two minutes later, Barney would have found her dead.

She tried to lift her head off the carpet. She had something to tell him. She must before she went.

'I'll call an ambulance,' he said quickly, beginning to get up, but he was stopped by the slight movement of her head.

'No,' she croaked, 'too late for that.'

He could barely hear her but he knew what she was trying to say. He put his mouth up close to her ear, gently squeezed her hand.

'It's not too late, Mum, you've still got a chance. I'll get an ambulance.'

He started to get up again but she brushed his hand as she made an effort to grab it before he moved away. He looked at her; she said something to him which he could not make out. Torn between fetching help and letting her talk to him. Didn't know what to do. Knew deep down that it was already too late. Bent down, put his ear close to her mouth. Fighting back the fear; his mother was dying.

'The fre...' she whispered, her voice on the point of expiration.

'Sorry, Mum, I didn't hear you. Did you say *frisbee*?'

It hit him; he was listening to the last words of his mother. Her dying words. He put his head nearer, as the tears started to form at the sides of his eyes.

'Free...' she croaked, her voice barely audible.

He screamed within his head. These were his mother's dying words, he had to hear them. She was making the grand effort, so must he. This could be what stood forever on her headstone. He had to understand.

'Frisbee, Mum? What about a frisbee?'

She summoned up the juices of life for one last great effort. Held her hand out, grabbed the sleeve of his coat to pull him closer. She paused to conjure up new energies, then spoke slowly and powerfully into his ear.

'Not frisbee, you dunderheid. Freezer! It's in the freezer!'

The words 'what's in the freezer, Mum?' – pointless words for he knew well what she meant – hung suspended on his lips, half uttered and then forgotten, as his mother folded from her last great effort. Having said what she must, the will was gone, and her body settled lifelessly on to the floor. Her fingers remained gripped to his jacket. A death grip. He grabbed her head, pressed his cheek against it and wept, his other troubles forgotten.

He stayed like that for a long time, unable to let go, as if by hanging onto her body he was in some way hanging onto her life. Finally he pulled himself away and, after having trouble detaching her gripping fingers, he sat wearily down beside the telephone and started making calls.

*

Two hours later, Barney and his elder brother Allan sat and blankly stared at the carpet. They didn't see each other much, had never got on particularly well. And here they sat, sharing something for the first time in over twenty years.

Allan lived a moderately opulent existence on the periphery of Perth, in a house which Barney envied, with a wife that Barney yearned for. Three children and a dog completed the picture-perfect life and Barney would never know that Allan was even more miserable than he was himself.

'Well, my brother, I'd better be getting back. Barbara will be wondering what's happened to me. I didn't leave much of a note.'

Barney's grief was marginally pushed aside for a second. He hated it when Allan called him 'my brother', which he always did, and the mention of Barbara – attractive, intelligent, delicious Barbara, who had never watched a stupid soap in her puff – had pangs of jealousy thumping loudly at the doors of his grief, demanding entry.

'I'll be back early tomorrow morning to get on with the arrangements.'

'You can stay the night with Agnes and me, why don't you?' said Barney. Something within him wanted Allan to say yes, some basic fraternal thing which made him want to hang on to his brother, even though he knew that there was no way he would accept. And would he not be ashamed to take his brother back to his flat in any case?

'No, that's all right, Barney, thanks. I'd better be getting back. Thanks all the same.' He stood up, started to put his jacket on. 'Will you be going to your work tomorrow? You know, it's all right if you do, because I can take care of everything.'

Like the unwanted belch of curry back into your mouth, four days after you've eaten a vindaloo, reality kicked Barney stoutly in the balls.

His work. The shop. Wullie. The corpse. The freezer.

Shit.

He cleared the image from his head and looked at Allan. Maybe he could tell him everything. Allan, the older brother. The sensible older brother. He'd know what to do.

Phone the polis and get him locked up, probably.

'Aye, aye, I've got to go to work,' he said. He wasn't telling Allan anything. 'There's one of the other lads off at the moment, so there's only the two of us the now, you know. I'd really better go in.'

Allan nodded. 'No problem. Don't you worry, I'll see to everything.'

They said their farewells, Barney saw his brother to the door. Returned to the sitting room, hesitated. He had to go and look in the freezer, but he desperately didn't want to. Tried to persuade himself that he could postpone it until morning, but he knew he might as well get it over with.

His mother had a huge freezer, he knew that. Plenty of space for a body. He and Allan had always asked her why she bothered; now it had been of use. Had she known all this time that she might one day have need of concealing a corpse? Of course not, Barney, don't be so bloody stupid, he muttered.

He walked with some trepidation into the kitchen. The big freezer dominated the room, taking up one whole wall to the left as he walked in. Stopped and stared. Not just big enough to hold one body, he thought. Big enough to hold several.

He put his fingers on the handle and left them there. Whatever he was about to see, he knew it wasn't going to be pleasant. Wullie's body, hideously curled up, his face distorted in agony and shock; was that what awaited him?

He swallowed and slowly lifted the lid of the freezer. A plume of vapour drifted out to meet him and he stared into it, waiting for it to disperse. Suddenly it was all there in front of him. Meat. The freezer was packed with meat. And then it struck him, and he felt his stomach push at the back of his throat.

This eclectic array of packets, frosted over reds and browns. This was Wullie. Neatly packaged, easy to handle, ready to use, Wullie.

He prodded something. It was frozen solid. She must have worked fast, he thought, because it had all been in here a long time. The freezer was tightly packed, every inch taken with bones and various chunks of meat and flesh. He poked at a couple of things, his face a mask of horror and wonder, then wriggled something free from the frozen mass.

It was a foot, sweetly severed below the ankle. On the side of the package, neatly printed on a white label, were the words *W. Henderson / 11 Mar / Left Foot.* He dropped it back into the crowd, lifted another one. An indeterminate lump of flesh and organ. *W. Henderson / 11 Mar / Part of viscera (unsure which)* it read. Quickly put it back, lowered the lid. Didn't want to see any more.

He rested his hands on the edge of the freezer and stared blankly at the top of it for a while. Trying to examine his emotions to discover what he really thought about it.

'What were you doing, Mum? You labelled Wullie. Did you have to go so far as to label him? Was this thing not grotesque enough for you?'

He lowered his head still further. And as he stood hunched over the freezer, the thought which had been nagging away since he'd first looked inside, finally broke out into the open. It had been a distant nag, something he couldn't place, but then suddenly it was there; stark naked in front of him, screaming. The idea of it chilled his heart; hairs rose slowly on the back of his neck.

The freezer was full, absolutely full to the brim. There was no way that the whole of this huge compartment was taken up with Wullie.

He opened the lid again, looked inside. Started picking up bits of Wullie, dumping them on the floor out of the way. A femur. The heart. An arm. The head. Christ! the head, the eyes removed. Packages of flesh, all neatly wrapped and labelled. He quickly lifted them all and then dumped them noisily on the floor. There seemed to be hundreds of them. Untidily arranged in ill-fitting row after ill-fitting row. God! he thought, these couldn't all be Wullie. It couldn't possibly be as he feared, but his blood thumped through his body, his breath caught in his throat. What else could it be?

Finally he dared to look at another one of the packages. His heart froze, his mouth dropped in horror. The writing was neat and in his mother's own hand. *Louise MacDonald / 5 Mar / respiratory system.*

Louise MacDonald. The name had been in the newspapers that morning. The latest victim of the deranged killer.

He let the package fall out of his hand, back into the freezer. Landed with a metallic thud. Christ almighty! His mother. His own mother! What had she left him with? More than just Wullie. A lot more than just Wullie.

He closed the lid and slumped down onto the floor, resting his back against the freezer. Sat amongst Wullie, the frozen packets strewn about the floor. The closest they'd been in a long time.

Barney Thomson, barber, ran his hands through his hair and closed his eyes. His breath came in spasms. His heart thumped. The doorbell rang.

He jerked his head back and smashed it into the freezer. Bit his tongue. 'Christ!'

He stood up in a panic. The door! It couldn't be the polis already. Stared out of the kitchen into the living room as if he expected

Special Branch to come charging into the flat. Felt hot and cold; frightened.

The door bell rang again. Quiet, urgent, wanting.

He swallowed. Might just be Allan having forgotten something. Looked at the mass of frozen food on the floor, decided to leave it where it was. Kicked it into the centre of the kitchen then closed the door behind him. Down the hall, round the corner, looked at the door. Could see the outline of a man behind the frosted glass panel.

A man alone, although it was not Allan.

Barney hesitated, staring at the grey figure. Imagined Death standing there, come to collect his dues. But it was he himself who was Death. He shivered, didn't want to answer the door, but now the man on the other side might be aware of Barney's presence. The light behind him.

The doorbell was pressed again. Get it over with, Barney.

He stepped forward, pulled open the door. Stared at his tormentor. A young, nervous looking man stared back. Late twenties perhaps. Checked jacket; Kay's catalogue. Debenham's tie; small blue and red bicycles on a yellow background. Mole beneath his lower lip, skin like feta cheese. Big hair; a Marc Bolan. Faint smell of cheap aftershave. Apples.

'Aye?' said Barney, as the younger man clearly was not about to start a conversation. Felt the commotion of his heart dampen.

Young man coughed, continued to look embarrassed. Nervous curiosity. Eventually he spoke.

'Mature woman, looking for love?' he said in a small voice.

Dead Mum Stalking

Barney sat quietly munching his dinner, Agnes opposite him at the table, a mug of coffee in her hands. He was glad that she'd cooked him fish, because he didn't think he'd be able to face meat. Nor would he for a long time, he reflected, as he stuffed a huge chip into his mouth.

The thought of the freezer turned his stomach; he tried to force it out of his mind, concentrate on his dinner. He was hungry but knew he wouldn't be able to eat anything if all he could think about was Wullie and all those others.

Agnes was looking at him, attempting consolation, the memory of her own mother's death stirring within her feelings of sympathy for her husband which she hadn't felt for some years. The television was playing in the background but for once she was paying more attention to Barney. She did have one ear, however, listening out for what was going to happen when Chenise and Manhattan discovered that Blade had been doing nights at a working men's club.

Finally Barney gave up the ghost and pushed the plate away. The memory of Wullie's face, twisted and distorted under a clear plastic bag, was too much for him. And how many more distorted faces were in that freezer, he kept asking himself. What were the newspapers saying now? Five or six? Was the freezer really that big?

'You not feel like eating, Barney?' she said.

He blinked, stared blankly at his chips. Should he come clean? It was on his mind. He wanted to own up to the whole sordid mess. But then, how could he? Not now. Before, perhaps, when it'd been his mess. But now? How could he reveal to the world that his own mother had been the mad Glasgow serial killer? And who was going to believe him anyway? Would they not all just think it'd been him who'd been doing it?

No, he had to finish what he'd started. He was going to have to get rid of those bodies somehow. They were safe enough where they were for the moment, but sometime he would need to get on with it. Corpse disposal; or what was left of the corpses. Death or glory, he told himself. But he knew there was no real way out. However this thing finished, his life was never going to be the same again. Unless he could make the acquaintance of denial.

'I don't blame you,' she said, and they sat in silence for another few minutes. Every now and again she was tempted to look over her shoulder at the television, but at times like these, soap opera was almost incidental. Almost.

'Oh aye,' she said, 'Bill phoned earlier. Sounded quite anxious to talk to you, but I told him about your mum, so he says he'll get you in the next day or two, you know. Passes on his condolences, and that, you know'

Barney looked at his watch. 'It's only quarter past ten. I'll maybe give him a wee call the now.'

'Aye, why don't you do that?' said Agnes, relieved that she would be able to watch the television again. Things looked as if they were picking up, and she submitted to her addiction.

Barney raised himself from the table, slumped down into another seat beside the phone, dialled the number. It did not ring long.

'Hello?' said Bill. There would've seemed to those who knew him, a slightly anxious quality to his voice. The effects of his knowledge of Barney's murderous intent of two nights before had been preying on his mind; uneasy rest.

'Hello, Bill, it's me.'

'Barney,' he said. Sounded relieved. 'I'm glad you called.'

He paused, knew that delicacy was required; was as incapable of it as every other man in Scotland. You don't lightly accuse a man of murder at the best of times, and certainly not when he is racked with grief.

'Did Agnes tell you about my mum?' said Barney.

'Aye, aye, she did. I'm really sorry Barney, that must've been a great shock. She was always so lively for her age, you know. What happened?'

'Well, you know, Bill, it was just her heart. She was an old woman.'

'Aye, aye, you're right. Still, it's aye a shock.'

'Aye, aye, you're right.'

'I know it's a bit early, and all that, but have you any idea when the funeral'll be?'

'I'm not sure. Probably not until Monday now, you know. Maybe even Tuesday. We'll find out tomorrow. Allan's going to take care of most of the arrangements. Elder brother and all that.'

'Aye, aye.'

There was a pause. Barney didn't know what else to say; Bill wondered how long he could leave it before bringing up the subject of the missing Wullie. And just exactly how was he going to put it?

Barney interrupted the flow of his thoughts.

'Did you phone for something else earlier, Bill?'

Bill paused briefly, then tentatively stuck his finger into the honey pot. 'Aye, well, actually there was, Barney.'

Another brief lapse in the conversation, while Barney waited to hear what it was. Bill tried to decide how best to delicately probe the accused. He'd read plenty of Henry Kissinger; tried to think of hints on diplomacy.

'Em, Barney...?'

'Aye, Bill, I'm still here.'

'...I, eh, understand that Wullie's missing. His father was on the phone to me earlier the night,' he said, finally taking his clothes off and diving into the honey pot, completely naked.

Barney put his hand to his head. Of course that was why he'd phoned. He was bound to have heard about it by now. Shit, shit, shit. Be assertive, he told himself, it was the only way.

'I didn't kill him, Bill, if that's what you're going to ask,' he said, not quite sounding as hard as he wanted to. It worked however. Bill sprang onto the defensive; like Italy in the '94 World Cup final.

'No, no, I wasn't going to say that.' He stopped, reflected. They were old friends. He might as well tell the truth. 'Well, aye, I was going to say it. But what can I think, Barney, eh? A couple of days ago you were talking about killing him, and now he's missing.'

Barney tried to play the part. 'I know what you must think, Bill, but wherever he's gone, it's nothing to do with me. I was just havering the other night. You know me, full of shite sometimes, so I am.'

Bill tried not to feel guilty, but wasn't entirely convinced by Barney's protestations of innocence. Years of reading philosophy had made him wary of coincidence.

'Have you any idea what's happened to him then?'

Barney was starting to get annoyed, knew it was because his friend's questions weren't misdirected. But still, he hadn't murdered Wullie, as such. It hadn't been his fault.

'I don't know, Bill, I told you that. Look, my mother's just died for God's sake. Give us a break, will you?'

'Aye, aye, all right, Barney. I'm sorry. I'd better go.'

'Aye, right. Look, I'm sorry I lost my temper, Bill. It's been a long night.'

'Aye, Barney, don't worry about it. I'm sorry for suggesting what I did.'

'Aye, right enough. I'll speak to you tomorrow.'

'Aye, aye.'

Bill hung up, wondering if he should call the police. Maybe you shouldn't do that to your friends, but then you shouldn't commit murder either. Wullie's father was his friend also, and he'd known young Wullie since he'd been a bairn. Made his decision. Prevaricate; sleep on it.

Barney hung up, wondering if Bill would go to the police. Maybe it wasn't the sort of thing you should do to a friend, but then Bill was also friendly with Wullie's father. And besides, he had always thought Bill was a slimy, underhand sneak anyway; the sort of bloke who'd report his own grandmother for taping a song off the radio. He had never trusted him when they'd played dominoes. Kicking himself for telling Bill his thoughts in the first place, he saw conspiracy everywhere.

He lay in bed that night wondering how he could shut Bill Taylor and Charlie Johnstone up, stop them from talking to the police. So consumed was he by these matters, that he hardly thought of his mother's freezer, and of his mother herself.

An advert in the paper; young men enticed to her flat. The great Glasgow serial killer.

Last In Line

Holdall sat at his desk considering the new list of missing persons which had arrived with the dawning of Friday morning. Another five, the usual specifications. There would be nothing for them here. And of the eight they'd ended up looking into the previous day, only two remained unaccounted for. The barber, and a young seventeen-year-old lad from Milngavie. Only the missing barber troubled him. He expected MacPherson would be eager to get back to the shop, have another go at Henderson's colleagues. They would chase up another couple of things about Henderson that day, then return to the shop over the weekend if required. The two remaining barbers weren't going anywhere.

Friday, however, would also involve the usual round of concerned parents. Bloody marvellous, he thought, another day wallowing in the sewer of disenchantment. He needed coffee.

The door opened and MacPherson walked into the room. Holdall looked up, the two men nodded.

'Good news, Stuart?' said Holdall, not entirely sure what MacPherson could tell him that would qualify.

'I have news, sir, though I don't know whether it's good.'

Holdall sighed, rested his chin in the palm of his hand. 'Let's hear it then,' he said; resignation.

'It's about Jamie Lawson, sir.'

Holdall stared blankly at him, narrowly avoided asking who the hell Jamie Lawson was.

'One of the two unaccounted fors from yesterday, sir,' said MacPherson, reading his mind. Holdall nodded, tried to look like he'd known all along.

'Dead in a ditch, is he?' he asked, no sympathy and almost a little hope in the voice.

MacPherson coughed. 'As a matter of fact, aye, he is. Stepped in front of a train, sir. On the west coast line, near Dalry.'

Holdall shrugged. He didn't care. If these bloody stupid teenagers wanted to do that to themselves it wasn't his problem.

'Why on earth would anyone go to Dalry to kill themselves?'

'I couldn't say, sir.'

Holdall grunted, thought about the half hour they had wasted the previous day talking to the boy's mother.

'Don't suppose he left a note confessing to a host of murders in and around the Glasgow area?'

'Not as far as I'm aware, sir.'

'No, I didn't really think that he would.'

He looked at his empty coffee cup, thought of the awfulness of the day ahead. It lay before him like a rotting cow on the pavement.

*

Friday was a long day in the shop. Many customers came in, as was always the case at the end of the week, and the barbers were kept busy. Wullie's father, James Henderson, even returned to work for the first time in five years to help out for a couple of hours in the afternoon. Some old time regulars were glad to see him, but they were nevertheless wary of submitting to the whim of his scissors, most of them having been burned by an out-of-practice barber at some time in their lives.

His first two haircuts were indeed dangerously close to being suitable cases for litigious action. However, he was a past master of the water disguise treatment, so his initial embarrassments were well covered up. After half an hour he was back in form, cutting hair with the light-fingered panache of old. Like a spy called out of retirement to take one last covert dip behind enemy lines, he took to his task with a smile on his lips and a glint in his eye. The old magic was still there.

He was telling himself that his son had probably just gone on an incredible two day drinking binge; felt quite proud of him, having done it himself a few times in his younger days. Knew, however, that he would not be able to keep the worry at bay for much longer.

Every now and again Barney cast an eye over the work going on next to him and was suitably unimpressed. He had always thought that James was a lousy barber and, as he studied the work which he was now doing, concluded that five years' abstinence had done him few favours.

And this, his blighted mind kept telling him, was the man who wanted to sack him. However much guilt Barney felt about what he'd done to Wullie, he still felt hurt and betrayed that they'd been intending to let him go. And if Wullie had been the agent of the dismissal, if it had been Wullie's finger on the trigger, it would still have been James who bought the gun, the ammunition and the hours of practice in the shooting gallery.

He found that he couldn't work and think about what had to be done at the same time; did his best to push to the back of his mind the horror of what lay in front of him. Having to dispose of five or six frozen bodies. You just didn't get training for that in life. Was thinking that he should've done Pathology 'O' level. Could not even begin to think of what was to be done with them, so he concentrated on work instead. If the whim took him, he attempted some inane conversation. Anything to push away the thought of the contents of the freezer.

James left the shop at around four o'clock, saying that he would return in the morning if Wullie hadn't shown up. His parting words to Barney – come in early so that I can have a word – had had Barney almost cutting the ear off the customer beneath his trembling hand.

It was late in the afternoon, with the day seemingly drifting to a quiet conclusion, when disaster struck. The rush of customers to the shop had ended, the skies outside were grim and dark with foreboding, the March rains had returned with a vengeance having given the city a few hours' respite. Barney and Chris were cutting the hair of one last customer each when the door opened and a figure dashed into the shop out of the rain.

Flat cap pulled low over his eyes, the collar of his coat turned high. He shook himself off, removed his cap, looked at Chris.

Charlie Johnstone.

'I know it's late, Chris, but you wouldn't have time to squeeze in an old muppet like me, would you?'

Chris glanced at the clock, but was not really concerned with the time. 'Aye, no bother there, mate, I'm nearly done here. That old carpet of yours shouldn't take too long.'

Charlie laughed and removed his coat to sit down, nodding at Barney as he did so. Barney nodded back; wishing the floor would open up and swallow him. He returned to cutting hair, but he couldn't ignore the feeling of dread. Of all the people who could have come in.

Barney's stomach churned, great armies of nerves and fear stampeded through his body. The hairs on the back of his head began to prickle and stand to attention. He had to do something.

He glanced at Chris to see where he was with his haircut. If he could get his finished first then maybe he would be able to cut Charlie's hair, making it easier to control the conversation.

Too late. As he looked over, Chris removed the towel from the back of his customer's head and shook the fallout from the haircut to the ground. Barney was still minutes away from a conclusion. Cursed quietly, tried to concentrate on the job. Perhaps if he avoided Charlie's eye he wouldn't speak to him.

His penultimate customer sent packing, Chris invited Charlie up to the big chair and prepared for the final haircut of the day.

'Thanks for this, Chris,' said Charlie, upon his ascent.

'Ach, no bother, Charlie, no bother. Mind you, it's been a right long day and all, what with Wullie not being here.'

Charlie glanced around, noticing for the first time that Wullie wasn't present, as Barney disappeared inside his pullover.

'Oh, right. Away on holiday or something?'

Chris shrugged. 'Tell you, we don't know, Charlie. Don't know what's happened to him. He left the shop on Wednesday. It was about quarter past five, that not right, Barney?'

'Aye,' said Barney, the presence of his heart lodged firmly in his mouth making it difficult for him to talk. If Charlie said something now, Barney was in trouble.

'And no one's seen him since. He's just disappeared off the face of the earth. Even Moira hasn't heard anything.'

Charlie slowly shook his head. 'Aye, aye, that's right strange, so it is. Right strange. Ach, he's probably sitting on a park bench somewhere, drunk out of his face. You know what Wullie's like.' And he laughed, but there was no humour or comfort in it.

'Aye, we know Wullie.'

Barney's hands trembled, the sweat beaded on his forehead. This was going badly. Then, out of the corner of his eye, he saw Charlie turn towards him. Knew what was coming.

'Here Barney, that wasn't him in — '

'What d'you make of those Rangers, eh, Charlie?' asked Barney. Smooth, cool, natural. And desperate.

Charlie looked quizzically at him. 'What are you on about? You ken I'm not interested in the Rangers. I was going to say — '

'Aye, I know, it's just, you know, it's getting near the end of the season, and I thought you might be going to the odd game.'

Charlie shook his head the best he could, given that Chris was now at work in and around the area of his left ear. 'I haven't been to see a game of football since my playing days finished, Barney, you know that, for God's sake.'

Chris looked up from the waves of hair. 'What's this great

interest in football all of a sudden, Barney? You're talking about the Rangers to just about everyone that comes in here.'

Barney attempted nonchalance. 'I just like to take an interest in what's going on. Football, that kind of thing. You know me.'

Aye, I do know you, thought Chris, that's what's so strange.

Barney stared at them to see if they were about to add to the conversation, but neither of them looked likely. He breathed a sigh of relief. The danger seemed to have been averted.

Charlie started up again. 'As I was trying to say, Barney — '

'So, how's Betty and all that, Charlie? You were saying something about her the other night.'

Shit! Barney, you stupid idiot. Don't mention the other night. Don't remind him, and don't give him the opportunity to ask.

'Aye, well she's not so bad. But you know, it was the other night I was going to mention. Was Wullie not still in the shop when I saw you? I thought he was and I couldn't get a straight answer from you. Head in the clouds, I thought, you know.'

'No, no, Charlie,' said Barney. Big relief – he'd thought Charlie had been about to mention the plastic bags. If he didn't say anything else, Chris needn't suspect anything. He might yet get away with it. 'He'd already gone a while earlier.'

There was near silence. The mellow clink of scissors. Barney felt the beating of his heart. He was getting to the end of his job and, surprisingly, it didn't appear to be going too badly. Don't mention the plastic bags, Charlie, he thought, please don't mention the plastic bags. Or I'll be forced to kill you.

Charlie nodded suddenly, grunted too. 'Aye, of course. That was about six o'clock, was it not? He'd have been long gone by then, so he would.'

The time! He'd forgotten about the time. Started cutting frantically with nervous fingers to cover up the panic. His customer semi-dozed beneath him, unawares.

Chris looked over. 'Six o'clock, Barney. What were you still doing here at that time? Couldn't have been that busy, surely? And not if Wullie had gone.'

Barney stared intently at the back of the head in front of him, as if trying to sort out some intricate piece of hair sculpture. Tried desperately to think of what to say. He believed himself to be a great barber, but he was crap in a crisis and he knew it.

'Oh, aye, well you know, it was stupid, but I just sat down at the end of the day, after Wullie had gone, and fell asleep. Who'd have thought it, eh? Woke up about six o'clock, feeling like a right eejit, so I did.'

Glanced over at Chris, saw the doubtful look in his eye. Chris looked away, returned to Charlie's hair. Barney could still get away with it if only Charlie kept his fat gob shut. Should have done it when he'd had the chance. What difference would one more corpse have made now?

The shop lulled into silence again. Barney relaxed; the conversation might be over. If he could just finish this haircut and get out of the shop, there had been nothing said to arouse the suspicions of Chris too greatly.

With a final couple of snips and an unsteady sweep of the comb, Barney was done. He lifted the towel, drew off the cape and the bloke was free. A final glance in the mirror, the customer was happy that the cut hadn't been as awful as he'd first suspected it might have been, then, with a brief exchange of cash, he was gone. Barney busied himself with clearing up, hoping he could make it out before anything else was said.

'You were sleeping, Barney?' said Charlie suddenly, as if he'd just been plugged in at the mains. 'I thought you were getting together all that — '

'What d'you make of yon serial killer, eh? That not terrible?' said Barney, but the words stuck in his throat. Knew he was beyond stalling tactics.

'What? No, I wasn't talking about that. Yon pile of garbage you were taking out on Wednesday night, that I helped you with. I thought that was what you'd worked late to do.'

Chris looked up. Curious. Pile of garbage? Penny did not yet drop. 'Oh, aye? And what pile of garbage was this, Barney?'

Barney swallowed, desperately trying to think of what he could say. There wasn't much for it, though – there was nothing he could say. He was going to have to disappear.

He looked up from where he had been busy arranging his scissors neatly on the counter and started to walk backwards. Trapped cat – without the claws.

'What? Oh, aye, well I've got to be getting to the toilet, if you'll just excuse me a second.' And with that he vanished through the door at the back of the shop, hoping that by the time he emerged the conversation would have been dropped.

Charlie watched him go, looked quizzically at the closed door.

'Bloody heavy, so it was. I had to give the lad a lift with it to get it into the back of his motor, so I had. Jings, but it was heavy. And big too. Long.'

'Is that right?' said Chris. The idea had come to him; comprehension slowly dawned. But it couldn't be. Barney? Mild-mannered, boring as you can get, Barney?

'Aye, it is right. What kind of garbage do you lot produce in here, anyway?'

Chris avoided the question. This was to be between Barney and him. 'Well, you've got to work in a barber's shop before you know the kind of things that we have to put in the rubbish.'

Charlie nodded gravely. 'Aye, I suppose you're right. The ways of many men are indeed mysterious.'

The conversation lulled once more, Chris was swift coming to the conclusion of his business. Barney skulked in the back room for a couple of minutes and then to his horror, as he emerged to make a quick exit, it was just in time to see Charlie put on his coat and head for the door.

'Oh, there you are Barney,' he said. 'I'll be seeing you.'

Barney had no words, returned the farewell with a lame nod.

'Right, Chris, thanks a lot for squeezing us in,' said Charlie. 'I hope Wullie turns up in the next day or two.'

'I'm sure he will.'

And with that Charlie was gone. After he had stepped out into the street, Chris slowly closed the door behind him, locked it and slipped the key into his pocket. He turned round and faced Barney. Barney stood with his back up against the rear wall; frightened eyes, muscles tensed.

It was time.

Jolene Stabs Billy Ray Bob Billy Bob

The two men stood face to face across the shop, the tension of unstated convictions thick in the air, Chris's finger twitching at the trigger of his suspicion. He stood in the centre of the shop, hands steady, eyes narrow, stance broad. Gary Cooper.

Barney pressed against the rear wall, where his hand fell on the broom which he had just been using to clear up the detritus of the day. Grabbed it tightly, held it to his side, his knuckles white. Beads of sweat appeared on his forehead; his face was pale. Knees weak, heart thumped, hands trembled. Gollum; he wilted under the persistence of Chris's gaze.

Neither man yet felt confident enough to say anything. Chris didn't know what to say, still incredulous that Barney could have had anything to do with Wullie's disappearance. Barney waited only to react to whatever Chris might say, for he knew accusations would soon fly. He should've been desperately trying to think of excuses or stories to tell, but his mind was thick with fear. Clogged up. Needed a chimney sweep. His tongue flicked out to remove the moustache of sweat which had appeared above his top lip; a lizard surreptitiously reeling in a small insect.

Chris found his own tongue. He couldn't stand there all night, and although he didn't have a clue what to say or how this might progress, he knew he must say something.

'And what heavy bag of rubbish might this have been that you were taking out to your motor on Wednesday night? Eh, Barney?' he said. Spat out the name.

Barney cowered before the question, his eyes ever more fearful. Tongue darted out in quick jabs; his fingers took a feverish grip on the broom, a staff for fighting. Now he was Robin Hood. A frightened Robin Hood.

'Well?' Chris sneered at him, accusing finger pointing. 'You cut a lot of heavy hair on Wednesday, did you, Barney, is that what you're going to tell me?'

Barney spoke. 'It was just some of my own stuff.'

'What?' he shot back. 'What own stuff? You don't have any of your own stuff. What stuff of yours were you putting into rubbish bags?'

With the words came the doubt. What if it had been something of his own that he'd been taking out? Why should he tell Chris about it? It wasn't as if they were friends. He might do a lot of things that Chris didn't know about. God, maybe he was making a complete idiot of himself. What was he doing anyway? Nothing less than being on the point of accusing Barney of Wullie's murder; a hell of a thing to be doing.

It was not a throwaway line, a casual easily-ignored remark. Working late and carrying a heavy bundle to his car did not necessarily add up to Barney being a murderer. It was strange, and he was acting suspiciously, but it didn't make him a criminal. This was mild mannered Barney. Mild mannered, Barry-Manilow-with-scissors, Barney. Not some bug-eyed psycho.

'Look, it was just stuff, all right? None of your business.'

Chris had been walking towards him, now he hesitated, stopped. He was at an impasse. He couldn't force Barney to tell him what was in the bags and it was still a giant stretch of the imagination to assume that it had been Wullie's body.

Still, there Barney stood before him, clutching desperately onto the broom handle. Would he be acting so suspiciously if he had nothing to hide? Why be so defensive if his actions were innocent?

And the consistent interruption of Charlie when he'd been trying to speak to him. Obviously he hadn't wanted Charlie to mention what he'd been doing on Wednesday evening.

He got there eventually; arrived at a conclusion. Barney was hiding something. Definitely. Perhaps it was nothing to do with Wullie, but then perhaps it was. It wasn't going to cost him anything to make the accusation – not his friendship, that was for sure.

And Barney was due for the chop, he knew that. Not a friend, not a colleague.

Chris's mind was made up.

'Did you kill Wullie?' he said.

Barney reeled, squeezed the broom handle ever tighter. 'No!'

'Well what was in they bags then, Barney, what was in they bags? Eh? You think I'm some heid-the-ba' or something?'

Chris walked slowly towards him again, finger jabbing out, the aggression on his face far greater than the confidence he felt about Barney being rightly accused. But the closer he came, the more he saw the fright in Barney's eyes. Knew he was right.

'You did kill Wullie, didn't you? Didn't you? You knew he was going to sack you, didn't you, you miserable bastard?' he shouted, his voice consuming the small shop.

Barney bent his knees, almost squatting. 'No!' he squealed, a scream of pathetic denial. 'I didn't mean to. It was an accident!'

The words fell dead in the air.

Silence enveloped the shop. Barney was down on the floor, pressed against the wall as much as he could be. Chris stood three or four feet away, amazement on his face. So Barney had killed Wullie! He was right.

Now that the information was out there, neither of them knew what to do next. Chris stood over him, astonishment and anger growing on his face; Barney cowered beneath, awaiting his fate.

Several things were flying around Chris's head. He wanted to kill Barney. He knew he shouldn't. He should call the police, make sure Barney didn't escape – that's what he should do. But what then? What if he tried to keep Barney in here until they arrived? Barney was a killer, he'd just admitted to it. What if he went for Chris as well? God, he looked pathetic enough, but he'd killed Wullie somehow. Maybe he was *the* killer. Perhaps he should just get out while he could, go straight to the police. And what might this bastard have done to Wullie's body? Chopped it up? Christ almighty. A piece of Wullie could be sitting in the post waiting for delivery to Moira's house the following morning.

His wrath rose once more within him; the fire blazed in his eyes. Barney saw it, knew what was coming. Held the broom handle tightly in his grasp, prepared to defend himself.

Finally, Chris's temper snapped. He leapt forward, hands outstretched, searching for the killer's throat. Barney was ready for him however, did what he could in his pathetic, overtly-defensive position. Thrust the broom hard at Chris as he dived towards him, hitting him square in the chest with the thick brush. The broom was old but the handle held, and such was the force of Chris's onslaught that the full weight of the broom on his chest unbalanced him; sent him toppling backwards. He grabbed at air to try and right himself, but there was nothing to grab hold of. His feet slipped from under him and he fell back.

His head cracked off the sharp edge of the counter with a strange thud. Almost hollow, thought Barney, as he watched in horror. In a flurry of arms and legs, Chris collapsed to the floor, his head thumping down onto the ground; and there he lay. Motionless.

After the brief commotion, silence descended. Barney still cowered against the wall, the broom clutched in his trembling hands, staring at Chris. Chris was silent and unmoving on the ground. And then slowly, from where his head lay on the floor, a pool of thick blood began to spread out, stealthily creeping across the tiles. On his face could still be seen an expression of surprise, but his features would not move again.

Slowly Barney rose and crawled over beside him. He gingerly placed his ear on Chris's chest, held his breath as he listened.

Nothing.

He sat back on the floor, staring at Chris. Couldn't believe it.

'Christ, not again,' he said.

★

Barney ate his dinner. Once again he was practising a good deal of denial in order to be able to eat, as it was the last thing that he felt like doing. But he was temporarily trying to forget the previous three days, to relax before he had to face the awfulness of what was to come.

He had read somewhere once that the best way to rest the mind was to think of some idyllic and peaceful setting, to concentrate on it, imagine that you were there, smelling the aromas, hearing the sounds. So, as he sat at the dinner table, Agnes's tinned beef stroganoff – beef, by God! – flitting quietly between plate, fork and mouth, he imagined himself to be at the foot of Ben Ime, where the forest track comes to an end beside the small dam with the beautiful clear pool of water behind it.

The sun was shining, there was a crispness in the air, the snow still covered the top half of the hills. He was sitting back after a hard day's walking, a cup of tea in one hand, a roast beef sandwich in the other. All of a sudden a small grey rabbit, its nose snuffling, overcame its fear and emerged from its hiding place in a nearby bush. It stood on its hind legs and sniffed the air, attempting to fathom what it was that Barney was eating. 'Ah, roast beef sandwich,' it said to itself. 'I like a bit of cow.'

Barney looked away from the rabbit and back up the hill. The last section was steep and tricky in the snow but hardly treacherous. He could still see the footprints he'd left, stretching back up the mountain. He sighed a contented sigh and turned to the rabbit. 'Would you like some sandwich?' he said, and the rabbit nodded its head, its nose twitching in anticipation. Barney tossed the remains of his sandwich high into the air towards the rabbit, a few inches above its head. It leapt majestically up to grab the bread and seemed to pause in mid-air while it plucked the flying sandwich out of the sky. It could not keep its balance however, and fell backwards, landing flush on its back, impaling itself on a broken beer bottle.

Barney had killed the rabbit.

He snapped out of his idyll, jolted and unhappy, and stared once again into the abyss of real life. He had accidentally killed his two work colleagues and his mother had died leaving him a freezer full of butchered corpses. Maybe he'd be able to keep his job now, but only if he could keep out of prison.

Chris's body lay dumped in the boot of his car, where he'd left it half an hour previously. Barney had no idea what to do with it. Or Wullie's body for that matter. Or any of the others. Maybe he could just mail them all to the relatives, bit by bit.

The one small piece of breathing space that he had was that Chris lived alone. It might be a while before anyone reported him missing. Perhaps it would even have to be Barney himself, when Chris didn't turn up for work the following morning.

He thrust a contemplative lump of potato into his mouth. If he was lucky, he thought with a smile, the police might think that Chris had killed Wullie and had done a runner. Not much chance of that, though. More like, they'd have him for both.

He glumly stared ahead as he speared the final potato, popped it into his mouth and contemplated his fate. And he did not even notice Agnes squealing with delight, as Jolene accidentally stabbed Billy Ray Bob Billy Bob in the throat with a pencil.

Russian Toilets

Saturday mornings were always busy. They closed at lunchtime, there being football matches to attend, and usually had a rush of people to deal with before twelve-thirty. They were especially busy this morning because Chris hadn't shown up for work. Old man Henderson was there, and in Wullie's continued absence he had also called for their occasional Saturday girl, Samantha, which clearly went down well with all the men who came into the shop. Samantha always dressed for the occasion. Some consolation for not having either of their preferred barbers there. Few were those, however, with enough of a neck to sit it out and wait for her in particular, most preferring instead to leave it to chance, scowling disconsolately when they were called by Barney or James.

James had been disgruntled when Chris hadn't arrived and had made a few phone calls to his apartment. Had decided he wouldn't bother Chris's parents with it, not yet. But with Wullie having seemingly vanished, it was giving him an uneasy feeling. No believer in coincidence either, Old James Henderson.

He was by now exceptionally worried about his son and the family were convinced that something must have happened to him. Whatever the case, he was upset enough that morning that he hadn't felt like telling Barney that he wasn't wanted anymore; deciding to leave it until the following week. He was still trying not to contemplate the *what if* of Wullie not returning.

Barney was cutting hair with robotic repetition. In trying not to think about the freezer, he found he had to think about nothing at all. He cut hair as if in a dream. Consequently, he gave some strange haircuts that morning, but such was the peculiar glint in his eye that few complained.

However, that's not to say that some of those strange haircuts were not dream tickets. Indeed one chap, as a direct result of the haircut he received from Barney, pulled a sensational woman that night. A babe, if ever there was one in Glasgow. And it just so happened that two weeks later she murdered him in cold blood. So it could be said that Barney was responsible for another murder, but that might have been unfair.

All morning, however, something niggled at his mind. Something which he'd thought about the night before. Whatever it was, it had been a good thought. A useful one. He couldn't remember it, but he was aware that it'd been helpful; but every time it was almost there, something snapped and it was gone.

The morning dragged on, haircut after haircut, a busy and endless stream, and fortunately a long line of people who were not interested in conversation. He'd had to briefly concentrate when one chap asked him for a *Brad Pitt-Vampire*, but that hadn't proved as difficult as he'd thought it might. After that, things had pretty much been plain sailing. There was one customer who was used to seeing Wullie, and who had wanted to talk about football. He'd asked Barney what he thought about Rangers' game against St Mirren in the Cup, but Barney had only looked at the Premier League table; he'd never even heard of St Mirren. The bloke realised quickly that he wouldn't be getting anywhere and fell into silence.

Finally the long morning drew to a close. The *Closed* sign had been posted on the door and each of the barbers was left working on their final job. As the hour had approached, Barney's stomach had begun to churn. Realised that something was going to have to be done with this great weight of dead bodies. He could no longer afford to simply not think about it.

Unfortunately, for his last job he got what all barber's hate to get when it is not looked for. A talker. A man with no particular favourite amongst the barbers and whose hair Barney regularly cut. Something in computers as far as he was aware. At least with this chap he hardly had to say anything. His concentration drifted in and out, catching the odd word or sentence. He'd started off on football, which Barney had completely ignored, then had moved on to the weather, and now, as Barney delicately negotiated the ears, he was on to the subject of toilets.

'And Russian toilets! Let me tell you about Russian toilets.' He stopped, caught Barney's eye in the mirror. 'You ever been to Russia, Barney?'

The question sank in only a second or two behind schedule. Barney shook his head, mumbled a negative.

'You wouldn't believe it. Me and Wendy went there last year. I'm like that, you think the toilets in Buchanan Street are bad? The smell in these gaffes hits you from about twenty yards, and then you go down the stairs to them and there's just shite everywhere. The floors are covered with it. Then there's these stalls with just a small swing door, with a hole in the ground. There's pish and shite everywhere, and there's no bog paper. And there's always some huge fat Slavic bird sitting there, and you've got to pay her for the privilege of wading through gallons of weapons-grade excrement!' Paused for breath. Barney nodded at what he presumed was an appropriate moment. 'And the toilets on the trains! Unbelievable. There's no bog paper, of course, there's pish everywhere, they're minging, and you get pubic hair in the soap because these people have never seen soap before, so they have a bath in the sink. Bloody awful country. And I'll tell you another thing,' he said, 'it's the same wherever you go, the minute you cross the Channel. These people just have no conception. The French, the Belgians. They're all the same. Maybe the Germans are all right, but they've got plenty of other deficiencies to make up for it. And the further south you go, the worse they get…'

Barney switched off, left him to it. The annoying nag at the back of his mind was right there, right on the cusp, waiting to be plucked out of the air; then it was gone and he'd lost it again.

He vaguely turned his attention back to the inane ramblings in his last victim of the day, who had made another quantum leap of subject matter.

'…and then he downloaded the whole bloody lot. So you know what he did then?'

Downloaded? He wasn't still talking about toilets, was he, thought Barney. He shook his head and feigned interest, as he applied the finishing snips to the back of his hair.

'Well, I must admit, I wouldn't have thought of this myself. You see, there was a guy called Johnson who left last week. Bit of a muppet, no one's ever going to see him again. So Ernie works out what the guy's password was, don't ask me how, gets into his computer and fixes it so it looks like it was Johnson who cocked it up. Brilliant! So when the Big Man finds out about it, which he did yesterday afternoon, he doesn't suspect a thing. Just assumes that it was Johnson all along. Ernie gets off scot-free, and Johnson's name is mud. But he doesn't care 'cause he's buggered off and is living in Switzerland or some shit like that. Amazing,' he said, laughing quietly to himself. 'Switzerland! Now there's a place where you'll get a decent toilet, if I'm not mistaken. Mind you, try flushing it after five in the evening and you'll get arrested. Think about that.'

Barney nodded, then with a swish of the comb and a pat or two of the top of the head to ease the hair into its final, respectable shape, he was done.

He had only been half listening to him, but there was something in what he'd said that had brought the irritating nag back to his mind. What was it for God's sake?

He removed the towel, then the cape, and stepped back. The man rose, brushed his hands over the shoulders of his jumper, then searched his pockets for the cash. The money and tip safely thrust into Barney's hand, he put on his jacket and headed out into the Saturday afternoon rain, cheerful goodbyes all round.

Barney slumped down into his seat. Thinking. God, what was it? It had to be so simple.

And then, like a pebble falling from someone's hand and splashing easily into the water, it came to him. Simple indeed, so very, very simple. Like taking candy off a wean, or sticking the ball into an open net, thought Barney the neo-football fan.

He shot up out of his chair, quickly clearing up the remains of the day, and soon he was on the verge of leaving the shop. Turned to James. He had to know how much time he had.

'You want me to go round and see if Chris is in, James?'

James hesitated. It had been a long morning for him. His hands were tired, he was scared. 'It's all right, son, leave it to me. I'll give his parents a call when I get in, see if they know anything. We'll give the polis a call later, maybe. See what his folks think. Jings, but I've got a bad feeling about this.'

'I'm sure he's all right,' said Barney. James had no answer.

Barney nodded, said his farewells, and walked out into the cold of early afternoon. He wasn't going to have too long, so he had to get on with it.

Quick pace, steady hand, glint in his eye. Gary Cooper.

The Obvious Freezer

The phone rang; Holdall snapped out of a deep sleep. His eyes opened and he was looking at horse racing on the television. Couldn't immediately tell how long he'd been out of it. There had been a horse race on when he'd drifted off in the first place, but there'd probably been another ten in between. Bloody horse racing, he thought, the bane of Saturday afternoon sports programming.

Looked at the clock as he struggled out of his seat. Half past three. Stoatir. There would at least be football commentary on the radio – he wouldn't have to suffer this damned horse shit any more. He could fall asleep in front of the radio instead.

'All right, all right, I'm coming,' he grumbled to the insistent ring of the phone. This bloody well better not be work, he thought. Lifted the receiver, knowing as he did so that it was bound to be work.

'Hello?'

'Afternoon, sir.'

Buggerty-shit-farts. Bloody Scottish Cup on the radio as well. This had better be good.

'Stuart, hello.'

'Sir.'

'Now, what could be so important that it requires you to rouse me from an afternoon of quiet slumber in front of the TV?'

His voice was level but he was daring MacPherson to make it

interesting. Too often, he always thought, some idiot thought that every time there was a crime committed, the obvious thing to do was to call a policeman who was off duty, as if, by definition, being on duty rendered you totally ineffective.

'I thought you might like to know, sir. We've had another report of a missing person.'

Bloody hell, he thought. Bloody hell. Another pointless teenager runs away from his parents because he thinks it'll be cool to hang out in London and sleep in a bin liner. For God's sake!

'Bloody hell, Stuart, it's the Scottish Cup this afternoon. What are you thinking? Tell me something I might be interested in.'

MacPherson was well used to his Chief Inspector's outbursts. Quite enjoyed them sometimes; had been known to incite him.

'Well, you might like to know that the Rangers are getting beat one-nil, sir, but the main thing...'

'What? By bloody St Mirren?'

'But the main thing, sir, is the person who's disappeared.'

Holdall slumped further down into his seat. He didn't like the sound of this. Getting beaten by St Mirren. What next? It was bad enough losing to Mickey Mouse sides in Europe every year, they didn't need to be losing to Mickey Mouse sides in the Cup as well.

'All right, Stuart. Who is it? The Rangers forward line, by any chance? They certainly appear to be missing.'

'No, sir, I think they're all present and correct.'

'Present at any rate.'

'Aye, well you know they're a load of pish, so I don't know why you should be surprised.'

'Stuart...'

'It's another of they barbers. The ones we talked to on Thursday. The younger one, Porter, hasn't been heard from since yesterday. His parents called up to report it half an hour ago, and the local boys passed it on. Thought we might be interested.'

Holdall was suddenly awake. 'We certainly bloody are, Sergeant. Hold the fort, and I'll be there shortly.'

And with a few more bloody hells muttered under his breath, he readied himself to go out.

*

Holdall and MacPherson sat in their car in the midst of a splendid traffic jam in the centre of town. They had visited old man Henderson and now were on their way to see Barney Thomson. The radio played quietly as they sat, while MacPherson continually annoyed Holdall by attempting to discuss the case. Not until he had heard that Rangers had moved into the lead, was he able to relax and give him any kind of attention.

'That's better. Two-one,' he said, pointing at the radio. 'Still can't believe they don't have commentary of the game, though. Who the hell is interested in Aber-bloody-deen. Even people in Aberdeen don't give a shit about them. Average crowd, two and a half.' Drummed his fingers on the steering wheel, looked with irritation up the line of traffic. 'So, what was that you were saying, Sergeant?'

MacPherson had been looking at some notes in his book. There was nothing which he couldn't remember, but he liked to be sure.

'Well, there's an obvious link here. On both days, at the end of the day, the two missing men were alone with this Barney Thomson. That two barbers should find themselves alone together at the end of the day appears to be a rare thing. And yet, after these two occasions, the men go missing.'

Holdall looked at the couple in the BMW in front of them. Angry words were being exchanged; was delighted he couldn't hear them. Everyone's got a story.

'You think Barney Thomson is a killer, Sergeant? Did he strike you as such?'

'He was nervous, certainly.'

'The way you talked to him, I was nervous.'

'I just questioned him like that because I sensed something. He wasn't sure about what he was saying. I think he might've been lying.'

Holdall nodded and shifted into first gear so that he could crawl forward another few yards. The rate they were going, if Barney Thomson was going to try and run from them, he could be in the Bahamas by the time they got to his house. The woman in the car in front lifted a fist at her husband; a child in the rear seat raised his ugly head.

'A bit stupid though, surely, if you want to kill your two work colleagues, to do them both inside three days.'

MacPherson shrugged. 'I don't know, sir. Maybe he kills the first one out of malice, and then this Chris Porter finds out, and he kills him to keep him quiet. Who knows?'

Holdall shook his head. 'No, no, I don't think so, somehow. Not this man. He just looked like a quiet, boring middle-aged fart to me. The sort of guy who picks spiders up and puts them out the door, instead of squashing them to bugger like the rest of us. No, I don't think Barney Thomson's a killer. And certainly not our killer, this bastard that's been taking the piss. No way.'

MacPherson rubbed his chin. Not convinced, but beginning to see another possibility. Even more far-fetched, perhaps, but you had to cover the bases in this job.

'What if we're completely on the wrong track, and someone is after all three barbers in the shop. It could be that rather than Thomson being our killer, he's the next victim.'

'You mean, a sort of mass revenge from someone who's had a stinker of a haircut, or something like that?' He laughed at the thought. 'That's a fucking bad haircut, by the way. I like the sound of that. Still, I think we're getting a bit ahead of ourselves, Stuart. We're not even sure that these men are dead yet, never mind that they've been murdered. Their disappearances could be entirely coincidental, and entirely innocent. Although, I have to admit, I don't think Henderson'll be coming back. Not now.'

Suddenly a gap opened up ahead, a clear lane of traffic appeared.

It was lined with plastic cones, but whatever road works were due to take place over the next three years, they had not yet started. Seeing his opportunity, Holdall went for the space and the free lane; passing by the attempted murder of the man in the BMW; wife's hands at his throat, while child giggled.

Holdall was in a plain car, and he considered putting his light on top to let the people past whom he was driving know that he was on police business. Then he thought, bugger it. If they didn't like it, they could clear off. And if it incited a whole bunch of others to do the same, well, it'd be someone else's problem.

'So, how do we treat Thomson when we talk to him, sir?' said MacPherson. Knew how he'd like to treat him.

'Oh, I don't know, Sergeant. I think maybe you should treat him much the same way that you did the last time. Let's see how he handles it. You never know. You might be right.'

'Very good, sir.'

MacPherson smiled, wondered if he'd be able to get away with using a truncheon.

*

Barney stood in the middle of the kitchen in Chris's flat, wondering what he was going to do next. It was a good plan. Deposit all the bodies around Chris's place, except the body of Chris himself. Make it look as if he was the killer and had fled the city. Simple, genius; jejune even. All great plans have their logistical problems, however.

Plastic bags containing the bodies of seven people lay in his car out on the street. Individually wrapped, a mass of limbs, organs and general viscera sat waiting to be disposed of. Fortunately it was cold and damp, the winter chill still lingering in the air. They were not about to begin to defrost. Still, he had to get rid of them quickly, and as he surveyed Chris's freezer, he realised he was in trouble. It currently contained two packets of boil-in-the-bag chicken supreme, half a bag of chips, an insubstantial carton of ice cream and three fish fingers. And it was full. Whatever else he could do with the frozen meat, he wasn't going to be able to put it into this freezer. Part 1 of his plan was down the toilet.

What had he been expecting? Rubbed his forehead; tried to get his brain to function properly. Of course Chris didn't have as big a freezer as his mother. Who the hell had, for goodness sake? Nobody had freezers that big. Nobody. Not even frozen food shops.

Frozen food shops! He could casually walk around them, depositing bits of meat into their freezers as he went.

Don't be an idiot Barney. That would hardly incriminate Chris. And anyway, it'd take forever. No, he was going to have to do something here. He couldn't just leave them all in the bags, because it'd be obvious they'd been sitting in a freezer somewhere else. It must be two months since that first one died; murdered by Barney's own mother. If he hadn't been in a freezer all that time, he would be fairly pungent by now. Were corpses still *he*, or were they *it*? Wondered.

He could cook them. That was a thought. Maybe if they were cooked they wouldn't smell so bad.

He pulled a chair out from under the kitchen table, slumped down into it. That wasn't going to work either. Even if they had been cooked, these people were still going to be off after this long. And there was no way that he had the time to cook God knows how many pieces of meat. The police would be called shortly, if they hadn't been already, and then they would very probably come around here.

And then there was still going to be Chris's body to take care of. That was bad enough, never mind all this extra baggage that had been dumped on him by his mother.

He buried his head in his hands, trying to think of a way out of the hole. Knew he just didn't have the imagination for it. Barney Thomson, barber, he was; not Barney Thomson, screenwriter.

★

Agnes Thomson opened the door, a look of annoyance on her face. Coralie and Cordelia were about to be sucked into a lesbian lovefest by Cassandra, who was only doing it to wreak revenge upon Cosmo and Clovis. It was the steamiest thing to happen on *Aardvark Road* for years, and she had known for months that it was coming. The videotape was running, but she was annoyed all the same.

The expression on her face changed when she saw the two men, heavily-coated and serious. There was one in his forties, the other maybe ten years younger, and whatever they were doing, they didn't look happy about it.

'Mrs. Thomson?'

She nodded slowly, not sure what the actions of her tongue might be if she attempted to speak.

The younger man held out his identification card. 'Detective Sergeant MacPherson, ma'm, this is Detective Chief Inspector Holdall. Is your husband at home?'

The look on her face changed again. Folded her arms across her chest. 'No, he's not. What's he been up to now?'

'As far as we're aware, he's not been up to anything. We'd just like a word with him. May we come in?'

Her expression told the story – why should they? – but she held the door open, beckoning them inside. There would be no cups of tea offered, however.

They followed her into the sitting room and sat down. She only partially turned down the sound on the television, but then, noticing that they appeared to be interested in what was going on – it seemed that Candice and Clarabel were being drawn into the whole sordid business by Coralie, who had never really loved Clint – switched it off altogether. She could watch it later in peace.

'Could you tell us where your husband might be, Mrs Thomson?' asked MacPherson, suppressing his disappointment, hoping Mrs MacPherson was taping the same program.

'Aye, I could tell you where he is. What's all this about, anyway?'

'Oh, it's nothing to worry about, Mrs Thomson. Just a routine enquiry. It appears that a Mr Chris Porter, who works with your husband, has gone missing.'

'No, no, you dunderheid.' Already on the point of reaching for the TV control, if this was all it amounted to. 'It's not Chris that's missing. It's Wullie, the other yin. And Barney spoke to a couple of you muppets two days ago. Says they were a right couple of old farts, whoever they were. So, get away with yourselves and don't bother me on a Saturday afternoon.'

MacPherson shook his head, deciding not to indulge in police brutality. 'No, Mrs Thomson, you don't understand...'

'Don't tell me I don't understand, you great lummox.'

'Mr Porter has now gone missing as well. They're both missing.'

Her high dudgeon vanished, she stared at them a little more warily. What were they after then? Better watch what she was saying.

'We'd just like to speak to your husband about when he last saw Mr Porter, that's all.'

'Why? D'you think he's got something to do with it?'

'Nothing like that. We'd just like to talk to him. You said you could tell us where he is?'

She thought about it. Barney had called earlier saying that he wouldn't be home because he was going to watch a game of football. It hadn't struck her as odd, because she hadn't bothered thinking about it. But now? Barney hated football, so what on earth was he doing? Unless, of course, he was lying. In which case, what on earth was he trying to cover up? Oh God, she thought, what's the stupid muppet been up to?

'Aye, he's away to the football.'

'Oh, aye?' said Holdall, speaking up for the first time. 'What team does he support?'

She thought about this for a second, trying to remember if she knew the names of any football teams, but none in particular came to mind. Shook her head, mumbled something incoherent. Holdall shrugged, stared at the floor, his interest once again extinguished.

'So you can't tell us when he'll be returning to the house?' said MacPherson.

She bit her fingernails. 'No, he didn't say. But I'll be making his dinner, so he better come home or I'll skelp his arse for him, so I will.' A thought came to her; an infrequent occurrence in itself. 'You don't think that if something's happened to the other two, that it might happen to him 'n all, do you?' Was he insured?

MacPherson stood up to go. Holdall, who was no longer paying any attention, absent-mindedly followed him.

'I think it's a bit too early for that kind of assumption, Mrs Thomson. We'd just like to speak to him at the moment. So, if you could get him to give us a call as soon as he gets back, thanks very much. I'll give you a note of the number.'

'Aye, fine. Whatever.'

MacPherson handed over a piece of paper, then he and Holdall made their way to the door. Before it was even closed behind them, they could hear Cruella and Candida arguing about Crevice's relationship with Collage.

They walked down the stairs to the car, Holdall with ill-concealed lethargy. He was fed up trailing round all these sad people. Perhaps there was some sordid story to be revealed in this awful barber's shop; maybe there were foul deeds going on between these men; but it wasn't what they were supposed to be investigating. They had a serial killer to find, and that was all he was interested in. Finding this bloody murderer, sticking him in Robertson's face, and then telling the stupid police what they could do with their stupid job.

'What now, sir?' said MacPherson as they reached the car. Looked around at the bleak row of tenements, damp and dreich in the rain.

'I suppose, Sergeant, that we should go and see if we can take a look at the flat of this Porter fellow. All might be revealed. You never bloody know, do you?'

'You didn't have any plans with Mrs Holdall this afternoon, then sir?' he asked, as they slumped into the car to escape the cold and deepening gloom.

'Knowing my interest in football, Sergeant, Mrs Holdall moves house every Saturday and takes up residence in Marks and Spencers for six hours. I expect I'll see her around seven o'clock this evening, heavily laden with goods, but light of cheque book.'

'Ah. Just like Mrs MacPherson.'

The Set-Up Comedian

Barney stared at his handiwork, considering all that he'd done in the previous couple of hours. The freezer compartment in the fridge was tightly packed with one small body part, suitably labelled, from each of the deceased. It wasn't much, but it was all he could squeeze in, and it linked Chris with every one of the murder victims.

To add some grotesque effect, he had left some of Wullie stewing in a pot, to make it look as if Chris had been in the habit of cooking his victims and had fled the city even as the last one boiled. After partially cooking the body parts, he had replaced the water with cold to ensure that no one would come across still hot water in the kitchen. It had been mildly disgusting when he'd removed the hand and the melange of viscera from their plastic bags, but a couple of hours of transferring body parts from the freezer to his car had toughened his stomach beyond reason.

Still he was left with seven bodies to dispose of, and quickly too, before they began to stink his car out; before Agnes noticed that the rear seat was piled high with black plastic bags. He would have to sneak out that night on this gruesome errand, but first he had work to finish in Chris's flat, making it look like he had made a hasty exit. Clothes left lying around, a bag half-packed but left behind, another bag and some clothes gone. Someone might know that they were missing. Thought of leaving a meal half eaten on the table, but that would have been unnecessarily dramatic. And time consuming. Perhaps he had another couple of hours to spare; perhaps he didn't.

On his way to the flat, he had gone into Central Station and purchased a one way ticket to London using Chris's credit card. He was unsure of how quickly the police could check up on that kind of thing, but it would be an effective red herring if they did. Rather pleased with himself for having thought of it.

He walked around the house, doing what he thought was necessary to make it appear that Chris was in flight. Found a set of three travel bags of different sizes, perfect for his requirements. Removed the middle one, hoping that it would be noticed, while he half packed the bigger one with a random selection of clothes. The bed had been made, so he ruffled the sheets, lay down in it for a while to give it the correct appearance.

After twenty minutes of stalking around the flat, deciding what else he could do to precipitate the belief that Chris was a killer in flight, he was done. Gathered up the bag with whatever articles from the flat he decided should be removed and prepared to leave.

A good afternoon's work was complete.

*

Holdall parked his car outside the tenement block where Chris had his flat. In front was a car with black plastic bags piled high in the back seat. Stared at it for a second or two, mildly curious, then let the thought pass.

They got out of the car and stood on the pavement in the lightly falling drizzle, looking up at the third floor. It was a typical West End block; huge rooms, large bay windows looking out onto the street, not far from the university. The lights were out in the flat, as Barney had toiled on in the ever deepening gloom, frightened to illuminate the windows.

'Nice block,' said Holdall. 'How the hell can a sodding barber afford to live here? Tell me that, Sergeant.'

'Lucrative business, barbery, I suppose. There's always some bampot wanting their hair cut. Big tippers in this area too, I expect.'

'While we toil away doing the Queen's bidding, working with the scum and filth of the world, and we get paid a bloody pittance. Bastards.'

'The Queen's bidding?'

'You know what I mean, Sergeant. I was being poetic. You've got those keys?'

'Aye, sir. Should do the trick.'

The door into the close was locked. MacPherson produced a huge bundle of keys from his pocket, started working his way through them. No point in letting any caretaker know the police were here, if they didn't have to. There would be time enough for all those obstructive bastards to get in their way. He was really hoping that they wouldn't be able to get into the flat itself, because that'd give them an excuse to kick the door down. Hadn't had to kick down a door for a couple of years now. One of the staples of a policeman's diet.

At the fourth attempt the door clicked open and the two men trudged into the dreary close, the door slamming shut behind them.

Upstairs, Barney heard the faint rumour of the door closing and jumped. Thought about it for a second, realised he had no reason to worry. There were plenty more people in these flats to be using the door, there was no reason why anyone should be coming here. Very likely the police hadn't even been called yet. And it wasn't as if Chris was going to be coming back.

He quickly looked around the dark of the room, the lights from outside sending strange shadows scuttling into the corners. A shiver drifted lazily up and down his back at the thought. Had seen enough horror films in his time to not even need to use his imagination.

Dismissed the thought, pulled himself together. It wasn't going to be Chris coming up the stairs, or anyone else coming here for that matter. Still, he'd better get a move on.

Everything was done that he could think to do, the bag waited ready at the door. He just had to hope that he'd done enough to incriminate Chris, without making it look like the set-up job that it was. All that remained was to dispose of seven bodies. Piece of cake. Wondered if they ever had to do that on any of his mother's game shows. *Lose That Corpse!*

Presumed he'd have to face the police another few times. If his nerve held, and the police were as stupid as everyone thought they were, he might get away with it. Piece of cake.

The doorbell rang.

Barney lost momentary control of his bowel and bladder functions, only managed to get them together after the initial damage had been done. Heart started thumping extravagantly – would it ever stop? – his head span into a frantic muddle.

God, there was someone at the door. Who the hell was it going to be? A friend of Chris's? Chris's ghost? His parents? The police? A host of seven dead bodies re-assembled to take their revenge?

Pull yourself together, for God's sake, Barney! Ghosts didn't ring the doorbell. The police? Would the police ring the doorbell? Probably not. Those bloody thugs would just barge the door down. It must be friends of his, someone like that.

A key! They might have a key! You can't just stand here like a lettuce, Barney. Hide!

He quickly dashed through the flat, trying not to make any noise with his footfalls, anxiously looking in every door to see if there was any cupboard space. Found it behind a door in the hall, next to the bedroom. There were shelves inside, with sheets and blankets, but there was enough space at the bottom to crouch down and pull the door shut.

He held his breath and waited, trying to think if he had left anything of his own lying around.

His heart jumped again as the doorbell rang once more, and then keys were pushed into the lock. Whoever it was seemed to be having some trouble because they couldn't open the door immediately. Funny if it was someone trying to break in, he thought. Even funnier if they then tripped over the bag he'd left just behind the door. Too bad he couldn't see it.

Shit! The bag. The bloody bag. He'd left it lying in the hall. He had to get it.

Closed his eyes and tried to think. Dare he go out? Every few seconds a key was inserted in the lock and then withdrawn. Whoever it was, they didn't have the actual door key; must be trying a bunch of skeleton keys. What did that mean? Think man!

The police! The police maybe. If that was who it was, then he had to get the bag. He had to risk it.

He waited until the latest key had been tried and failed, gently opening the door and poking his head round. The bag sat in the middle of the darkened hallway, about three or four yards away. One more attempt with the key, he thought, and hope they didn't get in.

The key fumbled in the lock and then was withdrawn. In the silence he heard someone curse at the door. Couldn't wait any longer. He got up out of the cupboard and dashed the few yards to the bag. As his hand fell on the handle, another key was inserted in the lock. There was a deafening, damning click, and if his pants hadn't quite been laid waste from the previous occasion, they were now. The door was pushed open, and he heard a 'thank God for that'. He dived back to the cupboard, the brief second that it took for the key to be removed from the door giving him just enough time to get back into hiding.

Gently he closed the door of the cupboard, just as the first man poked his face around the door.

MacPherson flicked the light switch and they looked around. It was a large entrance hall, several doors leading off. The walls were hung with various framed movie posters – *Brazil*, *Pulp Fiction*, *Casablanca* – and Holdall grunted as he looked upon a flat which was clearly going to be a lot nicer than his own house.

He wandered off to the front of the flat, where he presumed would lie the sitting room and possibly the main bedroom. Walked through the door, hit the switch. He was indeed in the sitting room. Cursed under his breath at the decoration and furniture. The three piece suite looked just like the kind of one which he would never be able to afford. Wishing to make himself feel worse about it, he slumped down into one of the seats to see how comfortable they were.

Unbelievably bloody comfortable, he reflected as he looked around him. There was a huge television, two video recorders (if the bastard ever turns up, he thought, we can probably get him for pirating), a music system the size of a small African republic, and a computer which had clearly been rescued from a space ship. Cursed, rolled his eyes.

'This bastard has got to be up to something more than cutting other bastards' hair.'

Stood up, walked out of the room and through to the one next door. The bedroom was equally huge, similarly extravagantly furnished, dominated by an enormous bed, the sheets ruffled and unmade. Above the bed, clinging to the ceiling, was a mirror covering the entire size of the bed. Holdall let out a low whistle; despite himself felt some admiration for Chris Porter. The guy had no class, but at least he had no class with style.

He stepped out of the bedroom, turned to the door next to it. Probably a cupboard which was going to be bigger than his house, he thought, as he put his fingers on the handle.

Inside Barney was tensed, waiting for the moment. Felt as much as heard the hand touching the door above, prepared to dash out. Guessed that if he hit the man in the face with the bag, just as he opened the door, he might be able to get past him and out of the front door before he could do anything about it. Had no idea what he would do when he got downstairs, because he couldn't afford to let them see him driving off in his car. He could worry about that when he got down there, however.

The door started to swing open. He tensed his legs, holding the bag up, ready to pounce. Cold palms, head thumping, nerves raw and bloodied. Last second decision; don't wait for the door to be fully opened – crash out, hitting the guy with it. Started his leap...

'Sir!' MacPherson called from the kitchen, 'I think you should take a look at this.'

Holdall held the door half open; Barney managed to stop himself hitting off it by less than a centimetre. Rested back on his haunches, chest heaving. The door was closed over in front of him. Not closed shut, however. It was left marginally ajar, so that he could hear the conversation that went on the short way down the hall.

Holdall trudged resignedly to the kitchen. He really didn't want to see it, because he presumed it was going to be one of those huge white kitchens that people have in adverts for floor cleaner, but that no one has in real life.

He was pleasantly surprised. It was tiny. Smaller than his kitchen by a long way. Small enough, indeed, to win small kitchen competitions. The thought would have struck him that a single bloke would probably be more interested in pulling women than in having a huge kitchen – if it wasn't for something else which grabbed his attention.

MacPherson was standing in the middle of the room holding up someone's left hand with an exceptionally large pair of tweezers.

The Pregnant Escape

Barney held his breath. They were not supposed to have found anything this quickly, whoever they were. His mind and body were disintegrating into a tangled mass of frayed nerves and gelatinous visceral substructure. This was awful; bloody awful. Wished he had turned himself in right at the beginning, as he listened to the voices from without.

'Well, bugger me with a pitchfork. And I thought they'd banned beef on the bone. Who d'you think that belongs to, Sergeant?'

'No idea, sir. It's male, certainly, but further than that I'd only be guessing.'

'Anything else in that pot?'

'Meat of some kind, sir. Who knows? Half cooked, too, but I wouldn't like to guess which part of the body it might be. Could be a bit of beef for all we know. I'm no pathologist.'

'Me neither. Looks like we've got a few phone calls to make.'

The voices continued, Barney stopped listening. He had recognised them; the same two policemen who'd been in the shop two days earlier. And they had found the hand a hell of a lot quicker than he had wanted them to. The place would be crawling with police within minutes, turning it upside down. He had to get out.

He slowly pushed the door further out, so that he could glance down the hall. The voices were clearer, but he was obscured from view of the action by a corner wall in the hall, between the kitchen and the front door.

He was just going to have to make a dash for it and hope for the best. He tentatively put his foot out of the door, and then, crouching, the rest of his body. Clammy hands, trembling with fear. If he was to escape it would have to be in the next few seconds or not at all.

He was into the hall and moving noiselessly and quickly to the door. He was at his most vulnerable, caught between hiding place and exit, should one of the police walk back out into the hall. And as he put his hand on the door handle and began its silent downward sweep, the conversation in the kitchen stopped. He heard footsteps coming towards him.

He froze. Still like ice. At least, you know, ice that's not thawing or anything. A voice screamed at him to run, but he knew it was too late. They would see the door closing as they came into the hall, there would be a brief chase and then he would be caught. That was all there was going to be.

And so, silently, finally, the flight and fear died within him and he stood awaiting his fate; awaiting his executioner.

The legs and then body of Holdall appeared at the corner, Barney released his breath, letting all hope fall from him. And then, as Holdall turned the corner and stood not three yards away from him, MacPherson called out again, having discovered the freezer, and Holdall turned his head away from the hall and Barney, before he had set eyes upon him.

So bereft of hope had he been, that Barney did not immediately dive out of the door. He remained frozen, before finally the impulse to move came to him, and slowly he opened the door, stepped out and closed it quietly behind him. His body disintegrated even further with relief. Stayed calm, because he was shattered of all emotion and anxiety.

He did not rush thereafter. The police were unlikely to turn up in droves in the next half minute and he didn't think he'd be followed down the stairs. So, with strange conviction, he walked quietly down the stairs, bag in hand, and out onto the street to his car.

As he started the engine he thought perhaps someone looked out of a window at him, but he didn't look back. Never look back. That was the way he would live his life from now on. And so he drove off down the road and disappeared into the gloom and dark of late afternoon.

★

The drive home was short and it wasn't until he was about to park his car that he thought to turn on the radio for the football results. He was going to have to tell anyone who asked that he'd been at a game, and it would be a good idea to know the score.

He had to listen for ten minutes before finally they gave a score from a match which he recognised as being in Glasgow. Partick Thistle versus Aberdeen. He wasn't sure exactly where Partick Thistle's ground was, but it seemed a fair bet that it'd be in Partick somewhere. Lived in Partick all his life, had never seen it; how small could a football ground be?

There was parking attached to the flats in which he lived, but he had a lock-up for the car about two minute's walk away. Was glad of it now, as he could get the heaps of plastic bags out of sight. A short walk back to the flat, was reminded that he needed to change his underwear. Too exhausted and relieved to be embarrassed.

He headed straight for the bedroom. It was hardly likely that Agnes would be interested in his arrival anyway. A quick wash and a clean pair of trousers later, he walked into the sitting room. Found her watching the television; the table set, awaiting dinner.

'It's in the oven,' she said to him, not bothering with an *hello*, or to look over her shoulder. Flange and Fleurelise were trying to fit Gossamer's body into the back of a Mini, after he'd been stabbed by Luge for having an affair with Peppermint. Barney grunted, realising with some surprise, as he went into the kitchen, that he was very hungry. All that handling chopped meat, he reflected.

The usual unappetising fare greeted him, but twenty-five years of it had quite lain waste to his taste buds. He was happy to eat anything. As always, he forgot to put on oven gloves and burned his fingers on the plate. Eventually he proved equal to the challenge and retrieved his dinner.

He lost himself in thought, as he plunged into his meal. What was he going to do with the eight hundred pounds or so of dead meat? Maybe he should just have left it in his mother's freezer, and then brought it home bit by bit for Agnes to cook. By the time she'd finished with it, it would have been quite unrecognisable. Still, don't be daft, Barney. You were never able to stomach Wullie alive, he thought, and he smiled grimly. And it didn't strike him how easily the grotesque had become acceptable.

Then, somewhere between a chip and a mouthful of savoury pancake, he realised that while he had to take care of what he did with Chris's body, he could dispose of the others as he pleased. Jings, I should have thought of that earlier, he thought, stabbing another chip with a little more venom. So what if they found the other bodies? It made no difference. It was only Chris's body which would have to remain concealed for all time.

Agnes's sweet voice dragged him from his deliberations.

'Here you! I had the polis looking for you this afternoon.'

Bloody hell.

'The polis?'

'Aye, the polis. They said that Chris was missing. Did you know that?'

He stared at her, wondering if the visit had been merely routine.

'What did they say? What did they want with me?'

'Well, I don't know, do I? They probably just want to ask you the same kind of thing they asked you the other day. Right strange though, isn't it, Wullie disappearing and now Chris? You don't think something's going to happen to you, do you?'

He slowly shook his head, stared into space. So, the police had already been round, even before they'd visited Chris's flat. Thought he better remember that football score. Two-one to Aberdeen. Don't forget it.

'They left a number they said you had to call when you got in. I left it by the ph…Here, what's going on?'

She turned back to the television. Dexter had just stabbed Deuteronomy because it appeared that it was Pleasure who'd drowned Patience and not Leviticus as everyone had thought.

Barney looked at the phone with dread, but something lightened his heart. It was unlikely that those two would come flying round to him, having just found what they'd found. There would be no immediate reason to suspect him, after discovering the cooking pot in Chris's kitchen, and they might leave him alone for a while. They'd be back, but he had probably given himself some breathing space.

Whatever else he did though, he would have to report in or else arouse suspicion. He happily speared three chips and popped them into his mouth. He wasn't home and dry yet, but things could definitely be worse. Much worse.

Waste Disposal

The sweat poured down Barney's face, mixing with the light drizzle. His clothes and his skin were soaking. *Barber Drowns In Own Body Fluids*. He hadn't had this much physical exercise since he was twelve, and his body wasn't coping well. He was having to stop every half minute or so and it was taking him a long time to get where he wanted to go. Wasn't that just the mirror of life? He took another look at his watch – already nearly four o'clock. He had to get a move on.

He straightened his back once again and put his shoulders into the task, sinking the oars deep into the water and dragging the boat forward as fast as he could. The weight at the back of the small rowing boat, however, was dragging it down, and it would have taken a much fitter man than Barney to manoeuvre it with any speed out into the centre of the loch. He cursed himself for not bringing gloves, as his hands were numb with cold and he began to feel the first tingle of pain, heralding the arrival of blisters on his fingers. *Helter Skelter*.

Once again he had to stop after no more than a few strokes. He looked over his shoulder and was surprised to see that he was nearer to the opposite shore than he'd thought. He was as close to the middle of the loch as he was able to get. Almost immediately the pain in his hands and shoulders eased and he drew the oars into the boat.

There was another impending awkward moment and not the first of the night. He had to tip the bundle at the back of the boat into the water, without capsizing or without taking himself over the edge with it.

He paused to get his strength back, looking around him. The hills were etched black against the night, the shores of the loch were visible, dim and dark through the drizzle. He could remember when his father used to bring him here for picnics when he was very young. Loch Lubnaig, a mile or two past Callander. Distant memories. Hot summers, smiling father. It wasn't as remote as he would have liked, but he hadn't had the time to go driving away up into the Highlands.

He'd waited late into the evening to see if the police would turn up at his house, and when by midnight they hadn't, he'd decided to make his move. With the final soap of the day finished, and Smoke and Dandelion safely locked up for the murder of Blanchette, a story in which even Barney had found himself interested, Agnes had trundled off to bed and Barney knew that within minutes she would be blissfully snoring and unaware of his movements.

He had headed off on the Stirling road, not entirely sure where he was going. On a whim, however, he drove through Glasgow rather than straight onto the motorway, and just before he came to Glasgow Zoo – which had given him an idea or two – he came across what he had been looking for. A dump. A bloody huge dump. And there he had deposited Wullie's body, and all the others. They would be discovered at some point, but that wasn't really important. It was the body of Chris Porter which needed to remain concealed for a long time.

And now he sat in the middle of the loch, about to dump it over the side. He had pulled off the road beside the loch, into what he'd hoped would be an area of solitude, and got to work with heavy stones and rope and enough plastic bags to wrap up a very large horse. He hadn't been sure if it would all be sufficient to keep the corpse at the bottom of the loch, but it was all that he could think of at the time. It seemed the only thing he had left to chance was in finding a rowing boat lying conveniently at the side of the water, waiting for him; and there it was, almost as if he'd had an accomplice. Divine assistance. A bona fide miracle. God was on his side. Or just maybe it was the Other Guy.

As the day had worn on, the horror of manhandling corpses had slowly faded, and by now he was almost treating them like any other pile of garbage. That initial fear that any second a finger was going to move, or Chris's entire body would suddenly sit up, had passed, and now he could just as well be about to throw away a consignment of rotting chicken.

He braced his feet against the side of the boat, the bundle between his legs. He stretched forward and slowly tried to lift it onto the edge of the boat, which he managed without too much difficulty. Now he had to transfer the weight of the package until it toppled over, while at the same time keeping his weight far enough back to stop it dragging the small boat underwater. And with almost consummate professionalism, he failed to do it. Half a minute later, Barney slid slowly into the water, arms and legs flapping. The package immediately began to descend to the depths, sucking Barney with it at first, but he soon struggled to the surface, coughing and spluttering, arms flailing; desperately hoping that whichever hand of fate had left him the rowing boat, would now throw him a lifejacket.

The boat, however, stayed upright, despite taking in large quantities of water. He managed to grab hold of the sides, slowly pulling himself together. It was only then, when he had time to think about it, that it hit him. The temperature. Barney would later reflect that there were no adjectives in the English language of sufficient adequacy to describe the coldness of the water. But he had to get out of it as quickly as possible, and in doing so almost toppled the boat over. The fates were with him however, even if they had briefly mocked him by dumping him in the water, and he managed to avoid further excitement as he returned to the boat.

After that, the row back to the shore was a long and slow and hard one. And cold; very, very cold.

Half an hour after getting back to land he was driving home, completely naked, the heating up full, his clothes squeezed of water and drying on the rear seat. Hoped desperately that he wouldn't pass a police car along the way.

He'd decided to take the roundabout way back to Glasgow through the Trossachs, thinking that the roads would be even more deserted and that he would be more likely to find somewhere to get dressed before he returned to the city.

It worked well, a smooth drive home; with the exception of passing another middle-aged man in his car, who also appeared to be naked. The things you come across, Barney had thought.

And so, by just after seven o'clock on Sunday morning, he was back in bed, pyjamas safely on. He fell into an immediate and deep sleep, free of dreams and nightmares.

Minutes later Agnes awoke and mooched into the kitchen for the first soap of the day.

Where The Detectives Go

Monday morning. The room was thick with cigarette smoke, the air heavy with the rancour of aggressive argument. It seemed as if the five policemen each had differing views on the crime, although that wasn't quite the case. The two detective sergeants had taken a back seat, such was their lot, and had let their superiors get on with the argument. Still, they had managed to express their opinions without getting dragged into the open war which was developing.

McMenemy sat at the head of the table, watching over proceedings, asking pertinent and tough questions – so he believed. Gave his men free reign to indulge their tempers. Another dictum; a station divided, is a station easily controlled.

It all seemed clear cut to Chief Inspector Brian Robertson, a fellow of infinite lack of imagination. Chris Porter was the mad Glasgow serial killer and had fled town after committing a crime which had been a little too close to home. In fact, it was out of their hands now. They knew that he'd purchased the ticket to London, and now that they'd issued the countrywide alert, what else was there that they could do? Chris Porter was their man and it was just a matter of sitting and waiting for him to show his hand. And if he never did, well it wasn't their problem. As long as he never returned to Glasgow. 'QED,' he'd said at the end of one of the explanations, although he hadn't known what it meant. Hoped he hadn't made an idiot of himself.

Chief Inspector Robert Holdall was not so easily led by the glaring evidence. The whole thing reeked of a set-up, although he was not convinced of it, and unsure of how to play his hand. Robertson was in the ascendancy in the case and he had to be careful what he was doing. Still, there were things which had to be said.

He was airing his views, enjoying the disdain with which they were being treated.

'We spoke to Barney Thomson again yesterday. All right, so I've no idea what he's got to do with it, if anything, but he panics every time we walk into the room.'

'Aw, come on,' said Robertson, waving an extravagantly dismissive hand. 'This Barney Whatshisface. You really think this bumbling moron is a serial killer? I don't care what you say about serial killers, but there has to be some spark about them, surely. Something different, something to set them apart from the rest. This guy is about as interesting as a two hour Nescafé Gold Blend advert. Get a life, Holdall.'

'What's this difference you look for in your serial killers? A chainsaw draped over the shoulder? Maybe all their clothes are made out of women's skin? Come on. How the hell are you supposed to be able to tell that someone's a serial killer just by looking at them? Bloody hell, you can't work like that.'

'So what are you saying then, Holmes? That Barney bloody Thomson is our killer? That this poor, sad bastard, with no friends and a pathetic wife, is the type of guy to chop people up into little pieces and go scuttling down to the Post Office? The guy is just a dork, and that's it. He couldn't kill Jack shit.'

Holdall laughed. God, I want to punch him in the balls, he thought.

'Jack shit? Been watching *NYPD Blue* again?'

McMenemy finally held up his hand, although he was loathe to do so. Loved it when his detectives got into an argument, allowing him to appear even more statesmanlike and superior.

'Calm down gentlemen, please. Now then, let's consider all the facts. Stuart, if you could just run down all the relevant details for us please, and no asides gentlemen if you would be so kind.'

MacPherson looked quickly at his notebook, while Detective Sergeant Jobson frowned, wondering why he hadn't been asked to go over the facts. He believed MacPherson to be an all right copper, but couldn't stand him all the same. Guilty by association.

MacPherson started reading in a subdued monotone. 'Chris Porter last seen on Friday night by Barney Thomson when he departed the barber's shop in Partick. Reported missing by his parents early Saturday afternoon. On entering his flat later that afternoon Chief Inspector Holdall and I discovered a small freezer full of body parts, a bit from each of the victims of our serial killer. There was also a hand and some viscera lying cooked in a pot on the hob. These, as yet, remain to be identified. Checks made with travel firms and companies yesterday showed that Mr Porter had purchased a one way train ticket to London early on Saturday afternoon. We have yet to identify who might have sold this ticket but we should be able to do that today.'

'Yes,' interjected McMenemy, 'that might tell us something.'

'There are a lot more details, sir,' said MacPherson, looking up, 'but those are the most pertinent.'

'Exactly,' said Robertson, laying his hands in an expansive gesture on the table. 'It's bloody obvious. This Porter fellow is clearly our killer, he's buggered off to London and within a week or two people in Wimbledon and Balham will be having pieces of their children turn up on their doorstep, while they're getting tucked into their cornflakes.'

McMenemy grunted, hunching his shoulders even further. It just so happened that he agreed with Robertson, but there was no way that he was going to give him any encouragement. He was about to say something challenging and spymaster-ish, which he hadn't thought of as yet, when there was a knock at the door. He grunted loudly, bellowed a command.

The door opened and a rather dishevelled middle-aged man trudged in. His clothes were old-fashioned – designer stains on the shirt collar – the watch chain dangling from the tweed waistcoat setting the whole off beautifully. He was fiddling with his horn-rimmed spectacles and looked rather embarrassed, as he always did when confronted with a room full of more than two people.

The pathologist, Jenkins, had arrived.

'Jenkins!' boomed McMenemy. 'What have you got to tell us, man? Make it quick. Don't just stand there looking like a piece of pumpkin pie, for God's sake.'

Jenkins stared at the floor, fiddled with his glasses some more, put them on and finally looked at his audience. Coughed quietly, removed his spectacles again before he spoke.

'Hm, I'm not sure how you're going to take this, gentlemen.' Paused again, put his glasses back on.

'Get on with it, man!'

Took off his glasses, let a look of worry career with abandon across his face. 'Well, what I have to tell you all seems rather strange and I know you won't want to accept it.'

'Good God, man! You're not giving us the chance. Bloody well get on with it!'

Independently, Holdall and Robertson smiled to themselves. It was always the same. Jenkins would bumble and fudge, McMenemy would bluster and shout, and eventually they would get somewhere.

'Mm, well it seems, gentlemen, that it wasn't your Mr Porter who chopped and packaged these bodies so beautifully. And can I just say that, whoever it was, did a lovely job.'

Holdall couldn't stop himself clapping his hands together. Encouraged a raised eyebrow from McMenemy, a scowl from Robertson.

'Hah! I knew it! I knew it wasn't that Porter bastard.'

'It was an old woman.'

The words fell softly into the room and lay there, no one particularly keen to pick them up. The five men stared at Jenkins, who wilted under the glare, trying not to be too embarrassed. Wondered if he still had some of his breakfast on his chin. Finally, McMenemy exploded.

'What in God's name are you talking about? An old woman? How the bloody hell can you tell that from a few packets of meat?'

'Skin cells,' said Jenkins, voice even more of a mumble than normal. 'There are skin cells left on the outside of some of the packages. We found some that belonged to a man, but mostly they're of an old woman. A very old woman.'

The rest of them looked at him in amazement. 'You're joking, right Jenkins?' said Holdall. Aghast, angry, his moment of triumph rudely snatched away. 'How can you people tell that stuff? Why couldn't you tell it before from the packages that came through the post?'

'She wore gloves, presumably. This other meat was probably never meant to be found. We're not sure about this man's involvement, but certainly, almost all the work appears to have been done by the woman.'

McMenemy had temporarily lost composure. Covered his face with his hands, muttered about the press.

'And when you say old?' asked Robertson. Not smiling, because that would be out of place; still, very relieved that he wasn't the only one around the table looking stupid.

'Eighty. Eighty-five. Difficult to say exactly at this stage. Might know a bit more when we've done some more tests.'

McMenemy let out a loud groan, chin slumping into the palm of his hand.

'What the hell do we tell the press?' he said, question directed at thin air. 'They'll love this. The great granny from Hell. Christ almighty, we're in trouble. We've been farting around for the last two months looking like a complete load of bloody oafs, and all the time there's been some antediluvian witch charging about with a two foot butcher's knife. Jesus Christ.'

'But whoever's granny she was, how did all the stuff end

up in Chris Porter's fridge? Was it his granny, perhaps?' said MacPherson.

McMenemy straightened his shoulders, attempted to regain his authority. Looked around the room, the command back in his eyes.

'Gentlemen, we need to find out who this damn woman is.' Had the tone of a washing powder advert. 'Check out Porter's grandmothers, find out if he has contact with any other elderly women.'

'And Thomson,' said Holdall, 'what about him? There's got to be something there.'

McMenemy shrugged. 'Very well, do as you will. Just remember that Robertson's in charge of this one.'

Holdall nodded, couldn't keep the scowl from his face. The men rose and left the room. Robertson was out first, waited for Holdall to follow him. Delighted that his authority in the case had once more been asserted.

'Right, Holdall, you heard the man. I'm in charge, so you'll bloody well do what I say. Barney Thomson has nothing to do with this. Nothing. You leave him out of it. If anything, he was only likely to be another victim of this Porter and his vicious female accomplice, and if I find that you harass this man, you're finished. And don't think I won't have the authority. You're a stupid, wasted old fart, Holdall, and it's about time you got put in your place.'

Holdall stared at Robertson, fighting the urge to head-butt him. He'd never head-butted anyone before, but a football thug he'd arrested once had given him instructions on exactly how to do it – he still had the scar – so he was pretty sure he could carry it off. Forehead to the bridge of the nose. Straightforward enough. And the bastard was asking for it.

'So,' said Robertson, with relish, 'I'd like you and your monkey to go to all the old people's homes in the area. Find out if any of them recognise Porter. Think you can handle that, or are you not sure you can cope with the strain?'

The foosty moustache which crawled along the Robertson top

lip curled slightly, and then he was gone, seconds before Holdall could choose to make the career-ending decision of acquainting Robertson's nose with the inside of his head.

Holdall and MacPherson stood and watched him go, biting their lips and their tongues. They stayed like that for several seconds, as they each considered what other lines of work it would be easy for them to enter.

'You know, sir,' said MacPherson finally.

'What, Sergeant?'

'If I'd been you, I'd have head-butted that cunt.'

A Prayer For
Cemolina Thomson

A Hugh Grant. A Gene Wilder. A Jack Nance (*Eraserhead*). He grimaced. An electrocution special. A John Lennon (pre-Yoko). A regulation US Marine.

Barney reeled off the haircuts of the men as they walked past him, shaking his hand. He gave no thought to the hair of the women. He knew nothing of hairdressing, except that you could charge a lot more money for doing the same amount of work.

'She was a good woman, Barney,' said a mourner, clasping Barney's hand. Barney nodded, staring at his Sigourney Weaver (*Aliens*). Odd haircut for a bloke.

A good woman? What might the definition of that be? A woman who lured men back to her flat and then murdered them. Chopped up their bodies. Didn't like to think about the fact that maybe she ate some of them, but the thought kept intruding.

Another man walked by and shook his hand, another friend of Allan's whom he didn't recognise. He was surprised by the turnout at the funeral, but he hardly knew any of these people. They were all associates of his brother, all here for Allan, not Cemolina, and certainly not Barney. An endless line of them pouring out of the crematorium, shaking the hands of the bereaved brothers.

It might have been a good service but Barney hadn't been listening. A few words from a minister who'd never met her, a couple of hymns which Allan had chosen and which Barney didn't know

– what hymns did he know? – then a lengthy eulogy from the elder son, talking about his mother's good nature and her remarkable and amusing eccentricity had nearly made Barney weep, so he'd switched off.

A man with a completely inappropriate Michael Jackson '75 walked past Barney without even acknowledging him.

Eccentric? Is that what his mother had been? A loveable eccentric?

His immediate job was done. The bodies disposed of and the police fended off as best as he could manage. The interview on Sunday morning with Holdall and MacPherson had been uncomfortable, but he didn't think they were any closer to him. A few words about Partick Thistle and Aberdeen, eased by having had time to read a report in the morning paper, and they'd seemed satisfied. It had all been, as far as he could tell, routine. Little or no suspicion on their part. Holdall had seemed more interested in his description of the first goal.

And so now, with those unpleasantries out of the way, he'd had plenty of time to reflect on all that had happened. To think about the deeds his mother had committed.

An advert in the newspaper. No artifice about it. Mature woman, mid-80s. And there had been young men who'd replied to it. Could not begin to believe that, but it must have happened. He himself had had to dispose of the evidence. And the woman who had been his mother's final victim, what about her? How had she come to be sucked into it? Had she answered the ad in the paper?

A kid with a Soapy Souter shook Barney's hand and trudged off, looking miserable in his Sunday best.

And what would have happened once they'd arrived at his mother's flat? They could see the extensive range of butcher's tools and the five cut-throat razors he'd found in the kitchen. Had that been it? A cup of tea, perhaps something stronger, then what had these men been expecting? Not their little old lady suddenly appearing beside them, her hand poised with a razor, then *slice!*

the throat open and bleeding. Or had she waited until they were in bed?

Almost a more distasteful thought; his mother in bed practising her Eastern lovemaking. Barney shivered, accepted the condolences of a man with a Jay Leno.

The line was drawing to an end. Bill Taylor stopped in front of Barney, held out his hand. Their eyes met. Locked. The full horror of the police findings at the flat of Chris Porter were only at that moment being made public, so Bill knew nothing.

'Terrible business,' he said. Edge to the voice.

'Right,' said Barney.

Bill's suspicions of Barney were running rampant. Saw himself as some kind of defender of truth and justice. Superman! But he had no proof and had yet to do anything. Hadn't told anyone, had made no effort to discover what had happened to Wullie and Chris. Frightened perhaps. Not Superman at all. Vacillationman. Scaredypantsman.

He nodded. Barney nodded. Bill walked on and wondered. Barney remained distracted.

A final couple passed by, the woman with the hair of Queens, the man with an indeterminate eighties cut which Barney couldn't place. Then the line was over and the minister was with them, shaking them both by the hand.

'Thanks a lot, Michael,' said Allan. Allan wore an expensive dark grey suit. Bought especially for funerals.

The minister smiled.

'It was an honour. She was a most singular woman.' Extended his hand to Barney, who took it.

'I'm sorry I never got to meet your mother, Barney. Quite the eccentric by all accounts.'

Barney smiled weakly. Christ! He wanted to scream. If he heard that word one more time. Eccentric? She was mad! A killer! A freezer full of bodies now, and how many more throughout her life?

He'd spent the last couple of days examining the past. Could there have been earlier signs that he ignored? Madness and murder. And another horrible thought lurking at the back of his mind. The death of his own father; had she been responsible for that? A heart attack she'd said, but her boys had been on holiday at the time with their grandmother. It could have been anything.

All those strange jams and wines and pies she'd made all her life; what had been in those? Barney stared blankly back at the minister. He was getting carried away. Could not stop himself thinking of his mother handing over a fruit loaf for sale at a coffee morning. Everything he could remember her doing, and he had over forty years of a dominated life to look back upon, was now shrouded in suspicion, every act potentially barbaric.

Maybe he was doing her an injustice, or at least the memory of the woman she'd once been. Perhaps the eccentricity had given way to madness only in the last few months.

He realised he was still holding the minister's hand, shaking slowly. He let go and the Rev Michael Flood smiled awkwardly and was led away by Allan Thomson, who eyed his brother with suspicion.

Barney was left alone with the macabre landscape of his imagination. Endless debate on endless questions to which he knew he would never have the answers. Would one day rationalise it all, persuade himself that his mother's mental affliction had been with her for only these last few months. Might one day even see the funny side of it. An old woman luring young men back to her flat, then giving them so much more than they'd expected. But for now he was left to wonder who he was the son of, what evil had begotten him.

A soft hand on his shoulder.

'Are you all right, Barney?'

He awoke from the grotesque stupor, eyes wide open. Barbara Thomson stood in front of him, dressed in black. Auburn hair touching her shoulders. Autumn lips. Concern in her eyes, eyes pools of entrapment and impossible allure.

'Oh, Barbara, I didn't see you there. Aye, I'm fine.'

She smiled and he wanted to leap into her mouth and lose himself inside her.

'I was watching you during the service. You never heard a word,' she said.

He shook his head.

'Distracted,' he replied.

They stared at each other, nothing to say. Concern in the one matched by longing in the other. Barney had forgotten about his mother. Wished he could think of something to say. What smooth words had Allan first used to attract this treasure?

'You were a lot closer to her than Allan was. It must be difficult for you.'

'Aye, well, you know.' God! Barney, think of better than that. Stared stupidly at her. Suddenly had an idea. He could tell Barbara everything.

Of course, that was it! What had he been waiting for? Cool, sensible Barbara. She'd understand, she'd listen. She wouldn't immediately denounce him; turn him over to the police. Not Barbara. He could tell her now, where they stood. At least make the first noises about needing to talk to her. Get it all off his chest, the whole thing. She might not approve of what he'd done, but at least she'd listen. Sympathise.

Imagined her advising him to run away, head for the hills. Confessing to him that she was fed up with Allan and that she would come with him. They could disappear together to some remote corner of the world where Barney could set up his own shop. *Barney's Hair Emporium. Barney's Place. Barney's Cut 'n' Go – Haircutting While U Wait: No Children.* Had another thought. Maybe he could do what they'd done in olden times; become a barber surgeon. Haircutting one minute, surgical operations the next. That might be for him. *Barney's Cut 'n' Slice.* Saw a sign above the door; a pair of scissors dripping with blood. Just him and Barbara, together alone. No more Agnes, no more terrible soaps.

'You look upset Barney,' said Barbara, 'maybe I should leave you to your thoughts.'

He stared at her, mouth opened slightly. He could think of no words. His voice stalled, his brain automatically shut down. She smiled and turned away. Barney watched her go, his dreams along with her. He'd had his chance. Barbara alone.

She disappeared into the crowd. The image of his mother, cut-throat razor slicing into soft throaty flesh, returned.

He stared at the hard, cold ground, did not even fight the vision. A vision which should have been incredible, but which was so very easy to see. Never had been able to believe his mother's strength. Had always seemed so frail, and yet...

'Barney, you better come on.' He looked up. Agnes in front of him. Attempting compassion. 'There's another crowd here for the next funeral.'

Move 'em up, get 'em in, shove 'em out. The cattle market of the crematorium. Barney nodded.

'You all right to go to the hotel?' she asked. Tea; cheese and cucumber sandwiches; cake; polite chatter, sombre mood.

'Aye,' said Barney with resignation. 'Got to do it, eh?'

She smiled sympathetically and nodded. Took his arm as he walked away. Turning his back on his mother.

Agnes hoped she'd set the video correctly. Today was the day that Codpiece and Strawberry were to attempt to sabotage Zephaniah's hernia operation.

The Anthony Hopkins

The steady click of scissors and the gentle flop of hair to the floor were the only sounds in the shop. The three barbers went about their business, solemnly and quietly, each lost in their own thoughts and leaving their victims to theirs. The row of customers sat along the wall, a couple reading newspapers, silently resigned to their fate.

It was Wednesday afternoon. Word had got out from the police about the gruesome findings in Chris Porter's apartment and of the great supply of body parts which had been discovered on a dump on Monday morning. These had included the butchered corpse of Wullie Henderson.

There were some in the town who could not understand why James Henderson hadn't closed the shop, but only those with no conception of the Calvinist work ethic, which Henderson imagined himself to possess. If there were to be members of the public needing their hair cut, then the shop had to be open.

Had it been a women's hairdressers, the customers would have fled, and the shop would already have gone out of business. But men are lazy about hair, creatures of habit, and the previous two days had been business as usual. And besides, the word was getting out – there was a barber there at the top of his game. If Jim Baxter had cut hair at Wembley in '63, they were saying, this is how he would have done it.

The chair at the back of the shop was now empty. In the chair next to that James Henderson was working. He knew he shouldn't be. It was ridiculous, and his wife was furious, but he told himself that this was what Wullie would've wanted. What was more important to him was that it got him out of the house, took his mind off what had happened.

The next chair along was worked by James's friend, Arnie Braithwaite, who had agreed to start a couple of weeks early. His was a steady, if unspectacular style, a sort of Robert Vaughn of the barber business. He wouldn't give you an Oscar winning haircut, but then neither would he let you down.

And then finally, working the prized window chair, was Barney Thomson. He'd moved into it with almost indecent haste, the day before. Perhaps if he'd been thinking straight then James would've considered it odd, but everything was a blur to him at the moment.

Barney couldn't believe his luck. He hadn't heard from the police after his interview with Holdall and MacPherson on the Sunday, and while he still expected them to come marching back at any time and arrest him, it was now three days later and nothing had happened. And the interview which had appeared in the paper that morning with some policeman, Robertson, seemed to indicate that they were after Chris; not pursuing any other line of enquiry. It had all worked like a dream. And on top of that, the window seat had fallen into his lap.

Suddenly he was cutting hair with an extraordinary panache, now that he was free of his bitter rivals. If Arnie was the Robert Vaughn of the business, Barney was the Anthony Hopkins. Always good, frequently magnificent. He was cutting with verve and style, each hair pruned to perfection. He could taper the back of a head with ease and the flick of the razor; even ears were painless. Layering, perms, short back and sides, Kevin Keegan '78s, they were all easy for him now. In a matter of three days he had become quick, efficient and composed, and now, when he felt like it, he would happily chat away to the customers on any subject they chose.

So, it was Rangers versus Celtic in the semi-final of the Cup? No surprise there. Bill Clinton – dirty big shagger. Break-up of the Antarctic ice pack – the cause of Chernobyl, he would opine to anyone who listened. *Blackadder*? The second series was probably the best, but if you pushed him he might say the fourth. If someone wanted to chat, Barney was there.

The afternoon was drawing to a pleasant conclusion, the customers beginning to dwindle away, when the door opened and one last client, his collar pulled up against the driving rain, came rushing into the shop. It was Bill, Barney's dominoes partner; Barney's Nemesis.

He caught sight of him in the mirror as he walked through the door. They hadn't spoken since the funeral, and with all that had happened, Barney had quite forgotten about worrying whether or not Bill would go to the police. From the fact that they hadn't turned up on his doorstep jangling handcuffs and waving a search warrant, he'd presumed that he'd never made the call.

However, this was quite a bit out of his way, so he surely hadn't just come for a haircut. He must want to talk.

They looked at each other in the mirror. Bill nodded at Barney, Barney nodded at Bill. Bill sat down and waited his turn, steely determination in his eye. Bill the Cat.

Barney returned to his haircut, mildly perturbed, yet strangely confident. It was a simple and requested US Marine job, for a chap who'd said he was going hillwalking in Africa. Barney had been quickly knocking it off, but now that he hoped Bill would go to one of the others, he'd slowed down. No other customer awaited, Bill was next in line.

'So, whereabouts are you going walking, young man?' he asked, neatly executing an ear-bypass manoeuvre.

'Kiliminjaro,' said Malcolm Harrison. The new Cool.

'Oh, aye, that's near Cape Town,' said Barney, using his new found confidence and knowledge to its fullest.

Harrison paused briefly before answering, unsure exactly whether to tell a man from the *Barber Death Shop From Hell* with a pair of scissors in his hands that he was talking mince.

'Well, it's on the same continent.' Maybe sarcasm wasn't wise, he reflected. 'It's in northern Tanzania.'

'Oh, aye. Near that, what d'you call it, Zimbabwe, is it?'

The man smiled weakly, hoping Barney would shut up.

'You know, my friend, I was reading a book about Alexander the Great the other day,' said Barney casually.

'Oh, aye?' said Harrison, reflecting on the fact that any barber in the world would have been able to give him this haircut and he really needn't have subjected himself to this to get it.

'Apparently,' said Barney, electric razor poised and running in mid-air, ready to swoop, 'he was a total arse bandit. He spent all his time conquering other countries, so that he wouldn't have to stay at home and get married.' The razor dived down and bit hard, doing that razor thing. 'Amazing, eh?'

African Explorer mumbled something in reply. Vaguely remembered Wullie telling him something like that about five years previously. He knew, however, to keep his mouth shut and that Barney would be unlikely to go on. So he thought.

At that moment, however, James finished with his customer. The man rose, glumly handed over the required cash and gave a baleful look in the direction of the mirror. James turned to Bill.

'Hello, Bill. Bit out of your way?'

'Thought I'd pop by. You all right, James? I'm surprised you're here.'

'You know how it is. The show must go on and all that. Wullie would've wanted it that way.'

Bill nodded, thinking that that was one of the most ridiculous things he'd ever heard in his life.

'Well, I'm sorry about Wullie. It's a terrible business.'

James nodded, trying hard to think about something else.

'Aye, well, would you like to step up to the big chair, Bill?'

Bill shook his head, smiled apologetically. 'If you don't mind, James, I'm just going to wait for Barney. Heard he was cutting hair like Kenny Dalglish taking the ball past five defenders.'

James shrugged, didn't really mind. Barney smiled at the compliment. Assuming that it was a compliment, as he'd never heard of Kenny Dalglish.

Resigning himself to his fate, he hurried through the rest of the US Marine and sent the guy packing. And such was his relief at escaping earlier than he'd been expecting, Malcolm Harrison handed over an unusually large tip and ran out of the shop.

Barney pocketed the loot, turned with trepidation to Bill. He nodded at him, Bill took the few short steps along the long walk to the doom of the barber's chair.

Barney pondered the situation, decided he should play it cool. Innocent, appalled at what had happened. Confident that Bill was unlikely to loosely throw accusations in the shop.

Swishing the cape with a matadorial flourish, he placed it around Bill's neck and, resisting the temptation to throttle him with it, tucked a towel benignly in behind.

'What'll it be then, Bill, my friend?'

Bill was staring off into some far distance, shook his head to bring himself back. Looked at Barney in the mirror. 'What? Oh right. A Jimmy Stewart please, if you don't mind, Barney.'

'Right enough,' said Barney. 'No bother.' And neither would it be. The legendary and straightforward *Jimmy Stewart*, a staple of any barber's repertoire for the past sixty years.

Bill felt a little uncomfortable. He had come because he wanted to question Barney to his face. He wasn't sure what sort of set-up he'd expected in the shop, but now that he'd found James there, sitting forlornly beside them, he realised that there was no way he could talk about Wullie and Chris.

After he'd heard that Chris too was missing, he'd been on the verge of going to the police there and then. But something had stayed his hand; had made him want to see Barney. Then the reports that had started appearing in the paper on Monday night had just been incredible. He couldn't believe those stories of Chris, but then neither could he believe them of Barney, the man he'd set out to suspect from the first.

Perhaps that was always the case with serial killers. It wasn't as if they wore their chainsaw on their sleeve. Presumably, whoever it turned out to be, there would be people who would be shocked by their identity, thinking them all along to be normal citizens.

A shiver jerked down his spine at the touch of cold steel on his neck.

'Game of dominoes the night, Barney?'

Barney hesitated. Didn't want to get into any conversations about what had happened, which he obviously would if they went to the pub; but then, he had to find out if Bill suspected him of anything and whether or not he intended going to the police.

He was about to accept when another thought struck him. It might be better if he agreed to meet him alone, down some dark alley somewhere. A dark and dangerous rendezvous. Dismissed the thought straight away. How could he arrange that here?

The thought that he could kill all of them flitted through his head, but he managed to dismiss it before he set out on the road of giving it serious consideration.

No, it was going to have to be dominoes in a crowded pub, and if he didn't like what Bill said, he could take it from there. *The Domino Killer.* That had a ring to it.

'Why not? See if I can make up for last week,' he said, then laughed.

'Not much chance of that,' said Bill smiling, and to anyone watching it might have seemed like there was nothing amiss.

The Queen of Diamonds

Holdall sat in his office, feet on his desk. Idly tossing cards at the bin which lay three yards away. The floor was covered in them, while a solitary card sat in the centre of the wicker basket. The queen of diamonds; and if he wasn't mistaken, she was laughing at him.

It was Wednesday evening. The day had dragged interminably, as had the two which had preceded it. He had his ideas of where they should be going with this case and most of them led in the direction of Barney Thomson. He'd been trying to make a few discreet inquiries regarding the man, but it was proving difficult to find anyone who knew anything about him. Barney Thomson, the barber with no personality. A cipher. The task was made ever harder by Robertson making sure he constantly had trivial and useless tasks to take care of.

He knew fine well that Robertson didn't want him coming up with anything which might lead to the crime being solved. He was a credit-freak, needed it all to himself. Didn't care if Holdall spent his time going after the wrong man.

What they needed to do was find the body of Chris Porter. If all his years of detective work had given him any nose for a crime, the whole fridge business at Porter's flat had been a set-up, and a lousy set-up at that. But where exactly were they supposed to start searching for Porter's body? His idea was to keep a strict watch on Barney Thomson, the only lead that they had, but that would've involved plenty of man hours, something which required Robertson's agreement. Knew there was no way he was going to get it. Bloody-mindedly didn't want it.

The two of spades thudded off the back wall, plummeted into the basket. He held his arms aloft in mock appreciation of the crowd's applause, was still accepting their plaudits when MacPherson walked into the room.

'Just had a cohesive thought?' said MacPherson, smiling.

'Sod off, Stuart.' Lowered his hands, resumed aimlessly chucking the cards across the office. The five of clubs whizzed past the bin, flew in a wild arc, landed about four yards off target. 'Still here? Won't Mrs MacPherson be looking for you?'

'Late night shopping at M&S.'

'Thought that was Thursday nights just before Christmas?'

'And Wednesday nights just before the middle of March.'

Holdall grunted, narrowly missed with the two of diamonds. 'I wondered why I couldn't get hold of Jean when I tried earlier.' The king of clubs doubled back on itself, landed beside his chair.

'I've got something of interest,' said MacPherson.

'Oh, aye? Rangers managed to sign that big German full back?'

'No, sir. It's about Barney Thomson's mother.'

Holdall stopped, the three of hearts poised at his fingertips. 'What? The Rangers have signed Barney Thomson's mother?'

'No, sir. She's dead.'

Holdall released the card and it dipped narrowly short of the target. 'They definitely don't want to sign her, then. Maybe the Celtic might want her. They need a full back.' The five of clubs veered dangerously to the left, and had it been sharper of edge would have had the head off an hibiscus.

'Chief Inspector...'

Holdall stopped in mid toss, looked at MacPherson, laid his cards on the table, albeit not in any metaphorical sense.

'Very well, Sergeant, what is it you're trying to tell me?'

'Well, it seems that Mrs. Cemolina Thomson died last.'

'Cemolina?'

'Aye, sir, I know. Anyway, she died last week. Thursday night. Buried her on Monday. It sounded a bit far-fetched, but Jenkins did say that the packages had been handled by an old woman. So I did some checking.'

Holdall had a stab of guilt. MacPherson worked while he tossed cards into a bucket.

'And?'

'It ties up. I spoke to her doctor. Says she was long down the road to senility, but he thought her harmless enough. Didn't have a problem with her staying at home. Attentive son. She stayed in a flat in Springburn.'

Holdall turned away from MacPherson. The ace of hearts left his fingers and flew straight towards the centre of the bin. Veered wildly at the last second, missed by several feet. Next the ace of clubs missed right and his cards had been exhausted

'So what are we saying here? That this Cemolina Thomson...I can't believe that anyone is called Cemolina...that this woman is our killer. She dies, and so the son, Barney, has to dispose of the bodies?'

'There's more.'

'Oh, aye? Looking for promotion?'

'Yeah. Checked out a few things. Seemed she'd been placing an advert in a lonely hearts column. Mature woman, mid-80s, all that shite.'

'You're kidding?'

'Straight up. Skilled in Eastern lovemaking.'

'Cool. Was she a looker?'

MacPherson grimaced. 'She was eighty-five.'

'Aye, fine.'

'Anyway, checked her PO box, there were a couple of replies in there. Could be that's how she got the men back to her flat.'

'Jesus. There are some sick people out there.'

'Wanting to sleep with an eighty year-old bird isn't as sick as lopping someone's napper off and mailing it to their mother.'

'Fair point. What about the girl, though? Louise MacDonald.'

MacPherson shrugged.

'Who knows? Maybe she answered the advert 'n all.'

Holdall looked at the carpet, lost his thoughts in its plain weave. A young lesbian with a desire for an eighty-five year old woman. Was it so strange any more in these times of Gothic darkness?

Looked up, as MacPherson was not finished.

'And I also found out she was a member of some old women's group. You know these things where they bugger off around the country to eat scones.'

'And?'

'So far this year they've visited the salmon ladder at Pitlochry, Edinburgh castle, a distillery in Kingussie,' raised an eyebrow, 'Largs, for whatever it is the old yins do in Largs, some gardens in Aberdeen, and Ayr.'

Holdall let out a low whistle. The towns where the body parts had been posted from.

'Bloody hell, MacPherson. You're full of surprises. How long'd it take you to find all this out?'

'Few hours.'

Holdall stared. What had he done for the last few hours? Had had a cup of tea and a Mars bar; checked that night's TV schedule; tossed cards at a bin. It was about time that he got his hunger back.

'Good work, Stuart,' he said. Meant it.

'Thank you, sir.'

'Right. So what have we got? This old woman attracts young blokes back to her flat. Kills them somehow, chops up the bodies. Goes off on one of her day trips and mails a well-wrapped part of the body back to the family. Sounds plausible. But where do Wullie Henderson and Chris Porter come into it? They died, assuming that Porter is dead, either side of the mother, if she died on Thursday night.'

'Maybe Thomson killed Henderson completely independently of his mother...'

'But Jenkins said that the old woman had left traces of whatever the hell it was on Henderson's body parts as well.'

'Then maybe she just happened to kill Henderson as her next victim, and never got around to sending a bit of him off in the post. Whatever, one of them did for Henderson, and then Porter finds out about it and Thomson has to see him off 'n all. And then he hatched the plan to incriminate Porter. Or maybe he just bumped off Porter in order to incriminate him. Let's face it sir, if that's it, it's worked like a dancer.'

Holdall sat back, rubbed his chin. He liked it. It was all circumstantial, but it had a good feel to it. An honest feel about it, which Chris Porter running off to London leaving a hand cooking in a pot didn't have.

'Stuart, I'm impressed. I like this, and we've got to go with it, regardless of what that eejit Robertson says. We need to do some more checking on this mother, and I think we should have another word with Mr. Thomson in the next day or two.'

'Aye, sir.'

MacPherson smiled determinedly, walked out of the office. Holdall got off his chair to pick up the cards. Thank God for that. They had something to go on, at last, and a decent working hypothesis. No point in taking it to McMenemy yet, because he was as bad as Robertson, but in a couple of days they might have made enough inroads into the thing to be able to go public. Or they might have made complete idiots of themselves.

He winced at the thought, sat back in his seat and watched as the ace of spades flew straight into the centre of the bin. Then bounced out and landed four feet away in the base of a plant.

★

Bill and Barney were involved in another life and death struggle on the dominoes pitch. They'd both been putting so much concentration into it because neither man wanted to talk about what they were both there to talk about. So, apart from a brief argument about who should buy the first round, hardly a word had been exchanged.

Finally, after a few intricate stratagems involving double fours and threes, Bill had wrapped up his third game in a row. A little silent resentment from Barney and it was time to talk.

They sipped solemnly on their beers, waiting for the other to start. Barney had no wish to encourage him; Bill, the Great Diplomat, once again had no idea where to begin.

'So, Barney,' he said eventually, the art of subtlety still a mystery to him, 'any idea what's happened to Chris?'

Barney took a long draw from his pint this time.

'No, I don't. Or as much as you, at any rate, given what I've read in the papers. And if you're here to imply anything else, then you might as well get on with it.'

Bill held aloft a conciliatory hand. He had no desire to get straight into any argument but at the same time he saw no reason for delicacy. It was just over a week since they'd sat in the same bar and Barney had told him how much he hated Wullie and Chris.

'You really think that Chris killed Wullie, Barney? They were mates. Chris couldn't have killed anybody.'

'And I could?'

Bill shook his head, wondered again about Barney being so aggressively defensive.

'Calm down, Barney. Whatever happened, it's obvious that someone killed Wullie, and I'm just saying that it's right odd that it should be Chris of all people. Such a nice lad, and the two of them getting on so well and all that.'

Barney hesitated. Perhaps he had been overdoing it a little. He nodded. He was going to have to get into the persona of someone who hadn't killed his two work colleagues and disposed of six other bodies, and be convincing about it. The police had left him alone for the moment but it didn't mean they wouldn't be back. And if he couldn't convince Bill, he certainly wasn't going to be able to convince that bastard MacPherson.

'You're right, Bill. I know you're not accusing me of anything. It's just been an awful week, what with they two dying, and my mother 'n all.'

Bill nodded. Was feeling guilty enough about accusing Barney that the words didn't register. This man was his oldest friend after all. He had to stop so lightly accusing him of murder. Or worse, as it was now. It went a lot further than that, if the papers were anything to go by. There was some psychopath on the loose, and whoever it was, it surely wasn't going to be his old dominoes partner. But then surely it wasn't Chris either.

What was it Barney had just said that had been peculiar?

'The new lad's quite a nice chap,' said Barney, breaking his chain of thought.

'Oh, aye?' said Bill. 'Who is he exactly?'

'Friend of James's. Just moved over from Uddingston.'

'Oh, right. The south.'

'Aye. Just started yesterday. A steady hand, I think.'

'Smashing. That'll be just what you'll be needing.'

'Aye.'

'Aye, that's right enough.'

'Fancy another game? It's time I kicked your arse.'

'Rack 'em up.'

And so they settled down into another dour and tense struggle on the dominoes table. It wasn't until they were into their second hand that it suddenly struck Bill that Barney had said that both Chris and Wullie had died. There was a mild flicker on his face but he managed to contain it within the lugubrious whole. Perhaps it had just been a slip of the tongue. Or perhaps Barney knew something that he didn't.

The Haunting Of
Barney Thomson

Barney had had a good day in the shop. He liked Thursdays, always had for some reason. It was just some gut, barbetorial instinct, but he felt as if he always did good work on those days, and today had been no exception. Whether it was as a result of some fine work he'd done earlier in the week, or whether it was because the customers didn't like the look of the other two, he wasn't sure, but he'd never had so many people ask for him to cut their hair. And he had responded magnificently, customer after customer leaving the shop with dream hair. He'd not even been daunted when one man had requested a Byzantine Triple Weave, generally regarded as the toughest haircut in the world. He'd executed it with knightly splendour, his scissors swooping to cut like a majestic, unfettered eagle, his blow-dryer exercising consummate control over the intricate thatched patterns; his comb could have been forged in the Elven forests of Middle Earth, so smoothly had it been wielded in his hands. When he'd finished, he'd almost expected the rest of the shop to rise in calamitous applause, but instead there'd just been the usual rustle of paper, the soft fall of hair to the ground. The man had stuck an extra fifty pence into his hand and left; the meagre gift the Gods receive. Perhaps he wouldn't be mentioned in the Birthday Honours list for that haircut but at least he'd had the satisfaction of a job well done. Indeed, magnificently done.

And so the day had gone on. One dream haircut after another, all swiftly done and beautifully presented. Never before had a barber been so busy and Barney had risen to the challenge with a magnificence which clearly amazed his colleagues. And he was finding that the longer it was since the police had last been to see him, the more relaxed he was becoming about it. It had only been four days, yet it was enough to give him some breathing space, allow him to think they were off his trail.

Furthermore, there had been a wonderful item on the news the previous night, when some buffoon of a policeman had said that there had been a possible sighting of Chris in London. Heaven! They had obviously completely fallen for it. If he'd known the police were this stupid, he would've turned to crime years ago. He was thinking he might let all this die down and then try something else. Not grotesque murder, of course, something more financially rewarding.

He'd had a few worries with Bill the night before and he wasn't sure that he'd handled it all that well, but in the end he'd thought he'd got away with it. It was one thing for Bill to have his little suspicions, another altogether for him to go trundling along to the police. And anyway, would they listen, now that they were so consumed with the search for Chris? He wasn't out of the woods yet but he was standing at the edge of them looking at a beautiful green field with glorious snow-capped mountains in the distance.

Mentally free of his troubles, he had relaxed into the routine of majestic haircutting, and on occasion exercising his new found confidence with trivia.

His last customer of the day had asked for, surprisingly, an Argentina '78. It was the first one of those he'd had to do in over fifteen years, and normally it might have given him cause for trepidation. But not today, now that he was exercising all his new wiles and confidence to their fullest extent.

'What? What kind of muppet are you? You're saying that Tyson would've beaten Rocky Marciano? You're joking? All right, so he dominated boxing before he went to prison, but you've got to look at the quality of the opposition. Marciano was fighting against some of the greats, and he never lost to any of them. Look who Tyson beat. A bunch of glaicket, useless wankers! My mother could sort out most of the mob. Frank Bruno, for fuck's sake.'

Barney nodded at the chap as he went into the closing routine of the haircut – the sewing back up, as it were. He was a little out of his depth here, he had to admit. He'd just made the bold statement that Tyson would have floored Marciano, when up until the point that the customer had mentioned the name, Barney would've said that Marciano was a type of pasta. That's not to say that he wasn't just as likely to find someone who would have agreed with him about the Tyson-Marciano match-up, but when you're talking about boxing you usually have to count on an argument.

'I suppose you'll be saying next that Tyson could've beaten Ali?'

Barney thought about this for a second or two; had no idea who Argentina '78 was talking about, realised once again the folly of reading the sports pages for three days, then trying to discuss them. It was obvious from the way it had been phrased, however, what he was supposed to say.

'Ali! God, no, I wouldn't go that far. It's just, Tyson can punch, you know, and when you can punch like him, you can give anybody a go.'

'So what? Are you saying that Ali couldn't take a punch, is that it? Is that the crap you're coming out with, 'cause if it is, you're talking shite. You not remember the Rumble in the Jungle, Wee Man? Did Ali not take everything Foreman could give him, yon night? 'Cause he did. I suppose you'll be saying next that Foreman couldn't punch, 'cause that's about the level of everything else you've been coming out with. I'm telling you, Foreman could bloody punch but. And a damn sight harder than any of these namby-pamby muppets you get these days. Christ, the very fact that that old pudding was still taking them all on, even though he was in his sixties, surely to shite shows you what the talent's like in the modern era. So what does it mean if Tyson can beat most of them? It means dick all, especially when he couldn't even beat Holyfield, and remember that yon eejit wasn't even a proper heavyweight.'

Barney nodded a few times, grateful that the man had turned the argument into an aggressive monologue, for in precluding Barney from the conversation, he had prevented him from saying anything else monumentally stupid. He badly wanted to change the subject but didn't know how to just step into the middle of the flow and start talking about the weather. Still, he was going to have to do it before Argentina '78 moved off into territory even more unbeknown to him.

The telephone out the back of the shop rang and James, who was in the middle of a tricky Lennie Bennett '91, looked at the other two.

'Arnie, could you get that please? Probably just some numpty trying to make an appointment.'

Arnie had been doing a straightforward 'Groomed Oor Wullie' on an eight-year-old and was happy to down tools.

Whoever it was, Barney didn't care, but at least it had stopped the boxing fan's flow. Probably best not to talk about anything at all, Barney reflected, in case he wanted to get into some other impenetrable sport.

'It's for you, Barney,' said Arnie coming out of the back. 'Didn't say who it was.'

Barney creased his forehead, made his apologies to his customer. No one ever phoned him at work. He had no idea why, but suddenly he began to feel nervous; a shiver ran down his back, the hairs on his neck rose; body tingled.

He closed the door, lifted the phone. He paused for a second. Knew he wasn't going to like this.

'Hello?' His voice was quiet, almost unintelligible. There was no reply. 'Hello?' he said, a little louder.

'Barney Thomson?'

It was a man, a little younger than himself probably. Nothing much else to read into it. He remained hesitant.

'Aye.'

The voice came out at him, low and ominous. 'Perhaps you'd better check on that body you disposed of at the weekend.'

Silence.

Barney felt the shock of the words, a train thumping into his chest, crushing his bones.

'What?' His voice was weak, a child crying. 'What did you say?'

Silence. Barney's mouth ran dry, the sweat beaded on his face. Shouted *hello* down the phone another couple of times, but the line was empty. Then it clicked off, and he was holding nothing in his hands; alone in the small back room with his guilt and his fear.

He sat down in the seat, ran his fingers through his hair.

'Christ almighty. Someone knows about Chris. Someone knows. Jesus Christ, did they see me?'

He stared wildly around the room, as if expecting the person to be in there with him. Looked morosely at the floor. The police, it must be the police. But then, what were they doing calling up, leaving cryptic messages? If they knew he'd done it, surely they'd just come for him and beat him to a pulp, like they always did. It must be someone else. Must be. Mind raced.

And what had the Voice meant, *you had better check on the body*? Was it not there anymore? How exactly was he supposed to check on a body which was at the bottom of a deep loch? But then, maybe the loch wasn't so deep. He had just assumed it would be. It could be that he'd ineptly tied it all together and it had come apart. Imagined the body bursting up to the surface, floating ashore. God, it didn't make sense. Why would anyone call him up if that had already happened? Surely they'd just phone the police.

The fear grew within him; perhaps there was some higher force at work. Whose voice had that been? Should he have recognised it? Maybe it was Chris or Wullie? Began the descent into the throes of panic. Didn't believe in ghosts, supernatural forces, but maybe that's what was going on. God, he'd handled eight corpses over the previous weekend, could he be surprised if some weird things started happening?

So what was the Voice? Was it good or bad? It had given him a warning, but was it doing it to look out for him? If that was the case then he'd no idea who it might have been. Check on the body? God, he would have to go back out to the loch. What else could he do? He had to heed the warning, whoever it'd been.

The door opened and James stuck his head in.

'You all right, Barney? You've been in here ages.'

Barney tried not to display his turmoil, coughed roughly to straighten his voice out before he spoke.

'Aye, I'm fine. It was just Agnes about something, that's all. I'll be through in a minute. Just Agnes.'

James looked at him a little curiously, then returned to the shop. Barney started rubbing his forehead, trying to think. He had to go out to the loch, but then, what was the point in that? What did he expect to find?

Thought of the Voice. 'I can't ignore it. I can't,' he muttered to himself. Wondered if there would be someone waiting for him when he got out there. Chris, Wullie, anybody. A Satanic Host of the Undead; avenging angels. But whoever was going to be there, he had to face it.

He rose slowly, and walked back into the shop, half expecting everyone to turn and stare at him, pointing and shouting, *Killer*! There were a couple of half-hearted glances, but no one really paid any attention. Argentina '78 was reading the *Evening Times*, nodded at Barney as he returned.

'Sorry about that. You get these calls.'

'Aye, mate, don't worry about it.'

Fortunately he didn't lower the paper and Barney was able to concentrate on putting the finishing touches to what he considered to be the worst hairstyle of all time, even though, in a moment of weakness, he'd had one himself at one time. Every time he finished one of these he felt horrifically embarrassed, was always amazed when the recipient expressed satisfaction. And despite his shaking hand, sweaty palm and his mind being on some alien planet, this turned out to be no different.

★

MacPherson pressed the off button and slipped the mobile phone into his pocket. Outside the car the light rain increased, became a torrential downpour. He stared ahead as Holdall drummed his fingers on the steering wheel.

'Did he fall for it?'

MacPherson thought about it for a second or two, turned, looked Holdall in the eye.

'Crapped his load, sir.'

Holdall smiled grimly, clutched the steering wheel.

'And what would you say? Did he sound like he didn't know what the hell you were talking about, or did he sound as if he'd had to get rid of a corpse last weekend?'

'He sounded as if he'd disposed of about fifteen corpses last weekend.'

Holdall pursed his lips, looked out into the torrential rain.

'So, we've got the bastard then?'

MacPherson nodded, looked at his boss.

'Aye, I'd say we do,' he said.

And so the two men settled back and waited for Barney Thomson to emerge from the shop.

Let Me Die Right Here
In My Shoes

Barney headed out on the motorway to Stirling, Holdall and MacPherson keeping a safe distance. Holdall drove with a grim smile on his face, a smile he hadn't been able to remove since MacPherson's phone call.

They'd had a moment or two of doubt when Barney had returned home after work, but they'd waited him out and half an hour later he'd emerged. Had looked extremely nervous and had stared wildly up and down the street to see if anyone was watching him; something he'd done particularly badly as the two policemen were sitting twenty yards away and he hadn't noticed them.

'What's the plan, sir?' asked MacPherson as they drove past Stirling, the castle majestic through the rain.

Holdall had to drag himself away from the worst excesses of his imagination. In his mind, he already had Barney Thomson arrested and convicted, and he was receiving huge plaudits. Meanwhile, Robertson had been demoted to constable and was working nights in the worst area of Los Angeles. He had never been one to go in for brownie points and success on cases for personal gain, but in this instance, since it would get right up Robertson's arse, he was going to relish it.

'The plan?' He stared ahead into the murk at Barney's car, thinking about it for the first time. 'I don't really think we can have a plan. Just have to wait and see what happens when we get there.

If we're lucky, if we're very, very lucky, he'll have buried the body somewhere and he'll be so stupid that he'll dig it up again for us, just to check it's still there. That is, of course, as I said, if we're very, very lucky. At which point, we move in and make the arrest. After that, I don't know about you, but I'm going to go and find Robertson and piss on his shoes.'

MacPherson nodded. 'Stoatir. Think I'll join you. I might crap on them, though.' He was about to continue with his plans for Robertson's footwear when he saw Barney turning off. 'The Callander road,' he said.

Holdall started to slow, not wanting to take the turn off too close behind. 'Callander, eh? I tell you, Sergeant, it's always the same with these quiet little Brigadoons out in the sticks. Shortcake and knitwear shops on the outside, bloodied and chopped corpses on the in.'

'I don't think Callander's quite Brigadoon, sir. I've got a mate works out here. They've got the usual problems, you know. Drugs, the rest of it.'

'Aye, well, Sergeant, that's the modern Brigadoon for you. The next time the damn place crops up, there'll be someone round selling them E, or whatever it is the weans are popping these days, McDonald's will be wanting to set up a franchise, and at least five of the villagers will subscribe to satellite TV.'

'You never know. Ecstasy might help Cyd Charise with her Scottish accent.'

'But I wouldn't count on it.'

And so they wound on, through the twisty country roads towards Callander. Most of the time they lost Barney in the bends and if he had pulled off at some point, quickly dimming his lights, they might easily have missed him. They couldn't risk getting too close, although Barney hadn't spotted anything. Just as Holdall and MacPherson had not spotted the car behind them.

They got a good sight of him again as he came onto the straight road through Callander itself, but soon he was through the town and back onto the twists and turns of the road on the other side.

'So it turns out that Callander isn't the graveyard of horror after all. Better watch, Sergeant, I can't believe he'll be going too much further than this. Keep a sharp lookout for his car pulled into the side of the road.'

But as it was, when it happened they were on a straight section of the road, running alongside a loch; Barney was well within their sights. They watched him pull in, then they drove past him, around the next corner. Parked the car, dimmed the lights.

'This is it, Sergeant. Time to get our killer. Don't disturb him until we see the whites of the eyes of the corpse.'

'Aye.'

They got out of the car, let the doors quietly click shut. The rain had stopped but the air was cold and heavy with moisture. They crept along the side of the road beside the bushes, came around the corner where they'd left Barney. He was parked in a large clearing set aside for tourists; wooden benches and litter bins.

For the first time Holdall had doubts about what he was going to find. If Barney had buried the body, why on earth would he do it in such a public place? And then, as they crouched down in the bushes on the edge of the clearing, they saw him. He was standing at the edge of the loch, running his hands through his hair, constantly glancing over his shoulder. Even from fifty yards away they could see how nervous he was. Waiting for the Voice.

He began pacing up and down the edge of the loch, looking out over the water. Suddenly it struck Holdall what he was doing.

'Shitbags! Bloody shitbags!' he said under his breath.

'What?' whispered MacPherson.

'He hasn't buried the bloody body at all. He's dumped it in the bloody loch. Christ, we'll never get it now.'

He stopped as Barney looked over his shoulder in their direction. They held their breath but there was no need. It was just part of another anxious look around and quickly his eyes moved on around the rest of the clearing, then back out to the loch.

'Why did the bloody eejit listen to us? Christ, if he's dumped the bloody body into the water, how on earth would he be able to come and check it? What a fucking idiot. Christ, I tell you Sergeant, I've got a good mind to go down there and kick his head in. What an arse.'

'Don't give up yet. He's obviously scared and he's going to do something stupid.'

Barney cast another quick look around him, gave a little jump as he imagined he heard something. Started pacing up and down again, his head constantly on the move.

'Very obviously. So, Sergeant, what are we going to do?'

'Haven't a Scooby, sir.'

'No, neither do I. Shitbags. Absolute bloody shitbags.'

Barney stood at the edge of the water, wondering why he was there. What had he been expecting to find exactly and who the hell had brought him back to this place? In the cold, damp, silent night air he was constantly having to fight his imagination, forever throwing his eyes over his shoulder looking for the Voice. However, there was nothing in the murk.

It had suddenly struck him as he'd driven down that he might be being set up, that someone might be following him. *Barber Walks Into Trap Like Complete Idiot – Arrested For Multiple Murders.* As far as he could tell, however, he'd been alone most of the way. Certainly, there'd been the odd car or two behind him, but always far enough back for him not to worry.

And even if there was someone there, what were they hoping to discover? No more than he had been able to find by coming here himself. He knew he'd made a good job of doing up the body. Perhaps it wouldn't survive down there until the end of time, but it surely would be good for a long while, not just a couple of days.

Despite the cold he was in a sweat, such was the beating of his heart, such was his anxiety. His head was filled with a hundred ghosts, every one of them chattering away, every one stepping on stones and twigs, brushing through the bushes. Whispering.

And then, suddenly, to his dread fear, to his heart-stopping horror, he heard footsteps on the stones behind him. Real footsteps, not some frantic delusion of his imagination. And more than one set, by the sound of it – two slow, heavy footfalls were approaching him from behind. He froze, a whimper rose in his throat. Vomit not far behind, the fear was so strong.

They stopped three or four yards behind him, but he couldn't turn round, not this time when he knew that there really was going to be someone there. Once again, the mad desire to panic, to just lose control of every sense and every grasp on normal behaviour, was sweeping over him.

Tried to calm himself – think logically Barney for God's sake! Swallowed. There were two possibilities. Either they were ghosts, in which case he was going to die right here in his shoes; or they were real people, very possibly police officers. In which case he was going to die right here in his shoes. Either way, he really didn't want to have to turn round at all.

Whoever it was, they were just waiting for him, waiting for him to look over his shoulder. If it was the police, presumably it was going to be those two who'd been to see him a couple of times already. Holdall and MacPherson. If they were ghosts, then it was going to be Wullie and Chris.

Started to hope that it was going to be the police. Wullie and Chris would be really pissed off.

And then one of the footsteps scrunched along the stones a little nearer to him and he could almost feel the arm being stretched out, the finger reaching towards his shoulder.

He knew it was coming, but at the touch a shudder racked his body, his insides were tangibly gripped by fear; he almost had difficulty in standing up straight. Slowly, slowly, he turned, an almost impossible thing to do, so consumed with fear and dread was he. His eyes were almost closed, as finally he was able to look behind him and see the two men waiting upon him.

Suddenly there was a strange lifting in his heart. He didn't recognise either of them. He may have been standing in the pitch dark beside a loch on a cold and miserable March evening, confronted by two strange men in raincoats who he'd never seen before, but at least they weren't ghosts, and at least they weren't the two policemen whom he'd been expecting to see.

He was almost relieved.

Reservoir Frogs

The man who had tapped Barney on the shoulder stepped back beside the other; the three men faced each other in the gloom, as the rain once again began to fall; a few drops, instantly becoming a torrential downpour. Water bounced off stones.

While he was relieved at not facing a ghost or the police, Barney knew this wasn't going to be a good thing. Perhaps it'd be about the rowing boat he'd borrowed, and then not left where he'd found it. Maybe these were the Loch Police about to arrest him for dumping something in the water, even though they didn't know what. Nuclear waste for all they knew.

'Mr. Barney Thomson?' asked the older of the two, fishing inside his coat pocket.

Barney nodded. Had no idea what was coming, knew that it was going to be bad. *Barney Thomson, barber, this is your sodding life.* It might as well be. The man produced an identity card from his coat, held it up towards Barney.

'Detective Chief Inspector Robertson, CID. This is Sergeant Jobson. We're here to arrest you for the murders of Mr. Christopher Porter and Mr. William Henderson...'

Barney closed his eyes. God, of course he recognised him. This was the idiot who'd been on television the night before. Lying.

Robertson continued, but Barney didn't hear him. So they'd found him out. All his precautions hadn't been enough and they'd drawn him out with this sucker punch. All right, so he could deny it if he wanted to. They weren't going to be able to discover the body that quickly, if at all. But he was no master criminal. Just a barber, that was all. Lying would come no easier to him than disposing of bodies, or talking about football. They'd suckered him into this, now they had him by the balls. But whatever he did, he had to keep his mother's name out of it.

'This is where you dumped Porter?' asked Robertson.

Barney nodded, his eyes rooted to the wet stones.

'What on earth made you come back out here? All you bloody eejits are the same. Thick as shite the lot of you.'

Barney looked at him as the rain began to fall with even greater intensity. Would it never stop, he wondered. Realised for the first time just how cold it was, and he shivered and rubbed his arms.

'The phone call,' said Barney. 'Wasn't it you?'

Robertson looked at him, then at Detective Sergeant Jobson. 'I didn't phone anyone. What about you, Jobson?'

Jobson shook his head, looked stupid.

'That's because it was us that phoned, you bastard.'

Holdall and MacPherson strode out of the bushes. Batman and Robin. They had watched, incredulous, as Robertson and Jobson had appeared from the other side of the clearing to grab Barney. And they were pissed off.

'Ah, Holdall, just in time to be too late to make an arrest.'

'How the fuck did you get here?' demanded Holdall.

'We've just been keeping tabs on our man, you know, following him around, waiting for him to do something idiotic. You didn't really think I believed the Porter story?'

'I don't see why not. You're stupid enough.'

'You can make all the insults you like, but I was here first, and I've got the arrest, so you can go and piss in a poke.'

Holdall seethed. Gritted his teeth. Blood boiled.

'You bloody bastard. The only reason he's out here is because we phoned him and tricked him into it.'

Robertson nodded his understanding, smiled. 'Ah, so that's why he did it. Well, well, Holdall, you're not as thick as you look. You never know, I might mention it in the report. But then again, I probably won't. It's not as if anyone's going to believe that you used your initiative anyway.'

He turned away from Holdall and looked at Barney. Triumph! He had beaten Holdall to something for the first time in fifteen years and was absolutely delighted. That Holdall had actually turned up to witness it was all the more magnificent.

'Right you,' he said to Barney, 'are you going to come quietly or am I going to have to kick the shit out of you?'

Barney lowered his head, took a couple of paces forward. Of course he was going to go quietly. What else was there for him to do? He was no criminal.

Robertson and Jobson stood either side of him, took hold of his arms. Knew there was little point in handcuffs and both of them were privately doubting that they had the right man. Surely no killer this, despite his confession and what Bill Taylor had told them that afternoon on the phone.

Robertson stopped, looked at Holdall. The delight of victory continued cartwheeling around his face.

'Thanks for all your help, Holdie,' he said. Voice wet with sarcasm. Dripping. 'I'll try to remember you when I'm Superintendent. Maybe find some more old people's homes for you and your monkey to visit. If you're up to it.'

An insult too far.

When it happened, it was MacPherson who cracked, albeit only marginally before Holdall was about to.

He had heard enough. Took three steps forward and head-butted Robertson with superb mathematical precision. Had a vague feeling as he did it that it wouldn't do his career much good, but that was more than subdued by the delicious, hedonistic pleasure of retribution. His forehead met the bridge of Robertson's nose with a sumptuous crack, then Robertson fell, clutching his face, the blood already spurting and running through his fingers.

A gorilla in the mist, Jobson sprang to Robertson's defence, swinging his fist viciously at MacPherson, catching him full on the side of the head. Sent him reeling.

Jobson had no time to enjoy his pugilistic triumph before Holdall was on top of him, fists flailing, boots lashing out. Jobson reeled, stumbling to the ground under the onslaught, as Holdall assailed his head and body.

Barney stood back and watched. Amazed. Strangely, had no desire to try and flee the scene. What was the point? They knew where they could get him, and if he didn't go home, where exactly was he going to go? A life on the run wasn't for him. A brief vision of Brazil flashed into his head, beaches full of exotic women, but he knew it was fantasy. Prison, and a lot of it, that was what lay in front of him.

Barney started suddenly, took another two steps back, almost stepping into the loch. Robertson had produced a gun, and slowly Holdall and MacPherson, who had been beating massive lumps out of Jobson, become aware of him. They straightened up, stared at Robertson, leaving Jobson bruised and bloodied on the floor. But through the badly beaten face, he still smiled, picking himself off the ground. Then he too produced a gun from inside his coat.

Holdall and MacPherson stared them down, undaunted.

'You're finished after that, you bastards,' said Robertson. 'What the hell d'you think you're doing? D'you think you can get away with assaulting fellow police officers?' He laughed suddenly. Mocking, derisive. Took a pair of handcuffs from his coat pocket, threw them at Jobson. 'Cuff 'em, Sergeant, and make sure they're too tight.'

They did it slowly when they did it, daring Robertson to shoot, but almost in slow motion Holdall and MacPherson brought guns out from inside their coats, lifted them, aimed at the others. They flinched, but held steady.

Jobson and MacPherson aimed at each other, as did Robertson

and Holdall. A neat division between ranks. No one aimed at Barney.

'What the hell are you doing with guns, Holdall? You're in so much shit for this. And here was me saying that you weren't as stupid as you look.'

'We were chasing a suspected serial killer. We have guns for the same reason as you. We signed them out.'

'Well why didn't I know about it, when I'm in charge of the investigation? I should've been told.'

'I wouldn't tell you if your dick was on fire, Robertson.'

The angry words died away, the four men were left standing at gunpoint. The rain streamed steadily down upon them. Slowly, slight wisps of steam began to rise from the four bodies, curious formations dispersed under the weight of the torrential downpour. The heat of battle. Tension.

The guns remained steady. Barney took another pace or two back into the water. None of them were interested in him – curious, as he was the reason they were all there – but he didn't want to get shot accidentally. Couldn't believe anyone would be stupid enough to shoot in the circumstances.

Robertson's nerve was first to wither, making the initial attempt at reconciliation.

'Look, Holdall, this is stupid. We're supposed to be on the same side.'

Holdall didn't move, waiting to hear what else he was going to say. He was absolutely right, of course, and it wasn't as if he had any desire to shoot anybody, no matter how much he despised the man at whom he was aiming.

'We'll forget about all this, Holdall. Just put the guns down.'

They stood in doubtful silence. He was not a man to trust.

'What about the arrest report?' asked Holdall, not entirely interested. Wanted to keep Robertson going while he thought about how best to get out of the hole they had dug for themselves. Damage limitation. 'How's that going to look?'

'I don't know, Holdall. Did anyone else at the station know that you were on to Thomson?'

Holdall slowly shook his head.

Robertson smiled, Holdall knew what it meant. 'Same here, actually, couldn't afford to let you hear about it in case you got in there first. Too bad you were just too late.'

The spark was coming back to Robertson, as the throbbing pain in his nose increased. This was a bloody stupid situation and there was no way that anyone was going to shoot anyone else. There was certainly no way that he was going to give Holdall and his ape any credit in solving the crime.

'Look, bugger this, shithead. None of us is going to shoot anyone, so let's all just put down our guns and get the psycho into custody. Then we can argue about the report but just think yourselves lucky if I don't mention your assaults. Don't think I'm about to start giving you credit for the whole damn thing.' Sneered, wasn't finished. 'You and your monkey'll be lucky if you stay out of prison. Fucking morons, getting in the way of decent police work.'

Barney wasn't sure which gun went off first. It might have been MacPherson's but he couldn't be certain. All he knew was that the instant one went off, there was a loud report as all the other guns were fired. He didn't see anything, however, as he immediately covered his head with his hands and leapt back into the loch.

He lay in the freezing cold under two feet of water for a few seconds, terrified, desperate, listening to the wild beatings of his heart. Slowly and fearfully he lifted his head, looked along the shore. The noise had died quickly in the rain and mist and low cloud, and now there was nothing but the sound of the rain falling on the four bodies that lay on the wet stones.

Barney got up out of the water, walked over towards them, his face still contorted in horror and disbelief, clothes clinging horribly to him, the hands of the insane. Robertson had been shot in the face, his body crumpled on the ground, his head a bloody mess on the rocks. Perhaps Barney had become immune to this kind of thing after the previous few days, but he looked at it, didn't even wince. Both MacPherson and Jobson had been shot in the chest and lay dead, their bodies thrown back with the force of the bullets.

Then he realised that Holdall was stirring and he walked and stood over him. The shot which had hit him was not so great, catching him on the shoulder and knocking him down. He had a dazed look on his face, still not taking in what had happened.

The brief glimpse of freedom which Barney had been afforded vanished in the dust. He looked at Holdall, bent to help him. What was he doing? If he finished off Holdall now, he could get away with it. He had just heard the two of them say it – no one else at the station was in on their suspicions. Perhaps there might be someone who'd come to talk to him after this, but no one who would know why these four were here. He could easily kill off Holdall, then walk away from it all.

He searched around on the ground, saw Holdall's gun. Picked it up, weighed it in his hands for a second, uneasily pointed it at Holdall.

Christ, he thought. This was a big step. Bloody huge. It was one thing accidentally killing your two work colleagues, another clearing up after your mad, psychotic mother. This was cold-blooded murder.

He stood over Holdall, the gun in his hand, his doubts careering around his head. Holdall opened his eyes, looked at him. Barney stepped back, immediately knew he wasn't going to pull the trigger. Barney was the man with the gun – and he was the one with the fear in his eyes.

Holdall eased himself to try to sit up, resting on his right arm, lessened the pain in his other shoulder. He looked at Barney, knew he wasn't going to shoot. So did Barney, and he lowered the weapon.

Holdall was already thinking. He looked around at the three other bodies. What the hell was there for him now? He'd just killed a police officer. How the hell could he explain this? His career had just vanished down the toilet inside two minutes; along with the rest of his life. Mrs. Holdall was going to be extremely pissed off.

'Looks like I'm in as much shit as you,' he said to Barney, looking up, away from the surrounding carnage.

Barney nodded, let the gun slip out of his fingers, fall to the ground. He hadn't thought about that.

'That was just about the stupidest thing I've ever seen in my entire life,' said Barney.

Holdall smiled, laughed. Bitter.

'Maybe we can do a deal,' he said, 'although, Christ, it'll have to be one hell of a deal to get us out of this.'

Barney nodded. Tried to think of something, but he didn't have a naturally devious mind. Completely out of his depth.

'It was your mother, right?' said Holdall.

Barney nodded again, surprise on his face. So they'd known anyway.

'And what about the other two?'

'I know it sounds hard to believe,' said Barney, 'but they were accidents. Both of them.'

Holdall nodded, smiled. 'You're right, it is hard to believe.'

There was a small noise behind Barney. A low groan. A wraith. The two of them turned. Jobson was leaning up on one arm, gun waving in his hand. It was difficult to tell which one of the two he was aiming at, and there was no time for anything other than the initial surprise.

The gun went off.

The shot caught Holdall full in the throat. He slumped back, his body a tangle of arms and legs on the rocks, finally dead.

Jobson aimed unsteadily at Barney, the gun still meandering from side to side. Barney could do nothing, feet of clay. Closed his eyes.

Again, the gun went off. The final explosion of noise in the night, and Jobson collapsed back onto the stones, his final effort.

Barney opened his eyes. It had been a wild shot, fired off into the cavernous darkness of night. He walked over gingerly, stood beside

Jobson. Kicked at him gently, bent over to feel his pulse. He was no doctor, but he knew this. Jobson was dead.

Barney looked out over the water. It was difficult to see more than a few yards across the loch; thick mist, thick rain. He shivered in the cold, was once again aware of the clinging dampness of his clothes.

Go and check on the body you disposed of, that was what The Voice had told him on the phone. Well, he'd done it. He'd looked out over the loch and he knew Chris was still there.

Dead and buried, and the secret had just died with the four policemen on the lochside.

He swallowed, shivered again, and turned towards his car. It was time to go home.

Epilogue

The cold weather had come earlier to Glasgow than usual, and although it was only the beginning of November, there was already a sprinkling of snow on the ground. However, it was unlikely it would last, as the cold freshness of night had given way to a harsh and bitter wind, bringing low cloud and drizzle.

In the shop there was a comfortable warmth, the gentle sounds of hair flopping quietly to the floor, easy chatter between barber and customer. There were three chairs being worked, and five people waiting, having succumbed to their anticipatory trepidation, along the bench.

Barney was on the window chair, as he had been for eight months, cutting with his now legendary verve and panache. Next to him was Arnie Braithwaite, as steady and unspectacular as ever. Then there was an empty chair, and at the end a young lad who was the only person whom James Henderson had been able to get to replace himself. The shop had a grotesque reputation to live down after the events of the previous spring, and it had been difficult for James to find someone willing to come and work there.

In the end he'd settled for a twenty-one year old lad named Chip Ripkin, fresh from Ontario State Barber University. His hands were erratic, his style occasionally wayward. Some might have said he was the Marlon Brando of the shop, but even at his best he could never achieve that level of intensity. He could be great and he could be dreadful, but never was he magnificent and never would he produce the hair of kings.

No, if you were looking for that in the area, there was only one barber; one man; one pair of scissors. Some were saying that he was giving the best haircuts in Europe – although there was always someone else to point out how easy that was, as the second you crossed the Channel you were accosted by limp-wristed, rubber-lipped French faggots, brandishing hair-dryers and family-sized cans of mousse. However, whatever his merits on the European stage, there was no denying that Barney Thomson was cutting hair like a dream. There were few who had tied it to the time when Wullie had been murdered and Chris had fled from Glasgow, although it had been noticed by one or two. Not that they minded or commented to anyone – they were all just happy to be able to get their hair cut by a man whose prowess was becoming legend. If Mohammed Ali had cut George Foreman's hair in Zaire in 1974, they were saying, this is how he would have done it.

Barney had walked away from the scene at the loch, stunned and disbelieving. He hadn't been sure that there would be no one else from the police to suspect him; had spent weeks waiting for them to turn up at the shop, or at his house, but it had never happened. Attention had been distracted from the serial murder case by the horrific – and as far as the press had been concerned, singularly impressive – events at Loch Lubnaig. Then, as attention had shifted back to catching the murderer, there had been more sightings of Chris Porter in London, and even, Barney had been delighted to see, in a small town near Brussels. It had all been more than he could have dreamed of. Now here he was, eight months later, cutting hair like the British conquered colonies of unarmed indigenous peoples in the eighteenth and nineteenth centuries, and in charge of the day to day running of the shop.

Of the five people sitting along the wall waiting to get their hair cut, he could be pretty sure that at least three of them would be waiting for him, and possibly all five.

Consequently, he now cut hair as slowly as he could, making as much inconsequential chatter as he could manage along the way. Just because all these bastards were coming to him now, didn't mean that he'd forgotten the resentment of the past twenty years. It was a small gesture, but it was all he could do to make them pay. He hurried for no man, and every man waited on him.

Caught sight of himself in the mirror, felt pleased at how good he was looking these days. There was a light in his eye that hadn't been there since he'd first picked up a pair of scissors.

He turned his attention back to his customer. It had been slightly tricky to start with. A young lad had come in, asking for an Anwar Sadat '67, a haircut of which Barney had no conception. The Anwar Sadat *'Camp David'* was one of his old specialities, but this had been new to him. However, it turned out to be the same haircut under a different name. Piece of cake. And now he was slowly making his way through it, taking as long as possible around the ears, even though he could have done them in under twenty seconds, such was his new-found skill and confidence.

'Did you know,' he said to the chap, deciding that although he was going slowly, he wasn't going quite slowly enough, 'that the average male life expectancy in Russia is fifty-nine? What d'you make of that, eh? Fifty-nine!'

Kazem Al-Sahel smiled, trying to look interested. He had read this stuff in a newspaper a few months earlier. Barney was probably going to mention the abortion rate next. '*You want an Anwar Sadat '67?*' they had said to him in Cairo. '*Go to Barney Thomson. But be prepared to wait. And be bored shitless, be prepared to be bored shitless.*'

'And you know, there are twice as many recorded abortions as there are births. And that's recorded abortions, mind. Jings knows how many actual ones there are.' Shook his head, waved the scissors about in the air a little. 'That not amazing? You wouldn't have thought it, now, would you? These folk can put people in space, after all.'

Kazem smiled, thought about the weather. They had told him it would be cold but this place was incredible.

'But I'll tell you something. The life expectancy might be fifty-nine and all that, but have you noticed the age of all they senior politicians, eh? There's none of them died at fifty-nine, that's for sure. And you know why, don't you? Because they'll all get perfectly good medical facilities, won't they now? Aye, bloody right they will, while all their people are dying at fifty-nine. And that's just the average mind. Think how many must be dying younger than that.'

Kazem affected a serious face, nodded in agreement again. This was unbelievable; but as he studied the progress of the haircut in the mirror, he had to admit that it was worth it. With hair like this he could get the pick of the babes in all the seedy bars in Alexandria.

A seat was pushed back and to Barney's right Chip's customer stood up, started fishing around in his pocket for some money. He had been given a beautiful, regulation, geometrically precise, US Marine haircut. Barney smiled, wondering if it had been requested. Assumed otherwise and that Chip had had to fall back on one of the old safety nets.

The man walked out looking reasonably unhappy, although it could have been because of the rain and wind he was just about to face. Chip turned to the customer at the head of the queue.

'All right, mate, you're up next.'

The man shook his head, nodded at Barney. 'That's OK, thanks, I'll wait for this fellow here.'

'Sure,' said Chip, unconcerned. He moved onto the next and then the next until he had worked his way down the line. All of them were waiting for Barney. He shrugged, sat down in his chair, put his feet up on the counter, and lifted a copy of a two-month old *Toronto Sun* which his mother had just sent to him. It seemed a man in Flin Flon, Manitoba had transmogrified himself into a lizard and couldn't change back.

Barney looked along the array of men waiting on him, allowing himself an even bigger smile. This was what he'd always wanted. Recognised a few of them as blokes who would have previously waited for Chris or Wullie at his expense, consciously made the effort to slow down even more. He had made a good job of that ear he'd just finished, but perhaps he should just go over it again. If he malingered properly, he could take nearly forty-five minutes over this particular haircut.

Snipped at an invisible hair, stood back to see how much of a difference it made to the overall shape of the head. As he did so, he spotted another few invisible hairs he still had to remove. This could indeed take a while after all, he thought to himself.

*

The young man picked up a flat stone, skimmed it across the surface of the water. It bounced five or six times, came to a stop, rested for a fraction of a second on the surface, sank. He looked at it for a while, then picked up another stone, threw it at the wrong angle, watched it plunge straight into the water.

He turned, started to wander along the shore of the loch. The hills rose up on the other side, the early winter snow beginning to show on the top of them. Around him, large branches lay on the rocky shore, evidence of the devastation caused by the bad storms of two days earlier.

He pulled his jacket collar up, close around his neck against the biting wind, looked at the sky. It was going to be raining soon, judging by the great swathes of low cloud beginning to sweep across from the west.

His mind was not on the weather, however. He was too busy thinking about Amanda Bagel – the girl who'd just dumped him for some big city shopfitter from Stirling. He had turned up in the bar in Callander one night with his fake Gucci watch, a sunbed tan and a couple of twenties in his wallet, and she'd fallen for him like he'd been Brad Pitt. God, they'd made him look stupid.

He was walking his dog, an enormous smiley Labrador called Bond, attempting to tell himself that it wasn't all that important.

It would mean nothing in a couple of months. That was right, of course, but it was still difficult not to feel stupid and hurt. Particularly the way they had laughed at his *Tie A Yellow Ribbon* during the karaoke.

He lifted a large stone – short of a boulder but still heavy – and heaved it into the water. It hit with a satisfyingly loud splash, and he had to jump out of the way of the spray.

Away along the shore, Bond started barking. He spent most of his life barking, the big fella, but now it was with a little more gusto. He was pulling at a black bag, jumping around excitedly, frantically wagging his tail.

Andrew Marshall slowly walked along the shore towards him. He wasn't too interested, knew that Bond would bark excitedly if he found a prostitute in Bangkok.

As he approached, the dog sat down on the rocks beside the large, bound black plastic bags; tail going furiously, enormous grin on his face. Marshall stopped, patted Bond on the head.

'Good boy, Bond, what have you found here?'

Looked down at the large package, now loosely bound with thin rope. Didn't want to touch it with his hands. Kicked at it but it refused to reveal its secrets. Kicked harder.

The bag opened slightly, and then in slow motion an arm fell out, plopping onto the stones. Blue, deteriorated skin, but it was human.

Marshall stared at it for a second or two, then stepped back. Horror ran wild across his face. Wasn't thinking of Amanda Bagel anymore. Turned away and started to vomit heavily onto the damp stones.

On seeing the product of his discovery – such a magnificent reaction – Bond went into another frantic dance, bouncing around in circles, yapping loudly, his tail swirling extravagantly in the chill November air.